STAR-CROSSED IN THE OUTFIELD

Teri,
Chase needs a keeper.
He's accepting applications

STAR-CROSSED IN THE OUTFIELD

AN ALL ABOUT THE DIAMOND ROMANCE

NAOMI SPRINGTHORP

Star-Crossed in the Outfield
An All About the Diamond Romance (Book 4)
Copyright © 2019 by Naomi Springthorp
Published by Naomi Springthorp
All rights reserved.

Print Edition ISBN 978-1-949243-08-6
Cover Photographer: Tonya Clark
Cover Model: Matthew Carothers
Graphic Designer: Irene Johnson johnsoni@mac.com
Editor: Katrina Fair

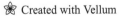 Created with Vellum

For the Naughties. Chase is here.

PROLOGUE

Chase

I spend the off-season looking forward to spring training, then I get there. I'm happy to be there, but talk about a grind! Every year it's back to the basics. Practice catching. Practice throwing. Practice hitting. Dive, slide, bunt, steal. Drill after drill. Long days with early morning workouts and afternoon games in the warm Arizona sun. It's always the same. All the younger dudes play with us until they get assigned to a lower camp and some of them are pretty cool. I was one of them and I'm still one of the youngest players on the big league team. I enjoy getting lost in that crowd during spring training and having fun. This season I've taken it to a new level because my best bud, Rick Seno, got married in the off season and all he wants to do is campout in his new wife's ass—figuratively, not literally, I think. The last couple of years he's watched out for me and even took the heat for me once to keep me in the lineup when I needed to be there or risked losing my spot on the roster. He invited me to stay with him and Sherry, and I took the room on the opposite side of the house from them because I don't want to miss out on Sherry's baking. Plus, I know he'll keep me out of trouble. Just because I have a room doesn't mean I have to use it. Our place has become pool party central for the team. The couple disappears into their side of the house at some point every night. Nobody even notices until they're gone. The problem with this is that I get out of control. Sadly, I need someone to babysit me sometimes. I've done some stupid things. It's not an excuse, but I'm only 23, male and single. The facts are that I'm a professional baseball player, have more money than anybody my age should be allowed, and women find me adorable. Shit happens.

CHAPTER ONE

Chase

Shit happens. I know I'm in the right place when I freak and immediately have Rick and Sherry both standing in front of me, focused on me sitting on my bed and their jaws both drop. Their view of the situation is worse than mine. I'm sitting front and center on the edge of my bed with my feet flat on the floor, buck fucking nude with a sheet wrapped around my good bits, my head bowed and being held up by my hands. I'm hungover and it's the mother of all hangovers. I have red splotches all over my chest, abs, thighs, and that's just the places I can see. There are three different women's bikinis on my floor and the tail from the team mascot seal costume. They stare directly at each other and laugh, full on belly laughs. They're laughing at me, not with me. Sherry stops laughing to make it worse, "Have you looked in the mirror yet, sweetheart? Looks like something bit you."

Seno shakes his head, "How the fuck did you get the tail of the mascot costume?"

A question I'd really like answered. I shrug my shoulders, not having a clue.

"Just relax and I'll get you some breakfast, maybe I can piece together what happened here." Sherry will always take care of me.

Seno shuts the door behind her and starts in on me, "Do you remember anything from last night? Do you know who you had in your room or how many? Do you know if you had sex? I thought you weren't doing this shit anymore! Who was hanging out at the pool last night?"

"Dude, just stop!" Still holding my head because it feels like that's the only thing keeping it attached to my body. "I don't remember having anybody in my room. I feel like I had sex. Mason, Stray, Clay, Bravo, and a couple of the minor leaguers were here late last night. Martin left earlier, not much after you went off to be married." I should know if I had sex or not and probably who I had sex with. "Pretty obvious there was someone in my room." I survey my room and hope I didn't manage to get bit everywhere while I was at the pool, though that would be kind of cool to get attacked by a bunch of women while I was swimming. I can see it now, skinny-dipping with women biting and sucking at me under the water, maybe even giving me head. My own personal kinky shark attack. Saving that one for later, filing it in my personal film collection.

"Sherry already thinks ball players are players. I don't want her having any extra stress or getting worried about me doing this type of shit. She needs to stay happy and relaxed. She's already dealing with enough and we want her to have a healthy pregnancy, so she can travel with me as long as possible. We're going to get this figured out. I got your back, but you need to work with me here."

"You're having a kid?"

4

"God damn it!" Rick shook his head. "Sherry!" He calls her and she appears a minute later with breakfast and coffee for me that smells delicious.

I don't know how she makes everything better with food. Waffles with bacon? It's like baked goods, but breakfast.

Rick gazes at Sherry and speaks sweetly, "Baby, I know you've been wanting to tell somebody. Why don't you tell Cross?"

Seno smiles when her face lights up. "I'm pregnant!" Sherry declares happier than I've ever seen her and everything starts to make sense. She turns to Rick, "And you need to be nice to Chase. He's just a kid and I know you'd never do those things. But, you might have to remind me of that when I'm eight months pregnant, look like a house, and can't travel with you."

"There's nothing sexier than you pregnant, my queen." Seno kisses Sherry and I can see where this is going.

"Congratulations. I can't wait to meet baby Seno. Now, take that, whatever you have going on out of my room." They leave me with my waffles and no answers about the night before.

I decide to text the dudes I was partying with and ask if they know anything, but I can't find my phone. I go for a swim to clear my head and look around at the pool for anything that might jog my memory. I find my cell phone in the planter, dead. I'm sure there were empty containers left out, but I don't find any. I'm guessing Sherry already picked up. I plug my phone in to charge while I shower and get another cup of coffee. I find Seno at the coffee pot.

"Bravo says the minor league guys were fucking with you and planted the bikinis in your room, but he doesn't know anything about the seal tail. Clay says he's hungover, but swears you were humping the seal. I thought the seal was a guy." Seno turns to me questioning, but gets distracted by Sherry walking

5

through the kitchen singing a mushy song by that Ed Sheeran dude. It's got this line about fingers and thumbs that's kind of sexy, but I don't know what it's called.

I get in Seno's face trying to get his attention back, "Dude! I need help here and you're doing your woman in your head."

"I was not." He grins and continues, "We need to get the tail from the seal costume back to the stadium somehow without causing a problem."

Sherry chimes in, "When do you want it at the stadium?"

"Earlier is better. Less people are there." Rick smiles and doesn't ask questions.

"I'll handle that right now. I'll drop it off and let them know I was helping clean it. I'll see if I can find out who's been wearing it. I've been making friends with the volunteers at the training complex. I need to go to the grocery store anyway. Barbecue this weekend, for you and the seal humper. I'll get enough for the team to come over. Last weekend of spring training there should be a party." Sherry smiles as she grabs the seal tail and leaves.

"I need a woman like that. Keep me wanting her and out of trouble. Fixes problems."

"You need a keeper, not a woman. The team knows it, the minor league guys played you!"

"Where did the splotches come from?"

"They look like hickeys. So, I don't really know what's going on with that. Maybe the seal is a vampire. Did you see the ones on your neck? You really don't remember anything?"

"It's weird. Maybe I got roofied or something." We talk as we walk to the stadium for our morning workout. The grounds are busy with fans because it's the last week of spring training and they all want to evaluate the product the team is going to put on the field. The fans are roaming the backfields, taking photographs, asking for autographs, and watching us run drills. There are women out here for completely different reasons. Yes, they're fans, but they want more. They're after a baseball player of their own and these women come in all ages, shapes, sizes, and colors. The gold diggers can be any age and usually appear to be perfectly put together with every single hair in place, typically they're under 30. The cougars are over 40, appear younger, and are only after sex. Baseball players are a conquest. For some of us younger players, we have pumas to deal with. They're in their 30s and still at least eight years older than us, but they're tricky. Some of them haven't given up on getting a player of their own, which makes them a gold digger. Others, are after the conquest and a small number of them are really potential girlfriends. Of course there are women of all ages that are truly fans, but most of them still spend some time gawking at the players or have a favorite player or something. The team front office passed information on to us about the fans now being more female than male. I hope they don't change the uniform to make it more appealing to the fans.

Text from Sherry - Seal tail returned no problems. A bunch of different people have played the seal in the last month, boys, girls, even retired volunteers. Still investigating.

Well, at least I don't have to worry about getting in trouble with the team. One problem handled.

Mason walks out to the backfield with me to warm up and throw the ball around, "What was with you and the seal last night?"

I focus on him, "I don't remember. What do you know? Help me out here. Do you know who it was or if the seal went in the house with me or anything?"

"You totally took the seal to your room with you. I assume it was a chick, but I never saw her face. She was wearing pink flip-flops, so you're cool because it was a girl." He nods coming to the female conclusion. "I still want to know how you got her in your room and did her without taking her mask off."

The power of a baseball player that's been hanging at the pool in swim trunks and no shirt, showing off his body unintentionally. Combine it with my non-existent will power and the need to get laid. I humped the seal. Seno's right. I need to be more responsible for my actions and stop acting like a kid. It's driving me crazy because I either had her out of the seal costume or there's another girl. There's no other way I would've gotten all these hickeys. Maybe the minor leaguers took a vacuum to me, but I don't think it's possible to be so drunk that I could have slept through that. I wonder if I left hickeys on the girl. Okay, so I'm watching for a girl wearing pink flip-flops that may or may not have hickeys.

Seal Girl

What was I thinking? I'm probably going to lose my internship over this. For what? A baseball player. Of course, they're always trouble. I can't keep a job as a volunteer! It's embarrassing enough that I dress up as the mascot and now I'm going to be known as the girl that was cut from the volunteer team for losing the tail piece of the costume. I can't go back in there and get it, can I? He's pretty wasted. He might not notice. No, I can't trust myself. I left because I want him too much. I can't even get a quick meaningless fuck right. It wasn't the alcohol. I couldn't help myself. I shed the seal costume and dry humped him for hours in my PJs. I wish I could be there to watch him try to explain the hickeys I left him with to the next girl. I kissed him all over his body, biting and sucking and leaving him spotted like a leopard. What kind of guy hits on a mascot anyway? Serioulsy? All he could see was my pink flip-flops and polished toe nails. Maybe he has a foot fetish. Worse, a seal fetish. Maybe he's into plush costumes and gets off on the anonymity of the whole thing.

I know three things.

One, he made me hotter than I've ever been. If I didn't get out of there when I did, I never would've left. His hands were warm and inviting. His body solid and sexy. His kiss owned me. His hard naked cock? I wanted it and had to rub on it. I still want it.

Two, I can't let him get in the way of my goals. This internship may sound silly, but it's the stepping stone I need to get into media at the major league stadium. I can't mess this up. This can't happen again. Chase Cross is not an option for me no matter what.

Lastly, baseball players suck.

CHAPTER TWO

Chase

I chill at the pool and relax as much as possible for the rest of the week, doing my best to stay out of trouble and not get released or reassigned to the minors. I'll party when everybody comes over for the barbecue after the last spring training game, and Sherry has invited everybody. I mean everybody, including the people who work and volunteer at the stadium, even some of the groupies. I think she wants to know who was in my room with me. You'd think it was the only chick I had in there, but it wasn't. Nobody noticed the others. I know I shouldn't, but I'm single and horny. I had two girls over together on two different nights, the same two girls and they apparently like to work as a team—I'm not complaining. One night I had three girls over, but I was sure I was going to get caught. They were so loud! It was fun to have them all in the pool together with me, but they were too giggly and I took them to my room and turned on some music to drown them out. "Train in Vain" by The Clash was playing. It was like hiding them from my parents, though I knew I wouldn't get in trouble. I don't disrespect them. I try to give them what they want. I've been told they like my blonde hair that's almost shoulder length and tries to curl around my ears, and that I'm tall and skinny and "have shoulders that go on for days." I'm not exactly sure what that means, but the chicks think it's a good thing and I'm going with it. Some of them like the way I play, I do put it all out there. I'm not afraid of diving for the ball. I've heard that chicks dig scars. I'll lay it all out there for the game and my team. I want to win and I refuse to be the reason we lose. The chicks say I'm the same way when it comes to sex, but I've never really thought about it like that. Game rules are that she's getting some and so am I. But, it's always just sex. Well, not just sex. Sometimes we do other things. We might order a pizza, or sit in the hot tub. I guess my point is that I haven't found one that I like. They like me and sadly I'm using them, so I try to stick to the groupies because that's really all they want. Fucked by a player. That, I can do.

I've been thinking about women a lot during the off-season. I'd already started to think I wanted a real girlfriend before last season was over, but then my best bud got married and I was best man. I don't think they're the norm for a couple. I like what I see and want some of it for myself. It'd be great if she likes to bake. I need to find a chick I like, not just girls that want me. Seems like it's one of those things I don't have control over and it's hard to meet chicks that aren't trying to meet me. I need Sherry to help me with this, but she's so determined to figure out who the seal is. I guess it'll take some time and I need to work on keeping it in my pants.

I've been volunteered to help prep for the barbecue. I'm in charge of cleaning the grill, cleaning the pool, and I'm supposed to go to the store with Sherry to be her bitch boy a couple days before because Seno doesn't want her lifting anything, and he needs her out of the house to do something for her while she isn't there. The bitch boy duty includes making sure I keep her out of the house for two hours and text him when we're on our way home. It's a special day or something, so many months since their first date or some silly thing he wants to turn the romance up for. I'm sure Sherry will eat it up. Maybe I should be talking to Seno about finding a woman. You know, I found Sherry and gave her to him. I mean it was clear that she was interested and not a groupie type. Maybe he can help.

While I wander around at the baseball complex, I'm on the lookout for the pink flip-flops and hickeys. I feel bad that I don't know who it was. Not that it's the first time that's happened, but she works for the team and I probably see her everyday. I probably walk right by her and don't even acknowledge her existence. That's just shitty. Why did she have to wear the mascot costume anyway?

While I sleep, there's a movie playing in my head and I can see the whole thing unfold in front of me. Shit, I can feel the whole thing. There she was with long dark hair, olive skin that's been tanned by the Arizona sun, warm green eyes with little gold flecks sparkling in them, and perfect curves on her slender frame. I see the seal costume on the floor in the background and I'm laying spread out flat on my bed and naked. We're making out and it's hot, I mean I'm hard and ready. Alcohol has helped her lose all of her inhibitions, or I think I would've noticed a girl that wanted to suck on my tongue like that sooner. She's wearing boxer shorts with pink sunglasses printed on them and a matching tank top that's stretched perfectly across her boobs that says "I wear my sunglasses at night." She wears pajamas under the seal costume, interesting. I remember things being a little blurry and I had drunk a lot. She asked if we could just kiss and I went along with her because I never push, it's always what they want. I suggested that we could kiss all over and she kissed me all over from my ears down my neck, across my chest, over my abs and I thought I was going to get a blow job, but she skipped that and went for my thighs, kissing and sucking and biting all over my thighs. Then she reversed and traveled back up my body with her teeth, biting and sucking until she got back to my mouth. She straddled me then and our kiss heated to the point where I really wanted her, and I absent-mindedly rocked my hips. It felt like she would leave if I pushed her, but she rocked back at me. This isn't the way I do things, it's always what they want. But, this girl was driving me, pushing me, making me want more. She was making me crazy.

I told her I wanted her and she whispered all sexy in my ear "I want you, too. You have to want me for more. You don't want me enough."

"I want you plenty. I want you now." I moved and took initiative, kissing her neck and sucking just below her ear. A little strange, since I don't put out any extra effort—I never have to. I held her tight against me when she tried to pull away. "I won't hurt you, baby. I won't do anything that you don't want me to." I pressed my lips to hers and took control of our kiss, sliding my tongue into her mouth and gliding it against hers. She tasted like cookies and then all I could think about was her "cookie." Fuck me, I had totally lost it. I rubbed my hard cock against her.

"Give me one second." She got up and I thought she'd changed her mind. But she put the costume back on and left in a hurry, leaving the tail behind. I don't think she's my Cinderella or anything, but a glass slipper would be easier to fit than a one size fits most mascot costume.

I wish I could remember the part at the pool, before I took

her to my room. Fuck she was hot and she told me no. She got up and left. Now I want her more and I don't even know her name. I don't think I've ever seen her at the complex.

I wake up the next morning hoping Sherry invited her. I get up early and sit at the kitchen counter chatting with Sherry. "Good morning, sweetheart. It's early for you." Sherry's surprised to see me.

I pour some coffee, "I went to bed early. Umm, did you invite a girl with long straight dark brown hair and green eyes, slender but with curves, maybe wearing pink flip-flops?"

She stops what she's doing and looks at me, "What's her name?"

Fuck! "I don't know."

"That's not a pretty name." Sherry torments me on purpose.

"I was drunk. At least I remember what she looks like now."

"Is this the Seal Girl?"

"I'm pretty sure. I remember how I got all the spots. Oh, I didn't have sex with her."

"You were naked. You have spots from her mouth all over your body. But, you didn't have sex with her?"

"Yes."

"That makes no sense."

"She said she only wanted to kiss."

"I suggested kissing didn't have to be limited to mouths." Proud that I didn't push her and then I remember that she left because I kind of pushed her. Damn it.

"And?"

"She got up and left, after she made me spotted and we made out for awhile. I shouldn't have told her that I wanted her. Sherry, I need help. I need a chick that I like and isn't after a baseball player."

"You need to talk to Rick about that. I'm good for other

stuff, but not the part that has to do with you being a player. You need to know their name before you stick your tongue in their mouth and get naked. That's the first step for you."

I listen to her. She's right. I need to know their name. I'll talk to Seno on our walk to the field this morning.

"You need to take girls on dates a few times and see if they're player crazy, not just fuck them as soon as you meet them."

"Didn't you have sex with Sherry the night you met her?" I know he did, he came to the stadium the next day wearing the same clothes he had on when he left and had a huge hickey.

"That doesn't matter. We're talking about you."

"What's the difference?"

"I'm older than you. I've got more experience than you. You just want to get laid. Look, Sherry broke all my rules. I can't explain why or how. She's different and I just knew. Fuck, you were there! You saw how fucked up I was over her. I still feel that way, but she's mine now."

"So, you're saying that rules can be broken?"

"Yea, I am. If you find yourself breaking personal rules, you need to pay attention to what you're doing and not be fucking around. You have no idea how many rules I broke with that woman. Fuck, she broke all my rules. I did some seriously stupid shit and I don't regret any of it."

"Got it. Don't follow my dick."

"I wasn't following my dick! But, for you, yea, that's a pretty good rule. Also, always use a condom and no sex until at least the third date, unless it's just one of your groupie fucks that you're never going to see again."

"Do the twins count as groupie fucks?"

"If you want a real girlfriend, you need to let that shit go."

Seno shakes his head as he walks into the clubhouse to get ready for workouts.

I know he's right. I guess it all depends on me. Am I ready to give up the groupies? I would give them all up for the right girl. I'll keep them until I find her.

CHAPTER THREE

Chase

Spring training is finally over. I'm cleaning the pool with a beer in my hand while Sherry sets out bowls of salads and sides that she made. Seno is manning the grill until Sherry takes the tongs from him and tells him to go have fun. It's going to be a good night. I know because I carried all the beer and ice in. Sherry has a display of jello shots out, too. She made some non-alcoholic just for her, so she can show us how they're done and drive Seno crazy at the same time.

People are everywhere for the next few hours. My team-mates, the ladies from the team store, the group who work in concessions, the retired volunteers, there's a representative from every part of the sports complex. The team had clicked together, it's great to hang out and have fun off the field. We're pounding beer and that turns into doing jello shots. We're challenging each other and, well, we're all very happy—even Seno's wasted, so I don't feel bad about my state of hazy desire. Some-body walks in wearing the seal costume and I head straight for it, I need her. I put my arms around the bulky seal and give it a squeeze, "I'm happy to see you. I've been thinking about you since you left the other night. Can we talk?" The seal stiffens and doesn't make a noise. "Please tell me I didn't just hit on another person in the seal costume." The team is watching me from across the yard and trying to hide their laughter. Sherry looks up and notices me with my arm around the seal.

Sherry walks up to us, "Welcome seal! How about I help you get changed into something more comfortable, so you can enjoy the party and have some fun?" I don't know if she's rescuing me or still trying to find out who the chick I had in my room was, but she drags the seal into the house with her and leaves me standing there. I didn't see the seal again and I still don't know who was in the costume.

There's music playing and when a slow song comes on, Seno grabs his wife and holds her close as they sway to the beat. Then our other teammates that have women do the same and I'm left standing there like a wallflower. It's different to witness all these big, tough guys be turned to mush for their women. Watching how they act differently with them and the expressions on their faces, the way they move together knowingly.

I want to dance, too. I want someone to look at me like that when I have my arms around them and want to dance with me, without me asking. Someone I belong with. I glance around and there's a chick making eyes at me from the other side of the pool. I smile at her and wave, then gesture to her hoping she'll meet me in the middle to dance with the crowd. I keep eye contact with her as we walk to each other and reach for her hand as soon as I'm close enough to reach it. She takes my hand willingly, glancing up into my eyes and blushing while she smiles timidly. She's shy and it seems like she hasn't been drinking. I pull her a little closer and kiss her on the forehead as we start to dance. I'm drunk, but trying to follow the rules. Don't push her. I need to know her name first. No sex unless I feel it's appropriate to break the rules. I wonder if she knows the girl from the seal costume with the pink flip-flops. I step back and look at her, wondering what shoes she's wearing and if she has any remnants of hickeys. Her skin is soft against mine and she has dark chocolate brown eyes. Her warm brown hair is tied up into a ponytail, revealing her long sexy neck. We dance until the slow songs stop and all of the guys are back to drinking, but the women are happier because of the personal time they had with their men. Interesting things I'm noticing while I spend time here with the Senos. I watch her as she goes back to talking with her friends and grabs a beer. She glances over at me and smiles a few times, but then she turns away to concentrate on the conversation she's having with her friends. I want to go over there and ask her out, but what if she's friends with the seal? I at least have to get her name. I'm not used to these rules, I'm really going to screw this up. I look up to catch Sherry pulling something out of the oven and go directly to the kitchen because she's baking. I walk up to her as she pulls chocolate chip cookie bars out of the oven and they smell delicious.

"Hey, Sherry. Are these for me?"

"Of course, sweetheart. I need to tell you something about the seal." Sherry focuses on me with a funny grin.

"Did you find out who she is?"

"It was a him tonight."

"Shit! I hit on a dude?"

"Maybe you just like the soft gray plush fur on the costume. He said he was flattered." Sherry laughs.

"Do you know who the girl I was dancing with is?"

"You danced with her and don't know her name? What did

you talk about while you were dancing?" I feel like I'm being scolded.

"We didn't talk. We were just quiet and happy. At least, I was happy."

"Okay," I watch Sherry cut up the warm cookies and put a few on a plate. She hands me the plate, "Now, you go take these to her and offer her a cookie. Or, lead her away from her friends somewhere you can talk—Not your bedroom. Find out what her name is. Maybe find out how old she is, what does she do, does she work at the stadium, is she a student, where does she live," Sherry went on and on with things I should talk to the chick about. She stops and stares at me, "Never mind. You're drunk again, aren't you?"

I smile awkwardly, trying to remember what she said. "I'm going to walk over there with cookies and find out what her name is. Maybe get lucky and bring her back for more cookies and milk. Or, something more adult like sitting on the couch and talking. Maybe kiss her on the forehead again. Her skin is really soft." Sherry shakes her head at me like I've lost it as I walk out the door with a plate of cookies as an ice breaker to talk to the brown-haired girl.

I walk up to her, "Hi, would you like a cookie?" All of the sudden I'm reminded of wanting the girl from the seal costume and her "cookie". I'm torn and I don't want to lead anybody on. I don't even know who she is.

She takes a cookie, "Thank you."

I start talking to her and I don't know what I said, something about baked goods. I step a couple feet away and she follows, so I lead her off to a corner of the yard with swings and sit with her sharing my cookies. "I'm Chase, you probably know that."

She smiles, "Yeah, kind of. Everybody knows who you are. I'm Syl, it's short for Sylvia."

"Hi Syl." I smile at her and we talk while we eat cookies. I hear Sherry in my head and ask thoughtful things like she suggested. I learned that Syl was a college student and hoped to transfer to San Diego in the fall. She's not a groupie and I'm not going to be in Arizona long enough to date her the required three times, but she didn't seem like a player chaser. She works at the sports complex. I get her number, since I'd managed to talk to her without fucking her and consider kissing her. But, that would be it. A lesson in restraint. I need lessons and practice. She gives me her number and I send her a text.

Text to Syl - You have beautiful eyes.
Text to Syl - I'm leaving tomorrow because it's time for baseball season to start.
Text to Syl - If I wasn't leaving, I'd kiss you.

I gaze into her dark eyes and she smiles as my phone vibrates.

Text from Syl - Please kiss me.
Text from Syl - Let's get out of here.

I stand up immediately and take her hand, leading her to the empty family room via the kitchen where I pick up more cookies. I sit in the comfy chair and pull her down onto my lap with my arms around her. I hesitate, trying to be a good guy and not wanting to take advantage of someone a couple years younger than me. She giggles and puts her arms around my neck. Then shy, sweet Syl surprises me. She leans in and kisses me, licking my lips and sliding her tongue into my mouth to seductively caress mine. I let her take the lead, she can decide what direction we take and how far we take it. I'm pretty sure she's not the girl from the seal costume. Her eyes are the wrong color and they don't kiss the same. I may never figure out who the girl from the seal costume is, so I have Syl right now. At least I got her name before I kissed her. That's progress, right? A step in the right direction. Syl moves her lips to my neck and her hands to my chest, running her fingers across my chest and digging her fingers into my shoulders. I move my hand to her back and the other to her head, so I can hold her against me and run my fingers through her silky chestnut hair. I bring her lips back to mine, tasting her and feeling her full soft lips pressed to mine. Her kiss wants more, but I wait for her to show me what she wants. She moves her hands under my shirt to touch my abs, but really she's trying to get into my pants. I stop her and bring her hands up around my neck, but she goes right back for it and rubs against my now hard cock. I whisper in her ear, "What do you want from me, Syl? Are you just after a ball player? Thrill of the chase?"

She moves her mouth to my ear and whispers, "I like you. You're gorgeous. I want to fuck."

Alarms go off in my head, even in my drunk state I know this is a bad idea. Seno had managed to get something to sink in and I'm tired of being the dude who has sex with different chicks all the time. That's a lie, but I want a chick that likes me, doesn't care if I'm a baseball player and sticks around for repeat performances—and I don't think I can have both. "How about we just kiss?" I hear myself say and I don't know where it comes from.

Syl pulls back, and looks at me with big eyes, "We could kiss all over." I watch her eyes heat, "You know, naked."

I'm pretty sure I should be keeping my clothes on, but I don't want to. Her breathy voice and hands all over me have my body ready and willing to do about anything. I've said almost the same thing to get chicks naked in my bed before and one step closer to sex, hoping to at least get head. That has to count as kissing all over. I love it when a chick sucks me off. Fuck! I need to get some distance. "Be right there!" and I get up carefully leaving Syl in the chair. She looks at me questioning, "I'll be back, Sherry needs help." I didn't hear her call for help, but in my head it was there and I needed to escape.

I walk into the kitchen to find Sherry leaning against the wall and sliding down slowly. "Sherry? You need help with something?"

"No, I'm just tired. I think I overdid it today."

I'm glad I came to the kitchen when I did, Sherry loves time in the kitchen and is apparently still learning her limits. She doesn't act like a pregnant woman, but maybe she should. "Let me help you get to bed." I walk toward her and she gestures for me to get her a chair. I slide a chair over to her and leave her sitting in the chair, with her head leaning against the wall. "I'll be right back." I run outside to find Seno before she can tell me not to. That woman is headstrong and wouldn't want to be a bother. Seno sees me walk out of the house and notices the look of urgency on my face. He's running to the kitchen before I can say any words. "I walked into the kitchen and she was leaning on the wall. She wouldn't let me help her get to bed, so I got her a chair and was going to get you," I fill him in as he goes to Sherry.

He looks at her and picks her up, carrying her off to bed, "It's okay, my queen, I've got you. I shouldn't have let you do so much today. You're fine. You just need some rest." I watch as they disappear into the bedroom, wondering which of them he's trying to comfort. "Thanks, Cross." I need to take over the party and I need to get to know Syl, not just fuck her.

I walk into the family room and Syl's gone. I should let it go and be done with it, but I can't.

Text to Syl - Hey… where'd you go?
Text from Syl - Getting a beer. Out by the pool.

I walk out and join her, but I'm done drinking for the night. I need to be the responsible one. We talk and I give her a good-night kiss, not anywhere kinky.

CHAPTER FOUR

Chase

I wake up the next morning and wander out to take a swim before packing up my stuff for the drive back to San Diego. My head is clear, I'm not hungover, and I don't have any regrets about last night. I'm looking forward to getting home to my little bungalow by the beach and hitting the waves with my surfboard. It's early for me, so I do a double take when Seno's sister, Sam, is in the kitchen. "Hey, Sam, what's up?"

"Just here to help. Rick wanted me to come help them for a couple days, get them back home, keep Sherry from doing too much. Duties of the older sister," she smiles.

"Give me a few minutes and I'll help you get them packed up to go." I swim some laps, thinking about what I need to get done today and know I'll be on the waves tomorrow morning. I wish I could find out who the Seal Girl was, and I'll probably never know.

After my swim I find Sam texting and laughing, she left me with instructions to pack up the food into the ice chest and left to take care of an errand. I'm left to my own thoughts and I'm not sure that's good. I think about the seal and when I think about the girl who wore the costume, I envision the seal and not her. Maybe I'm losing it. Maybe Sherry was right and I like the soft plush costume. I'm a sick puppy. I need to get home and everything will make more sense.

It's a five-hour drive to get home. I get my stuff loaded into my pick-up and stop at the stadium on my way out of town to clear out my locker. I have mail waiting for me, so I grab it and take it with me to deal with later. I hit the road and turn up my radio for the drive across the Arizona desert to San Diego. I listen to the new wave station on the satellite radio on my drive, I love that old British DJ dude and all the new wave music. I'm a bit eclectic, I like new wave and surfer music and a little punk, as well as current top forty and oldies. He was playing a set of Depeche Mode and talking about an upcoming tour as he played "Blasphemous Rumors," "People Are People," "Strangelove," and "Just Can't Get Enough." I needed something with more for driving, so I switch over to listen to The Wrecks on repeat for most of the drive home. Still, I find myself looking at the cars I pass and searching for the girl from the seal costume, hoping maybe she's going back to San Diego, too.

When I finally get to San Diego, I pick up my favorite pizza from Little Italy on my way home and sit on my patio eating the whole thing while I watch the waves roll into the shore. It's nice to be home. I'm tempted to hit the ocean and forget about unpacking, but the season is starting in a few days and I won't have any extra time. There's laundry to be done, or at least dropped off at the fluff and fold. Either that, or I really need to hire a maid that does that stuff for me. It would be nice to have fresh sheets more often and clean towels all the time. My patio is the reason I bought this tiny bungalow. It's a huge concrete slab that drops off into the sand and it's fenced with a worn out wood picket fence that's about three feet tall with huge gaps between the slats. It doesn't keep anything in, or anything out for that matter. You can step right over it and see right through it. But, it does have a gate that works and leads you to the white warm sand of Ocean Beach, and the Pacific Ocean just steps away. The bungalow itself is small. The realtor called it a two bedroom, but it's more like a master suite and a small office, den or maybe a large closet. It doesn't matter. It works for me. There's only one of me and I don't take much room. Yep, I have 800 square feet of living space with unlimited beachfront. It's a good thing the flat screen is mounted on the wall because there isn't even enough room for an entertainment center and a sofa in the living room. Then again, that's based on my standards and everybody doesn't require a sofa to be long enough for me to stretch out my 6'4" frame on for naps. My bedroom is a good size, I painted it myself and put in new bamboo flooring. It's exactly what I wanted with dark brown and teal throughout the room, on the bed, and covering the windows. It's my personal space and I've never brought a chick back to my place. It's rare I bring the guys over. Usually, I'm picking them up because they're on my way since I live farthest this direction from the stadium. Can't get any farther than the ocean. I get my things unloaded and put away. I end up sitting on the beach, letting the water come up to meet my toes.

Text to Sam - I'm home. Did you get the Senos home? Do you need help with anything?
Text from Sam - We just parked. Everything is fine. Thanks for the offer. Kris is already on his way.
Text to Sam - Cool. Let me know if you need me.

Interesting, I'm Seno's buddy. But, I guess this is Sam's show and she's always gotten along better with Martin. Sam thinks I'm a kid and, honestly, she's probably right.

When I finally go in for the night, I open the mail from my spring training locker. Mostly, it's fan mail, autograph requests, photos that fans have taken of me and letters from younger guys telling me how they want to be like me when they grow up, asking for advice and I think I'll always find that weird. I don't think of myself as a role model. Then I find the pink envelope that just has my name written on the outside and I open it to find a letter that's handwritten on matching pink paper.

Chase,

I didn't mean for it to end this way. I left because I didn't want to be just another baseball slut. I thought I was going to see you again, but I have to leave before spring training is over for a job opportunity. Probably better this way anyway. We didn't exchange numbers or anything. It would have just been sex and I'm being a dumb girl if I think anything different. Better that we didn't. No regrets.

Good luck this season.

The Seal

It even smells like her. I still don't know her name. I still don't have her number. I look to see if there's anything giving me a way to respond to her or contact her, but there isn't and I'm sure that was intentional. I need to get over it. Maybe I need a seal costume for my own personal use. What am I supposed to say? It's either her or the costume and I can't have her.

I enjoy the few days before the season starts and relax on the beach, spending hours floating on my board waiting for my wave to come. Can't beat surfing in early spring, only in San Diego is the weather always right for surfing.

I only leave the house to pick up food and I get fresh baked cookies while I'm out, dropping them off for Sherry so she doesn't bake. I want to do my part and she has always taken care of me.

CHAPTER FIVE

Chase

I t's opening day and we're playing LA, which is the same
most years. The stadium is clean, fresh, and shiny. The
field is manicured to perfection. All of the opening day
decorations are out, the paint on the field, the banners, the
bunting—it looks like there's going to be a party. All of our
lockers are full of uniforms, caps, gear, deliveries from sponsors
and endorsement contracts, everything new for the new season.
We've been briefed on opening day festivities. We know we'll
each be introduced as we run out to the first base line in front of
our home dugout and there will be fireworks shot off with each
introduction, which is better than last year and the attempt at the
smoke screen we were supposed to be magically appearing
out of.

The stadium is buzzing. The gates open early and season
ticket holders are able to come in and watch our early batting
practice. It's an attempt to make getting into the stadium easier
for the sell out crowd and reward the regulars at the same time

by making them feel special. Make no mistake, they are special. Without them, the seats are empty and nobody cares. We need the fans and we feed on their energy. I watch them swarm around the dugouts and behind home plate to get a good look at batting practice, they're happy to be here. I remember when I was a kid, going to my first big league game of the year always made me happy. It's something about walking into the stadium, seeing the field, getting the ballpark food I'd missed in the offseason and anticipating the win. I can only guess that's how all these people feel and they're the extremists being season ticket holders. Losing is not an option. They're in it heart and soul, committed to the team like they're in a marriage. Yea, that's exactly what its like.

I wander off into the underbelly of the stadium to get some quiet time and I swear I see the seal out of the corner of my eye. It kind of jars my state of calm before the game. It's weird. The seal isn't the problem, it's the memory that it gives me. I'm going to have to make an effort to not let the seal get to me. Fucking mascot. That doesn't help. No fucking the mascot.

I turn around to go back to the clubhouse. I need my safe place. I need to be with the team. I need to stay focused. I see a girl walking away quickly, as if it's only a shadow and I think it's her. The Seal Girl. I try to catch up and get a better look, but she's gone. That's it! I'm going to the clubhouse. We're winning this game. I'm getting laid tonight. This is bullshit. I should've jerked off.

The clubhouse is amped up. The team is getting pumped up for the game and looks sharp in the new uniforms. Everybody showed up today with clean haircuts, trimmed beards, just looking good overall. Well, except me. I'm not cutting my hair and I couldn't grow a beard if I wanted to, I don't have the facial hair for it. Skip gives us a quick pep talk and we all walk the clubhouse high-fiving. It sounds funny, but its team bonding. We're all loose and ready to go. Most of the starting nine go out on the field pre-game and get warmed up. Stretching, doing sprints, throwing the ball. Seno and the starting pitcher, Rhett Clay, walk out to the bullpen early. It's Clay's first opening day with the team and to get called for the start, that's a big deal. I know he'll be great, Seno has his back. Seno was cutting up about it this morning because Sherry called it after Clay had only played with the team a couple times last season, she said he was going to be an ace.

I check behind home plate to see if Sherry's here and she's in the first row center, sitting with Sam. She won't miss a game unless she doesn't have a choice. She lives for baseball and she knows Seno wants her here, cheering for him every game. Hell, I love to hear her cheering for me, too. She has spunk and she isn't afraid to use it. I can't wait to hear what she calls the LA pitcher and what creative things she has to say about their hitters. She has had the whole offseason, so it should be good. The expression on her face tells me she's happy to be here. She's the definition of Seals Fan. I'm sure it made her happy to walk into the stadium today, even knowing its just the beginning of the season and having already been to spring training games.

I keep seeing the seal and the Seal Girl out of the corner of my eye, but then neither of them are there. Focus Chase. It's almost game time.

I'm lined up in the dugout for my name to get called out as part of the starting lineup, announcing me as I run out on to the field to fist bump all my teammates. I'm pumped, listening to the buzz of the crowd and cheering for the players announced before me. I'm in the lead off spot today, that makes me the first hitter of the season. The coaches and players that didn't make the starting lineup today have already been announced and are lined up waiting for me. The fireworks will start with me. I feel the pressure and hope I get a good reception from the fans.

Then I hear it over the loud speakers as it echoes through the stadium, "And now your Seals opening day starting nine as written in by the manager Butch Hopp. Leading off, in center field, number 17, Chaaaaaaasse Crooossssss!" I run up the steps of the dugout and the stadium explodes, calling out my name and screaming. I smile uncontrollably. I'm not an attention whore, but who wouldn't like this? It's a total ego trip. Fans hanging over the railings like they're reaching for me from the upper decks. Lots of girls wearing jerseys with my number, 17, on the back.

Sherry is out of her seat, yelling and I can hear her, "Go Chase" She's holding up a sign that says "Chase #17 Home!" and wearing a shirt that says "Future Seals Fan" with an arrow pointing to her belly. I can't help but chuckle and I can't take the smile off my face. The rest of the lineup gets announced:

Hitting second and playing Short Stop, #28, Jones Mason

Hitting third and playing first base, #2, Kris Martin

Hitting fourth, your catcher, #6, Rick Seno

Hitting fifth and playing third base, #13, Lucky Lucine

Hitting sixth and playing in right field, #10, Mark Rock

Hitting seventh and debuting at second base, #29 Andrew Brandt

Hitting eighth and playing in left field, newly acquired Seal, #15 Cain Simms

And, hitting ninth, your starting pitcher, #20, Rhett Clay

Nobody gets the cheers like Seno and it all comes from behind home plate. You can hear where Sherry's biases fall. The cheers for Kris were louder than mine, but that was Sam adding in. It's funny how you can still hear Sherry over the rest of the stadium, even on opening day, or maybe we're conditioned to listen for her because we know she's here for us. I find myself scanning the stadium, wishing the Seal Girl was here cheering for me. I know she's gone and I need to forget about her. If she wanted to be found, she would've given me a way to contact her.

We get to our positions and I hear "Make it a win, Seno!" yelled out and followed by a "Wooooo!" as he gets set behind the plate. Yep, it's time for baseball and the team is ready. I take the minute I have in the outfield before the first pitch and look around, enjoying the field and taking in the full stadium. I always forget to take time to enjoy where I am and have fun. I'm consciously trying to change that. I've seen what happens to players over the last couple of years and there are no guarantees I'll still be here next season, or even tomorrow. It's my reality. I think it's why I play with the groupies, it all kind of goes together—nothing is permanent. The thing is, I want more. I want permanent. I want to be better at baseball, I want to be a record breaker, and I want to show everybody that I'm an offensive and defensive force. While I'm wanting things, I want more time for surfing and sitting on the beach, and it would be great if I had a woman to sit on the beach with me. Just one.

Clay handled the top of the first inning perfectly, he's on

point and I may never get a ball in center this whole game with the way he's pitching. Bottom of the first, time for my lead off at bat and I've never wanted to make an impact so badly. I want to be noticed. I want to give Clay some run support. My job is to get on base. That's it, just get on base. My teammates will knock me in. I've got the speed. I can outrun the throw. I'm aware on the base paths and I can steal, it's why I lead off. Mason and I get on base, then Martin and Seno bring us home to score. It's the plan. It doesn't change. The team roots me on as I step into the on deck circle, I hear my walk up music "Turn It Up" by the Wrecks and Sherry yells, "You got this, Chase! Knock it!" The whole stadium is calling out to me. I get my footing in the batter's box and eye the pitcher, ready for whatever he has to send my direction. The first pitch is way outside, ball one. The second pitch is down the middle and low, ball two. The third pitch is a curve and the bottom drops right out of it, I swing and miss. 2 - 1 count. Keep your shoes on, Chase. Chill out. You got this. The fourth pitch is on the outside corner, my favorite pitch location, and I ground it up the middle. I'm safe on first and I did my job leading off the game. Mason strikes out. Martin looks better than normal and I can hear that he's still getting the extra support from behind the plate, he's actually smiling and he's all business on the field. The first pitch to him and he knocks it out of the park. I run the bases and he's right behind me when I get to home plate, just enough time to turn around and high-five.

Sam and Sherry, "Wooooot! Go Kris!" He turns to look at them, especially Sam, and I swear it's a look I've seen between Seno and Sherry.

"Nice work, kiddo!" Sherry gives me a thumbs-up.

Seno was up to bat and I don't know what he saw, but he did

a repeat performance of Martin's hit. Home run. The score is 3-0 Seals at the end of the first inning.

I walked once, and didn't get any more hits. The 5th inning was a merry-go-round of Seals scoring 4 more on seven consecutive singles. Clay pitched a complete shut out. Seals won 7-0 and everyone was happy, well except for LA and they don't count in my world.

I hung out around the dugout signing autographs for the fans while Clay did the on field interview with Hannah. I caught Seno before he disappeared into the clubhouse and told him I need him to find me a woman, while he signed some autographs with me. The team wants to celebrate together and our regular place, the Batter Up, won't work on opening day, too many fans. So, I invite the team over to hang on my patio and tell them to bring their beach blankets. I have to get food, get beer, and clean before they get there. I quickly get out of the clubhouse and run to my truck in the garage, where I find Sherry and Sam waiting for Seno.

"You ladies need to make Seno bring you to my place. Party on the beach."

Sherry stares at me in disbelief, "There's no way you're ready for that."

Of course she'd know, "I'm making it work. Just bring your beach blankets, bikinis, towels, whatever." I stop and look at her, "Any suggestions for easy food?"

Sherry smiles at me, "Order pizza, pick up fried chicken and salads from the deli. Everyone will be happy. You're going to need a huge ice chest for how much beer you're going to get, or a few small ones and you can divide up the options—like one with sodas, water and non-alcoholic options." Sam picks up her phone and orders a bunch of pizzas. "We'll pick up the pizzas and hit the deli for you on the way to your place, but you better have a comfy place for my pregnant ass to sit."

Sam chimes in, "So, is everybody going?"

"You should come, Sam. You'll like my backyard. I think the guys are all coming and you'll need to make sure Seno doesn't decide they're going home like old married people." She nods and I'm happy they're helping me. Though I'm worried that I might get beat for letting Sherry go to the deli for me. I take off to get things ready and I'm actually kind of excited to have everybody over.

When I get to my neighborhood, I stop at the liquor mart and get three ice chests filled with ice. I buy all the beer that looks good and a few sodas and a case of water, my pick-up is loaded and I drive the few blocks home. I pick up inside and make sure the bathroom is clean. I get the ice chests unloaded and fill them with drinks. I pull out my few beach chairs and flip on the patio lights, which are Christmas lights that I hung up all around the fence and under the patio cover.

Text to Sherry - Plates? Napkins? Chips? Dip?

Text from Sherry - Already picked it all up.

Text to Sherry - Thank you

Text to Sherry - Is Seno bringing me a chick?

Of course she did. What was I thinking? She's organized and knows how to do these things. I'm still learning. No response on the chick.

A few minutes later the team starts showing up and I lead them through to the back, so they can grab a drink and relax on the beach. I hear Seno coming through the door, "Cross! Don't give my woman jobs to do, it makes more work for me." He looks around and walks through the house to the patio, leaving his armload of stuff on the picnic table and going back for more. "You need to help me unload. Sherry's going to love this place."

I go to help unload and find Martin leaning on the roof of Seno's Challenger talking to the two ladies, and very gallantly escorting the two of them into my backyard while Seno and I unload. When I get back to my patio, Sherry and Sam are getting everything set out. Everything's perfect except Seno, he's ready to skin me. "Dude, you can take her for a walk out to the ocean. Let her get her feet wet. Whatever it is that helps her relax and will make you both happy. Then come back and make a nice spot on the sand with your beach blanket. It'll be fun. All of us kind of camping out at the beach." I walk back into the house and get some music playing, I set my music library on shuffle and "Rock & Roll Queen" by The Subways starts to play. I grab a beer and mingle with my teammates. It's interesting watching how everybody responds to my bungalow and how they embrace the beach. The women enjoying the opportunity to relax on the beach while the team drinks and talks about the game. Some of the dudes split off to hang with their women. It's kind of sexy seeing these players get close to their women. All different and like they're in their own space. Some walking off hand in hand on the beach. Others stretched out together on a beach blanket, or wrapped in each other's arms. The food, beer, and people are disappearing, but nobody is actually leaving. It's cool and I think they like it here. The problem here is that there are no extra women. I want you to understand what I'm saying here, I don't have a woman and there are no single women here for me to get to know. That's making it hard to get laid tonight. I need to get laid to get the Seal Girl out of my head. I need to be able to focus.

I find Seno leaning against the outside of my patio fence with Sherry sitting in his lap and his arms wrapped around her.

"Dude, I need a chick. I keep thinking that I see the seal or the girl and neither are really there. I just need to fuck her out of my head."

"I'm not helping you get a chick when you're just trying to get laid. Call the twins or one of the baseball skanks." Seno was forceful with his words as he held Sherry tight.

"Twins?" Sherry questions.

"He's got this pair of twins that he's hooked up with a few times." I glare at Seno, thanking him for sharing.

Sherry looks at Seno, "I told you he wasn't ready. He's still just a kid. Give him a break." She turns to me, "Sweetie, you should call the twins. Twins sound like fun. Do you know their names? How can you tell them apart?"

I think I might die now. Then I realize that I can't remember their names. "The older one keeps her hair shorter and the younger one usually has her hair tied up in a ponytail."

"What if they change their hair?"

"They both have little tattoos. One has a baseball and the other has a heart. But, you'd never see those." I say and blush as I remember finding them hidden low on the inside of their hips. "I always call them Chip and Dale because they remind me of happy little chipmunks." I smile hoping that keeps me out of trouble and think that the twins might not be a bad idea. Except, I don't bring chicks to my place and I have the team over, so I can't leave. Why did I feel like I had to share all of that?

Text to Chip and Dale - Hi Ladies! Just wanted to let you know I'm back in town. ;)

But, there was no response from Chip or Dale. I move on to my other guests and enjoy the evening. I drink more than I should, but there are no girls so I figure it's safe. When I finally climb into bed, everybody's gone except for Mason who's passed out on my couch. It's a good thing tomorrow's game isn't an early one. I can't sleep. I'm horny and I'm tenting the sheets. I don't like being thought of as a kid. I know what I want. I just need to figure out how to get it. Maybe I can play that kinky shark attack in my head and handle business to get me through.

CHAPTER SIX

Chase

Over the next few weeks, I manage to stay out of trouble. The team is winning and my place has become the preferred post-game destination for early games. I'm cool with that, maybe a little flattered. I've got it down. I always have the drinks on hand and order pizza delivery from the place that does chicken, too. All I've done is play ball, work out, surf, hang with the team and spend time at home. No chicks. With the winning, and my hitting streak—it's going to stay this way. I know it's superstitious, but I never mess with a streak. I'm not going to wear dirty clothes or anything like that, but I'll keep my daily routine the same. Over the last eighteen games I've got a hit in fifteen of the games and the team has won thirteen of the games. We all know the games we won were the games with Seno behind the plate, Lucky on third, Mason at short and me in center, but none of us have said a word. That's not true, Sherry has pointed out that her lineup wins a couple of times. It happens to be the lineup that she shared with Seno while he was suspended last season. The other games had us moved around or gave one or more of us an off day. It all has to happen and every member of the team should get to play. If we can do it from first place in the division, even better.

I t's a Saturday game and we've been playing at home for over a week. I've gotten control of seeing the mascot roaming the park. I'm out on the field stretching pre-game when I hear the public address announcer's voice fill the stadium. "Welcome to Seals Stadium. My name is Kristina. I'm the gofer this year, and I'm covering as PA Announcer for Kenny who's out ill today. So, let's get this rolling!" I recognize the female voice, but I don't know why. It's different, our announcer has always been a dude. I look up to the control booth, but can't see anything. I look at the Jumbotron, and there she is. My Seal Girl, or at least my vision of the Seal Girl from my dream. She's here. She's the stadium gofer. She's probably been here all season and I just haven't seen her, or maybe I have and I'm not losing my marbles like I thought I was. I run into the clubhouse to send a quick text.

Text to Sherry - The PA girl—I think it's her. My Seal Girl.
Text from Sherry - Really? Let me see what I can find out.
Text from Sherry - Go play hard and stay focused! She isn't going anywhere.

That's what I needed to hear.

Text to Sherry - Okay :)

Kristina

I've been on a high since I found out I was covering the PA Announcer today. It's my dream job. It's the perfect media position for me. I get to announce and I'm never on camera other than an occasional shot on the big screen. The fact that it's at the baseball stadium is interesting. I know baseball very well and I'm comfortable with all the ins and outs.

I went to every high school baseball game from my sophomore year on, home games and away games. I dated a utility player and when he got switched to pitcher he asked me to be his girl. I was loyal and I loved him, even when I heard rumors about him with other girls. They were simply jealous and wanted my guy. I helped him with his homework and he knew I'd always be there to support him. We did everything together for the first time. He got a full baseball scholarship and went away to college, while I went to a school specializing in communications, media, and journalism a couple hundred miles away. He dumped me after his first homecoming week and then posted all the pictures of him partying with other women—even a couple from high school. Baseball players suck.

The worst part is that I should've learned the first time. I didn't. I love the game and jumped at the opportunity to announce at a little league championship game. I didn't consider that the volunteer coach played on his own college team. I adored that he was coaching the team of eight year olds, it endeared him to me and I let my guard down. Of course, he wasn't what I thought he was unless we were in the same zip code. Yes, he believed that he could have a different girl in every zip code. He had someone waiting for him at every away game and me at every home game, not to mention all of the little league games he coached. Well, until I realized he was also fucking a couple of the little leaguers mothers. He was into MILFs. Jerk. I love the game, but the players suck.

Baseball players aren't an option for me. I've learned my lesson. I need to stay focused on my stadium internship and achieve my goal. I can't screw up my chance to show them what I can do. I need to stay away from Chase, he can't be a distraction. He'd be my downfall. I'd end up blacklisted in baseball media and labeled a player chaser, or simply thought of as a silly girl that can't handle her own emotions. I need to remember, he's nothing but cheating baseball player number 3.

It's my first time and I thought I'd be nervous, but I'm not. This is my opportunity to shine. Stadiums need more female announcers. The Seals need me. I keep repeating this to myself as I'm directed through the process by the control booth staff. Everything is timed and typed out. It's basically reading clearly on queue. It's obvious they're making it easy for me this time and I hope they take me seriously. I read through the required greeting and emergency information on queue and wait for my next mark while the control booth runs the disabled list on the big screen to the theme of an old hospital drama. It's time for the visitor's lineup and I read through the names plainly, perfectly on my mark. I want to put my own spin on it and show them what I have to offer, but I'm told to speak clearly and not go crazy. Then I get my queue for the home team, "And now for your starting lineup as written in by your manager Butch Hopp." I'm told to stop and wait for a beat. I'm told when to announce each player in the lineup. Time is going slowly in my head and I don't want to be plain, I want them to remember me. Never waste an opportunity. I can be plain for everything else. But the lineup? No way! And I get my queue. "Leading off and playing in Center Field, number 17, Chaaasse Crooosss!" I get a thumbs up from the booth director as I'm looking out over the field and see Chase smiling up at me. No distractions. The beat between each player gets quicker and quicker, but I know its really just in my head. It's timed perfectly. I'm just falling into sequence. "Hitting second and playing at Short Stop, number 28, Jooonesss Maaaaasson!" The wait gets shorter between announcements, almost non-existent. "In the third spot, your first baseman, number 2, Krrrrisssss Maartinnn! Hitting fourth, your catcher, number 6, Rrriickkk Seeeenooo! Hitting fifth and covering the hot corner, number 13, Luuuckyyyyyy Luuuciiiiine! In the sixth spot and playing in Left Field, number 15 Caaaaaaiinn Siimmmmmms! Hitting seventh, your pitcher, number 8, Coooreeeyy Graaaaaaace! Hitting eighth, in Right Field, number 10, Maaaaark Roooock! And, hitting ninth, your second baseman, number 29, Aaandreeew Braaandt!" There's room to breathe now as I wait for my next mark and I glance around the stadium. They've got me on a small corner of the big screen and Chase Cross is focused on me, along with a portion of the crowd. He's just a guy. I don't like baseball players. I'm not interested. Clear your head! The stadium is full and buzzing, ready for the game to start. Ready for the Seals to get another win.

I follow along with the game and the scheduled announcements that are interspersed with introductions of the players coming up to bat. I have to be ready, but I get to watch the game and it's a great view of the field. I can see everything from the bases to the outfield wall and into the Seals dug out.

It's going well and I haven't caught any flack for how I announced the home team. We should all be excited for the home team.

It was a great game! Seals won 8-5. I hope I get a chance as PA Announcer again.

Chase

The game went well, and we won. I admit I was slightly distracted, but it was good to listen to her voice over the loud speaker for the whole game. Sherry was right, she isn't going anywhere. And, now I know her name—Kristina. I need to figure out how to talk to her, get her to go out with me. Yes, I need her to go on dates with me. I'm not screwing this up. Martin was the player of the day again, it seems like it's his year. While he's doing the on field interview, I walk over to the net to find Sherry.

"How do I get her to talk to me? I want to take her on a date."

Sherry stares at me like I just grew three heads, "What about the twins?"

"I haven't been with any women since we got back to San Diego. I don't want the twins or the groupies. I want my own chick. I want her. I still haven't stopped thinking about her."

"Are you sure? The twins sound like a lot of fun."

"I want to date Kristina."

"Are you allowed in the control booth or up in the press boxes?"

"I can get up there, but they might not let me in everywhere."

"Okay. We need help from somebody in the office or maybe Carter. Or, are you up for something kind of public?"

This could be bad, "Like what?"

"Well, you could go get interviewed on the field now and use the opportunity to talk to her and ask her to meet you before she leaves the stadium. It's the quickest way to get to her."

It sounds crazy, but Sherry's right. I've been waiting for her and I don't want to wait any longer. I walk over to the dugout and nod at Hannah as she finishes the interview with Martin. Hannah waves me over, "Chase, that was a great catch you made at the wall this afternoon and your hitting has been off the charts. What do you attribute your hitting success to?"

I check the control booth to see if Kristina's still there and paying any attention to me at all, "I've been more focused on the game this season, trying to do everything right to make my game better. I want to be a Seal permanently and I'm trying to make that happen. I'd like to compliment Kristina on a great job as PA Announcer today, it was nice to hear a female voice coming out of the control booth for a change." I glance up to see her sitting there stone cold and move forward with my plan. "Kristina, you should come out and celebrate with the team tonight, you earned it."

"You both were awesome today. Thanks, Chase." The camera goes off and Hannah starts talking to me, "I didn't think you guys paid any attention to people like Kristina."

I smile, "We don't notice everything. Some people stand out."

"I'm going to be talking to the control booth, would you like me to pass along a message?"

"Can you do that for me? That would be great."

"I'm happy to."

"Give Kristina my number and ask her to call me or text me,

please. Or, get her number for me?" I know I'm asking for too much, but she offered and I'm going with it. "Would it be easier to ask her to meet me somewhere in the stadium?"

Hannah looks at me like a horn is growing out of my head, "Let me call up and see what happens." Hannah turns away and makes the call. A couple minutes later, "She's not interested and she's getting ready to leave the control booth right now."

"How do I get up there? I need to talk to her." My eyes tell my story and Hannah's all in.

"Come with me." I follow her as she takes me to an elevator at the center of the stadium and uses her media card to get us to the control room door. She knocks and verifies that Kristina hasn't left yet. "This is the only door out, so unless she jumps to the field you'll see her come through that door. I'm leaving the rest to you." She winks at me as she turns and walks away, "Good luck, slugger."

I wish I had my phone, so I could text Sherry and find out what to do next. It feels like forever that I'm standing here, waiting for the door to open and see Kristina come walking out. I'm still in my dirty, game worn uniform and cleats. I probably smell like a stinky dude that's been working out in the sun all day. I know I've got dried mud on my pants and possibly a hole. My head is racing thinking about her and how it's been weeks since I've seen her. I try to ignore that she said she isn't inter- ested. Maybe she's not interested in celebrating with the team. That doesn't mean she's not interested in me. I start to get a little bit crazy and I'm afraid I'm going to do something I shouldn't, but I can't leave. I need to see her. I want to talk to her. I'd love to touch her. There's something about this chick. I get in my head and start to wonder if it's really her or if I'm making it all up in my head, as the door opens and a dark haired gentleman walks out, with Kristina a few feet behind him.

"Hi, Kristina? Can we talk?"

"We don't have anything to talk about, Chase." I can feel her voice as it touches my ears.

"Kristina, will you go out with me tomorrow night? You're welcome to join the team tonight at my place, too. Please let me take you out on a date." She stares at me blankly. "I'm sure this sounds crazy, but I've been waiting for you."

Kristina glares at me, "Why?"

"I want to get to know you and spend time together."

She stares at me blankly and I don't find any of the fire I could hear in her voice when she's announcing. I reach for her, putting one hand on each of her upper arms gently and I'm happy she doesn't back away. I gaze into her eyes and lean in, pressing my lips to her soft, full lips that are exactly as I remember except she tastes like chocolate chip cookies. I think it's her lip balm. I don't push further, I simply hold my lips to hers until it runs through my head that I'm kissing her and I'm not supposed to do that and it's basically like kissing a co-worker while you're at work. I needed to make sure it's her. I needed to know it's really her and not a chick I made up in my dreams. I pull back and search her eyes, "What do you say? Will you let me take you out?"

She stares at me blankly and I can see the no coming.

"The team is going to my house to celebrate tonight and you should join us, bring a friend if you want." I give her my address and my phone number. "See what you think and then let me take you out tomorrow night."

She's still giving me the "I really don't want to talk to you" look.

"Kristina? I don't know why you don't want to talk to me. Give me a chance. Come by my place and see who I really am." I lean in to whisper in her ear and end up smelling her hair,

"Please. I just want to talk. I promise all my clothes will stay on." I lean back and smile at her hoping for something positive.

"I'll think about it."

"At least text me, so I have your number."

"I'll think about it."

Better than a no. I give her a quick peck on the cheek and take off to the clubhouse. Hoping to see her at my place.

CHAPTER SEVEN

Kristina

I walk into my apartment and go directly to my room, tossing my bag into the corner and changing into my PJs before I plop down belly first on my bed for some alone time.

I turn the lights off and start to shut my bedroom door, but my roommate, Michelle, blocks my actions. "How was it, PA Announcer?" She asks all smiley.

"It was fantastic. It couldn't have gone better!"

"Then what's with the mood?"

"I'm not in a mood. I want to soak it all in and relax."

"I call bullshit."

I glare at her and force a breath out.

"Who is he?"

"Why does it have to be a guy?"

"Do we have to do this every time? It's always a guy."

"I don't know what you're talking about."

"Overly obstinate, nice. He must be a baseball player."

I screech at the top of my lungs and bury my face in my pillow.

"Why don't we skip to the chase?"

"How did you know?"

"Know what?"

"Chase."

"Chase Cross? Are you kidding me? The guy you jumped in the mascot costume? He's here?"

She laughs at me and the story I'm now wondering why I told her.

"Let's talk it out now, so we can drink tonight and get it out of your system."

"I don't want to talk about him."

"Oh, you like him. Like, really like him."

"Shut up!"

"You want to kiss him all over and jump his bones."

I swear I'm going to strangle her in her sleep.

"Oh, wait! You already did!"

"Stop! None of it matters! I'm not going!"

"Going where?"

Shit! "He invited me over to his place to celebrate with the team. I'm not interested and I'm not going."

"This is the hot blonde ballplayer that you humped for hours? I'd say you're interested."

"You know how I feel about baseball players. They're bad news. I don't want anything to do with any of them."

"They can't all be bad. It's mathematically improbable. So, you talked to him?"

"Yea, he was waiting for me outside the control booth."

"So, he went looking for you? Put effort into finding you? Waited for you to finish working? And asked you to come over?"

"Yea, and he asked me out on a date." I remember the kiss that accompanied the conversation.

"You kissed him!"

"I did not." I stop and look around my room smugly. "He kissed me."

"I knew it! This would be so much easier if you just told me what happened. Why do you always make me figure out the details?" She does this little dance she does when she's right. "Tell me about the kiss."

"It was just a kiss. Forget it."

"I saw your eyes glaze over when you remembered him kissing you. Your eyes don't glaze over for nothing."

"Look, it doesn't matter. I don't date or do anything else with players."

"Stop holding out and tell me about the kiss. What did he do with his hands? How did his lips feel? Was it hot?"

"You really need to get a dude."

"Whatever. Give me the deets."

"Fine, but only because I think it's the only male interaction you've had this year."

Michelle scoffs at me and waves me on for more details.

"He took me in his arms with passion and dipped me leaving me completely in his control while he kissed me senseless until I begged him to carry me off to my cubicle and have his way with me."

She glares at me and shakes her head, "Start with where his hands were."

I thought about his hands and how they felt on me. I'm reliving the warmth of his touch and the feel of his body.

"Hey!" Michelle snaps her fingers, "Out loud please."

"His hands are large and warm, slightly rough to touch yet tender in their actions." Michelle drops to my bed and makes herself comfy while she melts into my words, "He placed one hand on each of my upper arms and held me gently, making sure I was paying attention to him. His eyes," I stop as I remember the look in his eyes and gather myself.

"What about his eyes? Keep going. Tell me about the kiss!"

"His eyes were focused on me. I was the only thing that mattered and it was more than desire. Then he kissed me."

"He just kissed you, like a peck on the cheek?" she rolls her eyes at me in irritation.

"He leaned in slowly with need, completely focused on my lips. Softly placed his lips to mine and pressed against them gently, holding his lips on mine and not asking for more."

"And?"

"That's it. He asked me out again, reiterated the invitation to his house and told me I could bring a friend."

She raises her hand, "Friend!"

"I already told you I'm not going."

"Then tell me about the rest of the kiss."

"That's it. There's nothing else to tell."

"No tongue?" She looks confused. "Was it a good kiss? Did you like it?"

"No tongue." I consider the rest of her questions and realize there's no reason to keep it to myself. She already knows. She saw my eyes glaze over. I take a deep breath, "It was amazing. Electric with only his lips."

"Why aren't we going to his party?"

"I'm not interested in a baseball player. I don't need the drama. He thinks I'm that crazy seal girl. Forget it."

"Not interested doesn't mean you don't want him."

"Shut up."

"Don't you wonder what that kiss could turn into?" Michelle stops and waits for me to respond, but I hold my ground. "Get ready we're going. I'll be your DD. We need to find out more. Consider it a research mission. Hurry up!"

I stand up ready to go off on her and hold my ground, but why fight it. She's right, I want him. "Do you promise not to leave me alone with him unless I approve?"

"Of course."

"Fine. Get ready. I'm sure there will be other single guys there and you need a man."

"Whatever." She gets up like a shot, changing to go to the party.

Chase

A couple hours later the whole team is hanging out on the beach around my place, when Kristina shows up with a friend. "Hi, I'm happy you decided to come by." I smile at her and give her a quick hug. "This is my place. Food and drinks are out on the patio. We've got a bonfire going out on the sand tonight and some video games in the living room. Mostly the single dudes are playing video games and the couples are out on the patio or the beach somewhere." I walk them out back to show them where everything is and notice the couples have gotten closer to each other, all snuggling in their blankets on the sand and watching the waves while they're warmed by the fire. "I have some extra beach blankets if you would like to use them. Please make yourselves at home." I stop, focusing on Kristina, "I'd really like a chance to talk with you. I'm here when you're ready to talk or if you want someone to keep you warm out by the fire." I turn to her friend, "Hi, I'm Chase," and I reach my hand out to shake hers.

This warm girl with a sweet, innocent face takes my hand and shakes, "I'm Michelle. Nice to meet you." She smiles, "Thanks for inviting us over. So, can we play video games with the guys?"

Kristina shoots her a quick stare and I respond, "You're welcome to do whatever you like. Let me introduce you to the gamers." I lead them into the living room and point to each of my teammates as I introduce them, "This is Nathan Stray, Jones Mason, Rhett Clay, Cain Simms, Andrew Brandt, and Corey Grace. Dudes, this is my friend Kristina and her friend Michelle." Look at me getting names and making sure that everybody knows who everybody is. I realize Kristina hasn't said a word and I don't know if that's good or bad. "I can take you around and introduce you to everybody outside, too, if you'd like."

Michelle is still the only one talking, "No, this is cool. I'm comfortable with the video game crowd." She smiles awkwardly like maybe she shouldn't admit that. "Hey guys, do you mind if I join in and play?" She asks as she settles into a spot in the living room, making herself at home.

"What can I get you two ladies to drink?"

Michelle responds quickly, "An energy drink or a soda would be great, thanks."

Kristina wanders out to the patio to get food and pick a drink from the ice chests. Getting Michelle something to snack on, too. She settles in next to Michelle, quietly eating and watching everybody play games. When she finishes eating, she throws away her trash and walks off, checking things out around my bungalow and finally making her way out to the beach. I go after her when she gets to the beach, "Hey, did you want to go for a walk? May I escort you, so you aren't out here alone tonight?"

She glances up at me and we walk down the beach together, "I don't understand why you're paying so much attention to me. I told you I'm not interested. I'm only in San Diego to work for the Seals and I'm trying to get a permanent gig."

"We have that in common. I'm trying to show the Seals they want to keep me. It's an everyday thing, making myself better and proving myself," I say sincerely.

"Yea, but you're a player and I'm an intern that gets coffee for the media and fills in whenever I possibly can."

"You really did sound great as PA Announcer today."

"Thanks." Her accompanying smile makes my heart skip a beat.

I know I shouldn't ask, "Kristina, what happened between giving me hickeys all over my body and now? What made you not interested in me? I know I was drunk and that means I'm a jerk. I'm not doing that any more."

She glares at me disgusted, like I should know. "I'm just not interested. Girls can change their mind, you know."

"Maybe you're not interested in that guy who wanted you in the mascot costume. But, how about me now?" She turns away from me and starts to walk away down the beach, but I go with her because I'm not giving up that easy and it's getting late for her to be out here by herself.

She sighs derisively, "You know I was trying to walk away from you, right? I don't need you to walk on the beach."

"Yes." I touch her cheek and make her look into my eyes, "Give me a chance here, get to know the real me. We can start from the beginning and pretend we just met. I haven't had another chick in bed with me since you left me. I've only wanted you and I thought you were gone." I feel my emotions in my throat as I say the words. I did think she was gone and now that I know where she is, I'm not letting her go. I need to be clear with her, she needs to know how I feel. "I'm not just looking for sex. I can get that whenever I want it. It's more than that." I'm really not good at this shit. No wonder she left in the middle of the night. I suddenly remember her words from that night. "I remember what you whispered in my ear before you left me that night. You said 'I want you, too. You have to want me for more. You don't want me enough.' and you were probably right. But, you wanted me then. I want you for more. I want you more than anybody else. Please let me show you." My hand still touching her face, I can feel her warm breath and her pulse quicken. I want to kiss her, but I don't want to do the wrong thing. I don't want her to run off on the beach. The wind off the ocean is getting stronger and cold. I brush her hair out of her face and I can't help myself, I lean in to kiss her. She surprises me by meeting me halfway and kissing me back. Relieved, this tightness that has been growing in my chest releases. The touch of her soft full lips to mine are an adrenaline rush to my system. I try not to push the kiss forward and instead wrap my arms around her, holding her close to me. I want to keep her warm. I want to take care of her. I don't want her to leave. I have no fucking clue what I'm doing. I can't believe I'm even thinking these things. The ocean roars and the lights on my patio twinkle off in the distance. I feel her lean into my body and she pulls back quickly, as if she's burned herself. "I like it when you're close to me." My voice comes out low.

"I should go back and check on Michelle. I shouldn't have left her with a bunch of guys she doesn't know." Kristina pulls away from me and I grab her hand, intertwining my fingers with hers as we walk back to my bungalow.

The crowd has gotten smaller and the bonfire is dying down. We catch Seno wrapping a blanket around Sherry as they're getting ready to leave. "Kristina, this is Rick Seno and his wife, Sherry."

Sherry immediately reaches for Kristina and gives her hug, "It's nice to finally meet you. Chase is one of the good ones." Sherry stops and stares at me, "Give her my number." It's more of an order than a request. Seno smiles and leads his wife away to take her home.

I start to go inside and check on the other dudes, but Kristina stops me. "How does she know who I am?"

"Uh, Sherry's my buddy. She bakes for me. Seno is my best bud, so I spend some time with them." That's good enough, right? She hasn't pulled her hand away from me yet, so it must be okay so far.

We walk into my living room to find Stray and Simms sitting on the floor playing a game with headphones on, and Mason sleeping on my couch with his arms possessively around Michelle. I didn't think we were gone that long. I glance at the clock and it's been longer than I thought, but not that long. The rest of the gamer dudes are gone. I look at Mason and Michelle. They're comfortable together and kind of match. I think that maybe we could double date, that would be fun. But, my thoughts are interrupted by Kristina. I feel her start to shake and she takes her hand from mine.

"Michelle!" Obviously upset at her friend. "What are you doing? Get up. Let's go."

Hold on. What happened? It was good and now she's freaking out.

Michelle opens her eyes and looks at Kristina drowsily, "What? I don't want to go yet." Mason's arms tighten around her and she smiles. "I like it right where I am."

"You don't even know this guy. He's a player. He won't

even know your name tomorrow." Kristina throws the words at Michelle.

Michelle rolls her eyes, "You need to get over it. He's been nothing but nice to me. His hands feel amazing holding me and I like him. So, again, get over it. All of them aren't bad. Remember? Mathematically improbable?" She talks to Kristina like nobody else is in the room or she doesn't care if there is.

"Michelle, get up and let's go!"

"No, I'm staying right here. If I'm wrong, then it's my problem." Mason whispers in her ear and her face lights up, it doesn't look like she's wrong.

Mason looks to me for some help. I put my hand on Kristina's back, "Let me give you a ride home. I'm happy to do it." I want to tell her she's always welcome to stay here with me, but I don't want to push her and even if I promised that I'd just hold her—it would be pushing her. She looks at me questioning, "I didn't drink tonight. I wouldn't offer if I had." I wonder if that's what she's questioning, or if it's maybe something else. "You're always welcome to stay." I lean in to her ear and whisper, "That doesn't mean you have to stay in my bed. I have plenty of blankets and pillows, you can sleep wherever you want." I want her bad. I want her in my bed. I want her naked. I want to kiss her lips and feel her warm against my skin. What I would do to hold her like Mason is holding Michelle right now. That's what I want. What the hell is wrong with me? I just want to be with her.

Kristina goes back to Michelle, "When are you going to be ready to go home?"

Mason whispers in her ear again before she speaks, "I'm not going home tonight. Just crash here or let Chase take you home." Kristina's frustrated, but I can't help the smile on my face because both of those options work for me.

"I'm never taking you anywhere again." Kristina turns to me, "Please take me home."

I smile, "I'd be honored," I realize this means I get to know where she lives and I still don't know her phone number. I gesture to the door and follow her outside. I open the truck door for her and make sure she's in before I close the door. I'm going to drive her home. I'm going to walk her to her door. I may get to give her a kiss goodnight. I'm not going in her place. "So, where am I taking you?" She punches her address into my navigation system and doesn't say a word. "Is this going to be a silent trip? Are you mad at me or Michelle?"

I know she rolled her eyes and I didn't have to look, "Both. She ditched me to stay with a guy that she just met. You won't leave me alone."

"And, I'm not going to leave you alone. Isn't it kind of nice to be wanted?"

"Find another girl. It'll be better that way."

"First, I don't have to find chicks. Chicks find me and it requires no effort from me at all. Second, I don't want some chick. I've been turning away all the chicks. I want more and I only want you. I'm not going away."

"Whatever." She looks out the window while I drive her home.

This girl is driving me crazy. I know she kissed me back. "Will you go out to dinner and a movie or something with me tomorrow night? Or, I guess that's later tonight now."

"No."

"Can I have your phone number? How do I find you on social media, so I can message you while I'm on away trips?" Either one will work. Just give me something. Please don't leave me with nothing.

She does something on her phone and I hear mine beep. "I just followed you. I'm @Kristeeeeeena."

"And your phone number?"

"No. One thing at a time."

"How about breakfast in the morning before the game?"

"I have to be at the stadium at 9am. I'm not getting up early enough to go to breakfast."

At least that wasn't a no directed at me. "If you want to come by my place after the game, I'll be there. If we win, the team will be there and you can bring a friend with you or whatever you want. Doesn't have to be Michelle."

"I can't believe my roommate did that! She said she'd be my designated driver. That bitch!" Kristina is laughing now and I love the sound.

"Mason is a cool dude. Very chill. I haven't seen him with a single woman since he joined the team. Not that it matters. Michelle is the only one I've seen him even get close to. That probably makes him better than me, but I know what I want now and I'm not doing that shit anymore."

I pull up in front of her building and she goes to jump out, but I grab her hand, "Hold on, let me park." I find a spot quickly and hop out to go open her door.

She smiles at me, "Thanks for the ride," and turns to run into the building like she's trying to get away from me.

"Why are you running away?" I walk to her, "Let me walk you to your door." She slows down and I take her hand as we walk through the door and up the three flights of stairs to her floor. We get to her door and she unlocks it, reaching in to flip the light switch on. I want to touch her and kiss her, I haven't released her hand and she hasn't pulled it away from me. I whisper, "Kristina," sweetly in her ear as I pull her into me for a hug. She reaches her arms up around my neck and runs her fingers through my hair. I'm trying to be on good behavior and her mixed signals are confusing. I want to ask for permission to kiss her, but a kiss with permission isn't the same. She's gazing up at me and I can't help myself when I see those eyes looking at me. I lean down to her and press my lips to hers repeatedly, sweetly giving her lower lip a suck and holding her head with both hands. I want to inhale her into me. I want to be closer to her. I want to taste her. I lick her lips and she separates them for me like an invitation. I touch the tip of my tongue to hers and wait for her reaction before going further. She opens further and sucks on my tongue. I move my hands to her back and splay them across her, while I hold her to me. I don't want the kiss to end and my tongue dances with hers while I soak it all in. She's not pulling away from me and shows no signs of running. I hear her little whimper as I feel her lean into me and I feel like I can die now. She tries to pull me with her into her apartment, but I stop myself at the door, "I'm not having sex with you until after we've been on at least a few dates. It needs to be more with you and I want you to know that I want you enough. I want you to know you're special to me." I close my eyes because it's one of the hardest things I've done. I want to go in her apartment and fuck her senseless. I want her legs wrapped around me. I know she'd be tight and slick around my hard dick. My voice goes deep and raspy, "And, trust me, I want to. Very few things I want more than that right now." My head is spinning and I want to go in her apartment and see what happens.

"Tell me what you want more." Now she decides to talk.

I don't even think, I just spill, "I want your phone number. I want you to go out with me. I want you to be my chick. I want to know why you don't want me anymore. I want to hold you and maybe kiss you more." She puts her finger to my lips, so I'll quit talking.

"I never said I don't want you." She goes up on her tiptoes and gives me a quick kiss. "Goodnight, Chase." She slides into her apartment and closes the door, turning the lock behind her.

My phone beeps as I'm walking down the stairs.

From @Kristeeeeeena - Thank you for the ride home :)
To @Kristeeeeeena - You're welcome. Maybe you'll have a thank you kiss for me next time I see you?
From @Kristeeeeeena - It's waiting for you now, if you want to come back and get it ;)

I'm a fool, but I turn around and go back to her apartment. I find her changed into her tank top and boxers with the sunglasses on them, hanging out at her door. She smiles as soon as she sees me, like she wasn't sure I'd come back. The sight of her in the tank top and boxers brings back memories of our night in Arizona. I see visions of her all over my body, kissing, licking, sucking, and I can almost feel it. When I'm in her reach, she grabs me and pulls me into her apartment, locking the door behind me. She takes me to her bedroom, climbs into bed and holds the blanket up, inviting me to join her. I have will power, but I don't know if I have enough strength for this. Those short boxers with the easy access and her tits bouncing around all over.

"I came back for the kiss." I say as I take in the view of her lying in her bed and inviting me in.

"The kiss is here, you should come and get it."

"You make me want more." I walk over to the other side of the bed and lean over her, planting a kiss on her with passion and claiming her as mine. I'm crazy hot and my dick is hard, yelling at me to just fuck her. I suck on her lips and push my tongue into her mouth over and over as if it was my dick in her sex. I keep kissing her and dial it back to show her how much I want her. I kiss her tenderly with desire. I stand up. "Goodnight." I turn around and leave. Ignoring the noises my phone is making until I get all the way to my truck.

From @Kristeeeeeena - I can't believe you left.

From @Kristeeeeeena - I don't get it.

From @Kristeeeeeena - Just fuck me and get me out of your system.

From @Kristeeeeeena - Then you can leave me alone.

To @Kristeeeeeena - Not going to fuck you out of my system.

To @Kristeeeeeena - That's not possible.

To @Kristeeeeeena - I want you and I want more.

To @Kristeeeeeena - Goodnight, beautiful.

I get home to find Mason and Michelle still sleeping on my couch, but everyone else is gone, the party has been cleaned up and the house is locked up. I go to bed and fall asleep happy.

CHAPTER EIGHT

Kristina

I'm not a morning person and my phone is going off like crazy much too early. I've gotten at least three text messages, that I have chosen to at least attempt to sleep through and now my phone is ringing. I have to open my eyes and answer it, it might be work. I reach for my phone while I struggle to open my eyes and expose my relaxed sleep state to daylight. It wasn't a good night for sleep. I don't sleep well as a general rule, but it's worse when I'm home alone. It's only 7:00am and I'm ready to scream at whoever is calling me this early, but it's the stadium.

"Good morning!" I answer bright and cheery and not at all like I'm ready to strangle the person on the other end of the phone.

"Hi, we'd like you to fill the PA Announcer position again today," the human resources representative for the stadium states politely.

"Absolutely, I'd love to!" It's confirmation that I did a good job.

"Can you come in early enough to get your regular tasks done before the game?"

I pinch my eyes closed as tight as I can and suck it up, because I want to be the announcer, "I'm happy to do it. I'll be there in time to get everything set for the broadcasters before the game starts. Thanks for giving me another shot in the booth."

"You deserve it. Keep showing us what you've got. Thank you," he hangs up.

I check my texts and Michelle has been texting me for the last hour.

Text from GamerGirlM - Are you up yet?

Text from GamerGirlM - Of course not. Too early for you.

Text from GamerGirlM - Wake up!

Text from GamerGirlM - Are you still mad at me?

Text to GamerGirlM - What? You need me to pick you up?

Text to GamerGirlM - Jerk ballplayer ditch you after he got his?

Text from GamerGirlM - Get over yourself

Text from GamerGirlM - We're going to breakfast. Want to go?

I stop and think to myself, I'm up anyway and I have to go to work early.

Text to GamerGirlM - I'm PA Announcer again today.

Text to GamerGirlM - I'll be by if I have enough time

Text from GamerGirlM - Can you hear my eyes rolling?

Text from GamerGirlM - I'll see you at breakfast. Jones is asking Chase to go, too.

Text to GamerGirlM - Whatever

Text from GamerGirlM - You know you want him

Another text pops through with a string of emojis including a bunch of hearts and an eggplant. I respond with an eyeroll emoji and toss my phone to the side as I get ready for my day.

I find myself paying more attention to my appearance than normal. Why? I don't even know if Chase will be at breakfast. It must be for work. Dress to impress, though I don't think the control booth crew will appreciate my perfect fitting jeans as much as the outfielder. I don't want to date or do anything else with a baseball player. I guess there's an exception to every rule. Michelle's logic isn't wrong, they can't all be bad.

Driving to breakfast the radio plays his walk-up song and I can't help but think about him. Damn it! I want to see him.

Chase

Mason wakes me up early, "Cross, we're going to get breakfast before stadium time. You want to go with us?"

"No, I'm cool. Thanks."

"Kristina might be meeting us."

"No, dude, she said she had to be at the stadium early when I asked her last night."

"Schedule changed. She's PA Announcer again today."

I'm torn because I don't want to be the third wheel when she doesn't show up and I want to take her on a real date, not just hang out. I'm hungry. "Okay, I'm hungry now that I'm awake." I get ready quickly and we stop at the Yolk on the way to the stadium. We walk in to find Seno and Sherry, already sitting there eating their breakfast. This place is always good to us and makes sure to get us tables quick on early game days like today. Michelle is cool, doesn't seem crazy at all and definitely not a player chaser. Mason with a chick is different, he's always respectful and his midwest upbringing shows. But, with a girl, I don't know, it's like she deserves and gets all of his attention, almost like she's on a pedestal for him to look up at and desire. I can see it's working for him with Michelle. I wonder if Kristina will show up for breakfast and I go with the flow, ordering and talking with Mason. I really want to talk to Sherry and Seno for advice, but it's not the place. This girl has me confused.

I walk over to Seno's table, "Dude, want a ride today? I'll pick you up after breakfast. I need to talk."

"Sure. Come by and get me."

But, Sherry wants to run with it, "What's up?"

"I don't know. This chick has me confused. She won't give me her phone number. She won't go on a date with me. But, when I kiss her she meets my kiss and kisses me back. When I drove her home last night she called me back to her apartment and dragged me into her bedroom, wanting me to get in bed with her. I left and she messaged me asking why I didn't fuck her so I could get her out of my system. I told her I want her for more and it's not possible to fuck her out of my system. I don't get it."

Sherry looks at me and smiles, "And, she's here." She waves at her from across the restaurant. Kristina scowls at Michelle and walks right by her table without stopping, sliding

69

in next to me at the Seno's table. "Hey, Kristina. Did Chase give you my number?"

"No." Kristina trades numbers with Sherry.

"So, Sherry can have your number and I can't?" I protest.

"That's right." Kristina smiles, looks at Sherry and laughs, "I don't give my number to boys. I don't travel with the team and I'm happy to help you while the team is away."

"I appreciate that. We're not looking forward to that. I always travel with Rick and we never spend a night apart." Sherry confesses her dread.

"I know, I see you at the stadium early and for every game. It'll be an adjustment, but well worth it." Kristina states supportively.

The waitress brings the food over to me and we leave Mason some private time with his chick. I like that Kristina and Sherry get along. That should help me.

Sherry looks directly at Kristina, "So, what do you think about our boy here?" Gesturing to me as I pound my head into the tabletop.

"Sherry, we don't need to talk about this." I look to her pleading.

Kristina starts in, "He's a great baseball player. He's a good kisser. He doesn't listen well and I think he has a seal fetish."

Sherry continues on, "I don't know about the kissing, but the seal fetish is interesting. I think he associates the seal with you, so technically he can't stop thinking about you. I haven't experienced the not listening."

They keep talking like I'm not right there listening to everything they say. Seno is taking it all in and enjoying that it's not him they're talking about.

"I keep telling him to leave me alone and he blatantly refuses. I ask him to spend the night with me and he leaves. I decline a date and tell him I'm not giving him my phone number, but he keeps asking for both. Do you think he's mentally impaired?"

"Well, he's male." They both laugh like this is simply a fact. "I think he hears you and he's just persistent. Maybe you should try telling him yes to a date and see what happens."

"Maybe, but I don't want to lead him on and it's weird after Arizona. I know he's thinking of me as that drunk girl in the mascot costume that left him covered in hickeys. I don't want to be thought of like that. That's the only time I've ever done anything like that. I never get drunk. I'm not that girl and I know that's what he expects."

I look straight at her ready to tell her she's wrong, but Sherry stops me. "I don't think that's true. He didn't even remember the night, he was so hungover the next morning. You should've seen his face when he found the tail piece of the seal costume!" Kristina cocked her head to the side, like she was listening. "You should give him a chance. Don't worry about leading him on. He's a big boy and he can handle himself. I'll tell you, spending time with a professional baseball player isn't what you think and you won't want it to be any different once you've done it."

Kristina turns toward me and examines me. She turns back to Sherry, "I'll think about it."

The whole time they're talking, Kristina is eating my breakfast like it's her own. She gets up to leave and I walk her out to her car. My body humming just being near her. "I heard you're PA Announcer again today."

"Yes! I love it. I wish they'd hire me to the position permanently." Kristina gets a daydreaming look at the thought.

"Good luck. I know you'll do great today. I'll be listening to your voice while I'm playing. Can I see you after the game?"

"I might come by if you win today." I have my hands in my pockets, to keep my hands to myself. But, she doesn't. She reaches her arms up around my neck and goes up on tiptoes to kiss me. She presses her lips to mine softly and holds them there for what feels like a long time, but I know it's only a couple of minutes at the most. She pulls back and I see her drag her teeth over her lower lip as she looks at my mouth.

She turns to leave and I can't help myself. I grab her and hold her against me. I bend down and kiss her neck at her ear, breathing in her scent. "I know you want me, too. Stop fighting it. Give us a chance, Kristina." I kiss her on the lips with the intent of things that I can't even understand myself and turn away as I walk back into the restaurant. I look out to the parking lot when I sit down at the table and see that she's still standing there.

To @Kristeeeeeena - Are you okay? I see you standing there in the parking lot.
From @Kristeeeeeena - No. I need another kiss.

I smile uncontrollably and get up, running back out to the parking lot. She's watching me run toward her with a huge grin. I take her in my arms and swing her around, holding her up to my lips. I kiss her, letting her know how much I want her, it's almost a need. Fuck, I need her. I need to have her. Her lips are so soft and giving, she tastes like my waffles. Out of breath, I set her back on the ground, "We can kiss for hours after the game."

She gets in her car, "I'm still not giving you my number," and she drives away.

I sit back down with the Senos and eat the remains of my

breakfast while Seno chuckles and Sherry provides commentary.

"Well folks, she came and ate most of his breakfast. Then she kissed him. Then she called him to the parking lot wanting another kiss. But, she's not giving up the digits and won't go out with him. The only hope he has is if the team wins today, she might visit. I'd say it's a pretty good bet, what do you think Mr. Seno?"

Seno nods, "We need to make it a win for Cross today, so he can make out later. You should send her flowers or a note or something, so she thinks about you."

"I was thinking about changing my walk up song, like a message for her."

"I like that, too. You could do both. Maybe tie them together." Seno continues.

"Okay, take me home so you two can have some guy talk. I can't handle this right now." Sherry has had enough.

CHAPTER NINE

Kristina

Am I truly considering Chase Cross as a potential boyfriend? He's everything that I avoid. I can't be in the same room or the same parking lot with him and maintain control. And his kiss! It's like potato chips, I can't have just one. Or, maybe M&M's, except I melt in his hands when he kisses me. I need to stay away from him, but, what if I don't want to? His fucking lips! One touch and I'm willing to give him anything. Distance is the answer. How am I going to do that when we work at the same place?

Can I be with a baseball player? My body wants to. I can't let my head give in.

I'm sitting in my car in the stadium employee parking lot and don't remember how I got here. All I can remember is how his lips feel pressed to mine, soft and warm. The happy grin he had when I wanted another kiss and how fast he ran to me, like he was stealing second. When he kisses me, I'm the only thing in his world, and his job is to please me and protect me. He takes my breath away with his touch. I wish I had his confidence. He believes we belong together. He must be crazy.

Chase

Mason catches me and Seno walking into the clubhouse, "Michelle knows absolutely nothing about baseball. I'm fine with it, but she wants to learn about the game. I need help with this. What do I do?"

Seno and I reply at the same time, "Sherry."

"Get her the seat next to Sherry for a few games and she'll know more about baseball than you do." Seno smiles, "Make sure both of them know what you're doing and tell Michelle to check with Sherry for what is acceptable food to eat around her that day. Garlic fries have been making her nauseated the last few days."

"She wants to come to the game today and I need to get her a ticket."

The three of us invade Carter's office. "I need a ticket to the game today for my girl and I want her to sit next to Sherry," Mason starts.

"It's a day game, so she's going to need a cap. Get her the game day cap and have Mason and his number put on it for her. While you're at it, have a game day cap made up with Cross and his number on it, too, and have it delivered to Kristina in the control booth. Oh, and take Sherry some chocolate soft serve ice cream in one of those little helmets and a bottle of water around the fifth inning please." Seno takes control of the situation.

"And, can you take Kristina some flowers with the cap

please? I want to write a note to put with it, if you can. I want to change my walk up song, too."

"Hold on... Two caps, a ticket for the game, ice cream, water, flowers and change a walk up song. Is that everything?" Carter inspects the trio curiously.

Mason adds, "Can you get my girl a shirt with my name and number, too? And, do you think she can get in early to watch BP with Sherry?"

"No BP today, but I'll get her added to the early entry list. What's the new walk up song?"

"'I Want to Hold Your Hand' by the Beatles." I find a piece of paper and a pen, to write a quick note.

Kristina,

Hope you like the flowers. Listen for my walk up song, changing it for you. Please come by later, I have kisses waiting for you.

Chase

I get it folded up and sealed in an envelope, leaving it for Carter to deliver with the flowers and cap.

"Alright, I'll get it handled. Now, get out of here so I can get working on it all." Carter evicts us back to the clubhouse and we all walk away satisfied with ourselves.

I walk out of the dugout to warm up before the game, earlier than usual because there's no batting practice today. Some of the team have been in the batting cages down in the stadium, but I need to get outside. I need to get some extra stretch time in and run some sprints, plus I want to see what everything looks like on the social side of things. Sherry and Michelle are sitting behind home plate all chummy and talking. Sherry looks excited, so they're probably talking baseball. Michelle is proudly sporting a new baseball cap and a Seals shirt. I can't see the back, but I know she's marked with Mason. I look to the control booth wondering what Carter managed to get done for me and there's a bright colored bouquet of flowers laying on the desktop near the microphone, but no cap and no Kristina. The Jumbotron is on an automatic slide rotation and there's music playing, but no announcements yet. I check the time and scan the stadium, hoping for a glimpse of Kristina. I want her to be wearing her cap with my name on it as proudly as Michelle's wearing Mason's, but I never know how she's going to respond to things. She might hate it or not wear hats.

I hear a female yelling, "Jack ass!"

I hear Sherry calling me, "Chase!"

I turn to run over to Sherry and she's pointing to Kristina, so I change course for her. I'm happy that she's looking for me, but then...

Kristina

"Jack ass!" I can't believe he had flowers and a cap with his number on it left in the control booth for me. In the control booth! I've worked so hard for this and he's going to ruin it for me! Why can't he leave me alone? Damn it! The flowers are gorgeous and I want to wear his cap!

"What the hell are you doing? You know I'm trying to land a permanent gig here and you go sending me things to the control booth! Don't embarrass me! Don't make me look like a fool or a player chaser!" How many times do I need to tell him no? Why can't he fuck me out of his system and be done with me? Or just leave me alone!

He stands there in all his baseball player hotness, staring at me without a response. I'm entranced by his shining light green eyes and watch them darken as I grab his jersey and pull him to me. I yell at myself internally as I kiss him and feel him smile against my lips. What the hell am I doing? I can't help myself. I hate baseball players! I press my lips against his harder, needing more and needing to have him. My heart beats faster and I feel his energy run through me, pushing me to give him more. I slide my tongue into his mouth, needing a taste of him. Damn it! What am I doing! Baseball players suck! I break the connection and try to hide that I'm breathing hard. I whisper in his ear, "Thank you." And as I'm running through the stands so I can get to the control booth on time, I yell back at him, "Now go win, jerk!"

Chase

Her lips were on me like never before, she sent a new electricity running through my body and I feel like I can do anything. I've never been so happy to be a jack ass and a jerk and get shoved away.

I turn back to the field and walk to Sherry and Michelle. They're laughing and Sherry points at me, so I question my decision to go talk to them. "Hello, ladies."

Sherry can't maintain herself, "It looked like she just went off on you, then took a kiss and shoved you away, but I couldn't hear anything other than the jack ass part in the beginning."

"She did say thank you and told me to win, too." I smile at

the whole interaction. "She doesn't want me to have things delivered to her in the control booth." If she's going to kiss me like that when she gets mad at me, I'm going to keep pissing her off. I look to the control booth and see Kristina sitting there now, reading the note with her flowers while she wears the cap with my number on it backwards with the head-phones over the top. It's perfect, even if all she wants to do is kiss me.

The rest of the team comes out for warm up. Mason goes directly to Michelle and I hear giggling. Everything else is the way it's supposed to be, other than my distraction of Kristina as PA Announcer and that really isn't a distraction—I like to hear her voice. She announces the lineup and I love the way she says my name. I know she does all of them the same, but mine feels different to me. She reads through all of the pre-game and we take the field.

I'm first at bat for the Seals and as I stand in the on deck circle swinging my bat I hear "I Want to Hold Your Hand" start to play, my new walk up song. The other team is still throwing the ball around the field and I take the opportunity to glance up at Kristina and see if she gets it. It's pretty straight forward. It's one of the first things you do when you meet someone or start dating someone—hold their hand. I've managed it a couple of times with Kristina and I love the way her hand feels in mine with our fingers locked together. Her skin is soft and while she's not delicate, her hands and fingers are feminine and slender. More so in my large man hands that have been beaten up by the sun and the game. When I hold her hand, she doesn't pull it away from me. It's like when we kiss, she meets me halfway. Kristina's smiling up in the control booth, but I don't know if that's my walk up music or her happy to be the PA Announcer again today.

"Chase," Sherry gets my attention, "Did you change your walk up song on purpose?"

"Yea," I think to myself that at least Sherry noticed, "What do you think?"

"I like it and it's very sweet." She gives me a happy nod of approval.

"I hope Kristina feels the same way." I look at Michelle for feedback since she's Kristina's friend and roommate, but all I get is a shoulder shrug.

I step up to the plate, digging my cleats into the clay and I hear her announce my name. Her voice wasn't as stable as it had been and I want to think that I could detect some emotion there, but it could be wishful thinking. The first pitch comes in low, then the second is outside, the third was high and inside causing me to lean back quickly to avoid getting hit by the wild 96 mile per hour fastball. That's when it happened. I heard the audible gasp come over the loud speakers throughout the park. I knew it was her. I knew I was in trouble because she would think that she'd messed up her opportunity for a permanent gig and it's my fault. I don't want to make things hard for her, but her gasp is proof that she cares. It means the ball getting that close to me scared her or worried her. While I don't want to scare her or worry her, I'm warm all over knowing how she feels about me. I knew she wanted me. I step out of the batters box to get my head straight and swing the bat a couple times, then get right back in there ready to get on base. I hear Sherry cheering for me and Michelle is yelling, too. The next pitch is low and I walk to first base without even swinging my bat.

Mason is up to bat next and just slams the ball on the very first pitch, hitting a home run to the left field upper deck. I think it's his first homer of the season. It's gotta be Michelle and she's out of her seat, yelling at the top of her lungs, "Go JJ!" and clapping. I cross home plate and wait for Mason to catch up with me, celebrating with him as he jumps on home plate. 2-0 Seals. Mason is focused on Michelle, I can see them smiling at each other and flirting as we walk back to the dugout.

Mason got a hit at each of his at bats, scoring three times and bringing three of his teammates home. Final score 10-3 Seals. The other two runs were home runs from Martin and Seno with Mason on base. I wasn't much help at the plate today, but I was all over the outfield like a dog playing fetch and had to climb the outfield wall to keep a ball from getting out of the park.

The way Mason hit today, you'd think he's a new man. They slept on my couch last night, there's no way he got laid. Then again, maybe he's being smart. I should probably take a lesson. Hannah grabbed him for the on field interview and I check to see if Kristina is still in the control booth while Seno walks over to the net checking on his woman. Michelle's eyes are locked on Mason doing the interview, I guess it would be different if you'd never been to a game before. Playing the game and giving interviews are part of the day for us, typically nothing special. Kristina's still sitting at the microphone, watching the interview. She must not be done announcing yet. I wave at her and smile, but she doesn't acknowledge me. I know she wants to kiss me. Even if she's mad, she wants to kiss me. I go to the clubhouse to get cleaned up and change. It's early and the team is coming over. I want to talk to Kristina and make sure she's coming over, but I don't want to appear needy. I guess it's my turn though, she did come find me to yell at me and kiss me before the game. Is it a problem that thinking of her yelling at me makes me happy? I must be a sick puppy.

To @Kristeeeeeena - Will you go out with me?

From @Kristeeeeeena - Give it up

To @Kristeeeeeena - Can I have your phone number?

From @Kristeeeeeena - Why would I give you my phone number?

From @Kristeeeeeena - You sent me gifts to the control booth! Jerk!

From @Kristeeeeeena - I totally screwed up today and it's your fault!

I wonder if her complaints that no other chick would complain about are some type of foreplay. I can't help myself.

To @Kristeeeeeena - You should give me your number, so you can kiss me sooner.

To @Kristeeeeeena - Phone number = quicker access

To @Kristeeeeeena - How did I screw you up?

I know, the gasp at the high and inside wild fastball. I want her to say it. I wait and get no response.

To @Kristeeeeeena - When you kiss me, I feel like
I've won.
To @Kristeeeeeena - Your lips are soft and you taste
sweet.
To @Kristeeeeeena - I want to hold your hand.
To @Kristeeeeeena - I want to hold you with a blanket by
the bonfire.
To @Kristeeeeeena - Your hand just feels right when our
fingers are locked together.
To @Kristeeeeeena - Please come over. You can stay over
if you want to.
To @Kristeeeeeena - We can go surfing in the morning.
To @Kristeeeeeena - Whatever you want.

I'm ready to apologize for whatever I did to screw her up and I don't think I did anything. Why won't she respond? Twelve messages in a row. Shit, I look like a stalker. What am I thinking? I can't think straight with this chick. I shove my phone in my pocket and go home to get ready for the team. I don't want to play games with her. I want her. I hope she comes to find me.

CHAPTER TEN

Kristina

I refuse to lose what I've worked so hard for when I'm this close. I've replayed my reaction to Chase almost getting hit by the ball over and over in my head. Every time the shock and concern gets me. Every time I gasp louder than I did live in the game. I've watched the video replay and it looked worse from my vantage point, like it almost hit his chin. In reality, it was almost straight across the top of the Seals lettering on the chest of his jersey. Not much difference, but the difference of a potentially life altering injury and it didn't stop him. I don't want to be known as the announcer that can't control her emotions or isn't professional. This is my first big break and I can't screw it up. I can't afford the wrong reputation. I don't have any other professional experience to prove who I really am.

I really am this girl that can't help but be affected by the man she wants getting hit by the ball or injured in the game. It's expected when you care about someone. I don't have the luxury to show it and get where I want to be professionally.

Baseball players are out for me. I need to stay away from him. If I'm outside of his atmospheric pull, I'm able to maintain my composure. That's it. No going to his house. I need to keep my distance.

I get home and change into my PJs, plopping down on my bed. I have the apartment to myself and leave the lights off to watch the replay of the game on my laptop, fast forwarding through and listening to my announcements. I get distracted and watch Chase's plays, replaying them and admiring his skill in the game. He doesn't get shook by anything. He knows exactly what he needs to do and he does it dependably. He doesn't let his team down. I also notice the way he stands with a masculine authority and flexes his muscles while he's at bat. The way his legs stretch his pants as he runs to catch the ball. How his helmet flies off his head as he's running the bases because of his sheer speed and dedication to winning the game. I need to stay away from him. I still want him.

Text from GamerGirlM - Why aren't you here yet?

Text from GamerGirlM - Chase has been watching for you.

Text to GamerGirlM - Not going.

Text from GamerGirlM - What? Why not?

Text to GamerGirlM - It's better this way.

Text from GamerGirlM - He's a good guy. Not a jerk player.

I know she's right and that's why I need to stay away. I can't get involved with someone real. I knew he was real. I should've fucked him in Arizona and forgot about it. Damn it! I want him.

Text to GamerGirlM - It's a work thing. I need to focus.

Text from GamerGirlM - Don't wait too long.

Text from GamerGirlM - He may be the one.

Text to GamerGirlM - That's stupid. That's not real.

Text from GamerGirlM - I was there when you got home that night in Arizona.

Text from GamerGirlM - You told me why you didn't have sex with him then.

Text from GamerGirlM - I know the truth.

Text from GamerGirlM - Were you lying to me then or are you lying to me now?

I love Michelle, but sometimes it would be nice to have a best friend that hadn't been my roommate since we got out of high school and that couldn't read me like a book because we've known each other for so long. I need to walk away from Chase.

Chase

The team is relaxing on the sand and the waves are raging. Kristina hasn't shown up and I haven't gotten any messages from her. I need to surf and get it out of my system. I grab my board and head toward the water, stopping just short to watch the waves. I'm familiar with the surf break. I've spent hundreds of hours floating on my board here waiting for my wave and weeks sitting on the sand observing. I swim out, diving into the waves with my surfboard. I feel alive. The ocean always makes things better, even if it's only a temporary distraction. I swim out at least a hundred yards and lay flat on my board watching the surf as it rolls in, waiting patiently. Floating calm on the raging ocean and letting the waves break, while they allow me to ride them. The waves are coming in sets of six and about every other set has my wave. I catch a few rides in, making it up to my feet each time and needing the rush of adrenaline. It's addictive, I immediately turn around and swim back out for more.

I walk up to my bungalow, dripping wet and cold. I observe the couples snuggling at the bonfire, wondering why it can't be like that for me. Why can't Kristina be here? Or, maybe she could message me. Anything would be nice. I watch Mason with his arms around Michelle as I approach, "Anything from your roommate?"

"Sorry, she's not coming."

"Did she say why?"

"She said she can't be with you and get the job she wants, that it's better this way." Michelle leans her head to the side with kind eyes, "I'm sorry. I tried to get her here. I'll keep trying. I think she's just upset today and I'm hoping she'll come around for you. I believe you're a good guy."

"This morning she was kissing me and wanting to kiss me more. I don't get it." I shake my head as I walk off to shower.

Chase

After everyone has gone home, I climb in bed and lie there thinking about Kristina. Not that different from the rest of the evening when I was hoping she'd show up. I'm not crazy. I know she wanted to kiss me this morning. She called me to the parking lot because she wanted another kiss and I'll never forget that feeling. I was happy in a new way, comfortable with her as I swung her around and kissed her. I know she was happy, too. I heard her need for me in her voice, and her joy when I had her in my arms. Shit, I've never felt so good as when she planted that kiss on me at the stadium today—even if I was a jerk and an asshole. I need to make her think about me.

To @Kristeeeeeena - Sorry you couldn't make it tonight.
To @Kristeeeeeena - Goodnight

I didn't think I'd get a response, but a reply popped through immediately.

From @Kristeeeeeena - Goodnight

I don't understand this chick.

To @Kristeeeeeena - I was thinking about you.
To @Kristeeeeeena - Wish you would've come over.
From @Kristeeeeeena - It's better if I don't.
To @Kristeeeeeena - How's it better not seeing each other and not kissing each other?

I'm frustrated and turn the sound on my phone off before she can reply. I wish she were here with me and remember her kiss as I fall asleep.

Kristina

I want to be kissing him right now, but I can't let myself get lost in his world. He's not good for me. I have a goal and I'm going for it. I need to stay away from him. He just makes things harder. Chase is a distraction I don't need. I need to focus on the gig I want, not the baseball player I want nothing to do with.

To @RookCross - You're bad for me.

I expect a quick response, but there's not one. He's not trying to change my mind. He's not saying anything. He's gone. "He's already off with another woman!" I yell out and throw my journal against the wall. "Damn it!" I kick the blankets off my bed and pace around talking to myself. "I knew it! Baseball players suck!"

"Excuse me, I'm a baseball player," I hear through the wall.

Shit! I didn't know they were here. "Michelle! Do you have a guy in your room?"

"We're playing in my room."

"What?" She's never had a guy over before.

"Not like that. Perv." Michelle calls back through the wall.

"Baseball players don't suck." Mason adds to the conversation and I hear giggling. I can only imagine the conversation about what else he would do to make up for not sucking.

I shake my head, "I can't believe you have a guy over in bed with you."

"I'm an adult and I can do whatever I want, mother."

"You could've at least given me a heads up before you brought your boy toy over for a romp. Why didn't you go to his place? I'm sure he's got a nice ball player bachelor pad." I joke, continuing the conversation through the wall. I hope she gets laid.

Mason complains, "Hey, you're messing with our mojo here."

Michelle responds to him, "Just put it on pause." I hear her bedroom door open and her walking toward my bedroom. "Are you decent? I'm coming in there either way." My door opens and there stands Michelle with the coolest wireless gaming headphones I've ever seen wrapped around her neck, fully dressed in leggings and a Seals T-shirt.

"What the?" I look at her confused.

She rolls her eyes at me, "Where do you think we were? We were at his place earlier."

"Then why are you here now? I'm sure his place is better."

"He doesn't have my gaming machine. I want to play my games, not his." She turns to leave, but changes her mind. "Why were you throwing shit? What did you do? It's about him. It's always a guy. Why didn't you just go to the party?"

"I told him he's bad for me and he didn't respond. He's probably busy with another girl. No time for me."

"You're a nut job! What do you expect? You keep telling him to leave you alone. He does what you want and you freak out. We all saw you kissing him. You were happy and wanted more. Why wouldn't you want more? Chase is fuckin' hot."

Mason interrupts, "Hello. Current guy you're dating is right here in the other room. Also a baseball player."

"I know, Mase. You're hot, too. And, you smell good." Michelle closes her eyes and continues, "You can't have it both ways. He wants you." She turns to the wall, "Mase, any chance Cross is with another girl tonight?"

He groans, "I'm sure there's one available and trying to get his attention."

"Not helping," she yells back at him.

"He's not into that anymore. I haven't seen him so much as call another woman."

I add on, "So, you're a guy, right?"

He groans, "Yes."

"Why wouldn't he respond to me?"

"Maybe he hasn't seen your message. Maybe you should call him or actually go to his house when he invites you if you want to talk to him instead of staying home. Fuck, maybe he's sleeping."

Michelle looks at me, "He could be sleeping. You need to figure this shit out. Mase is right and Chase won't wait forever." She stops, but gets the last word as she walks out of my room, "Love you to the moon, Kristina, but he's a good guy and he shouldn't have to wait. Figure it out."

"Thank you, Michelle," Mason calls out proudly.

She whispers to me, "I was referring to Chase." Then louder while shaking her head, "I know, I'll be right there."

"Hey, wait! What's up with you and Mason?" I whisper, "Did you get laid?"

"No! We just met. Perv!" She slams my door behind her and goes back to her room.

I grab my phone to look for a response from Chase, but there's still nothing. Maybe Mason is right. I should sleep, too.

To @GamerGirlM - Did he kiss you yet? Or anything?
From @GamerGirlM - He's sweet and respectful.
From @GamerGirlM - Not an intrusive perv like you.
From @GamerGirlM - Details later... when there are some.

I laugh out loud and Michelle yells through the wall, "Shut up! You could be getting laid if you wanted."

I'm not sure she's right. Chase wants to date me and kiss me. He's turned me down for sex. It doesn't matter. He's bad for my focus and I need to focus on my goal. If he doesn't wait, then he isn't the right one. Listen to me! He's not the right one. Baseball players are never the right one.

CHAPTER ELEVEN

Chase

I wake up to a missed call and texts from Mason.

Text from Mason - Dude! Where are you? Going to breakfast.
Text from Mason - Kristina is with us.
Text from Mason - She was freaking out about you not responding to her message last night.

I check my twitter.

From @ Kristeeeeena - You're bad for me.

Text to Mason - Thanks for the heads up.

Text to Mason - Fuck! How am I bad for her?

Text from Mason - I don't get that girl. She was watching for you at breakfast and waiting for your response last night.

Text to Mason - I don't get her either.

To @Kristeeeeena - Good morning. :)

To @Kristeeeeena - Sorry I missed our breakfast date.

To @Kristeeeeena - I was sleeping and my sound was off.

To @Kristeeeeena - Let me make it up to you over late night dessert at the diner after the game tonight?

From @Kristeeeeena - I don't think it's a good idea.

To @Kristeeeeena - Okay

Text to Carter - Hey Carter! Is Kristina PA Announcer again today?

Text from Carter - Yes.

Text to Carter - Perfect. Can you deliver the game day color cap with my number on it to her in the control booth please? I want her to match the team and feel special.

Text from Carter - No problem.

Text to Carter: Can you take her one of those plush seals with the jersey on it, too? Please. The larger one?

Text from Carter - I'll take care of it.

If I have to piss her off to get her to come find me and kiss me. I can be the jerk. Now I simply wait for her to get mad.

Kristina

What doesn't he understand about not sending me things to the control booth? I thought I was very clear. Maybe he really is mentally impaired! I have a goal here and he's getting in the way. He makes me look like a girl instead of an announcer. His truck is in the player's garage. I know he's here. He's not on the field or anywhere I have access to. I'm going to rip him a new one! Jerk!

Chase

When I get to the stadium, she's already been looking for me and she's pissed off. I take batting practice in the cage and do an extra work out on the weights, staying in the clubhouse until its time to go out and do my pregame warm-up.

Sherry and Michelle are behind home plate again and wave me over. "Kristina's been looking for you again and she didn't look happy." Sherry warns me, but I smile.

"That's part of my plan. She finds me when she's pissed and I'm betting I get another kiss."

"Sneaky. I like it," Michelle chimes in. "That girl doesn't think she can get the announcer gig and the guy. She acts like it's one or the other."

"I don't know what else to do. I'm open to suggestions." I see Kristina out of the corner of my eye, "I've gotta go." I turn and walk toward the outfield to warm up just in time for…

"Don't go running away from me, you jerk!"

I keep walking and pretend I don't here her yelling.

"Chase Cross! What the hell are you thinking? Idiot!"

I turn like I'm just noticing when she says my name, and run toward her with a grin plastered on my face. "Hey! What's up?"

"What's up?" She stares at me like she's trying to bore a hole through my body. "You sent me another gift to the control booth! I specifically told you not to send me things to the control booth! Is the plush seal supposed to remind me of your furry fetish or my stupid decision to make out with you in your room? Jerk!"

I watch her go off on me and take the opportunity to gaze into her gorgeous green eyes. Her anger has the gold flecks dancing around the edge of her irises and her cheeks flushed. I'm prepared to respond, but I don't think I'll have to. I wait her out and let her finish yelling at me.

"I swear you either don't listen or you're just plain stupid!"

Sure enough, she reaches for me and pulls me to her by the front of my jersey. This time I'm ready and when she plants that amazing kiss on me, I wrap my arms around her and I take control. I lift her up and hold her against me. Kissing her with every bit of passion I have and not letting her go. She tries to push me away, but gives in to my kiss and melts into me. She's kissing me back and her heartbeat skips, beating hard against my chest. I press my lips to hers repeatedly, tasting her and drawing her into me. I push my luck, licking her lips and slipping my tongue into her mouth to stroke hers. I want more. I want all of her and it's not the place to go further. It's not the time. I need to prove I want her enough, but I have to get her near me to do that. I hold her tightly against me, so she can't get away and I whisper in her ear, "Feel us together. I want us. I know you want us. I can feel it in your touch and taste it on your lips. Let me show you that I want you enough. Please, stop fighting it. Give me a chance, Kristina. You're beautiful. You're everything I want." I don't know where it came from. It's not what I planned to say. I should release her and put her down, but I kiss her sweet lips and pull her head to rest on my chest.

She pulls away from me and gets to the ground. Glaring at me, she stretches up on her tiptoes and gives me a quick kiss on the lips. Then as she runs off to the control booth, "You're hot, but you're still a jerk and a ball player."

I turn away smiling uncontrollably and get ready for the game.

Kristina

His hands are warm and protective. His lips tell me his story and make me want more. His body against mine is solid and gives me his heart. His words and breath at my ear promise me the world—but I can't believe him. I want to. I want to go to him and be with him. It's not an option. My world revolves around me, not a baseball player who will ditch me as soon as he gets what he wants. Maybe I want the same thing. It doesn't matter. I can't have it.

Yet, I allow myself the indulgence of kissing him and I allow him to distract me when I need to get to work. He's bad for me and the first thing I do when I sit down in the PA Announcer's chair is put on the cap he sent me backwards and kiss the plush seal on the nose. I look out over the field as I put my headphones on and he's looking up at me, grinning from ear to ear and blowing me a kiss.

The field clears while I run through the scheduled announcements and lineups. Then as the National Anthem starts I notice a tweet.

From @RookCross - I hope you caught the kiss I blew
to you.

From @RookCross - I know you always want a second
kiss.

From @RookCross - Would you like me to come over after
the game?

To @RookCross - I'm working here.

From @RookCross - You look hot wearing my cap.

From @RookCross - Have I told you how much I like
hearing your voice during the game? Nobody announces
my name the way you do.

To @RookCross - Can you leave me to work? Go win, jerk!

I turn my phone to silent and flip it over, so I'm not interrupted during the game. It doesn't help. All I can do is think
about him. Do I want him to come over after the game? The
crowd starts to yell and Cross is running for the wall. He jumps
and reaches over the wall to snag it, getting the third out of the
first inning and leaving two runners on base for the other team. I
want to cheer for him and holler out his name, but I stop myself
and have some decorum in the control booth. Bad enough they
probably saw me making out with him on the field. I'm sucked
into the game and Chase is leading off for the Seals. I hear "I
Want to Hold Your Hand" play as he walks up to bat. I catch
myself smiling and my voice sounds different when I announce
his name. I hear Sherry cheering for him and wish I could. I
watch each pitch get thrown, aware of the microphone in front
of me and not wanting to make any noise.

First pitch: Low strike on the inside corner.

Second pitch: Swinging strike, low below the strike zone.

Third pitch: Ball inside.

Fourth pitch: He hits the ball foul.

Fifth pitch: Ball high and inside.

I watch his lean back like the 90 mile per hour fast ball didn't just miss his chest by an inch. I could see his jersey move from the force of the ball and I'm sitting up in the booth. Chase doesn't even step out of the batter's box, he simply waits for the next pitch. He has a calmness about him when he's at bat that I can't understand. How can you be calm when somebody is lobbing fastballs at you? The count is 2 and 2.

Sixth pitch: The ball is low on the outside corner and he smacks it, grounding it up the center. Base hit.

He's safe on first base, I don't have to worry about him getting hit by the ball anymore. I realize I haven't been breathing when I announce the next hitter, Jones Mason, and I sound like an out of breath frog. Chase has a large lead off first and he's leaning toward second when I see him communicating with Mason at bat. I hear Michelle chanting, "Mason, Mason, Mason, Mason." Mason turns his foot in the clay, digging in, and Chase takes off for second on the pitch. Mason chopper's the ball through the center of the diamond and over the second baseman's head. Mason's safe on first and Chase is running to third, diving in to reach the base before the throw from right center field. He's safe. He stands up and dusts off, shaking his pants to get the dirt out or rearrange his jockstrap. I've always wondered what they're actually doing and I've never asked. I assume they get dirt in their pants and that can't be comfortable. That could lead to dirty peen. Why am I thinking about his peen? Focus! I announce Kris Martin as he walks up to the plate and I hear "Lights Out" by Royal Blood rock the stadium. He's swinging the bat as he steps into the batter's box and the first pitch is wild, slamming against the wall behind home plate and caroming toward the dug out. Chase steals home, scoring the first run of the game and gets high fives from his teammates as he walks through the dugout. He turns and looks up at me, grinning. I don't know why he's looking at me. I wish he wouldn't. I'm trying to work. I simply smile, annoyed, and he blows me another kiss. Damn it, if I don't want to catch it! My mind wanders. Maybe he's right. Maybe if I was with him, it would be better. He wouldn't be a distraction, he'd be my—my what? Boyfriend? Fuck buddy? Booty call? Baseball player. He's always going to be a baseball player and I'm not interested in baseball players! Unless, maybe I am. No. No, I'm not interested in baseball players. I wonder if he has a brother who does advertising or sales or something other than being a baseball player. That's stupid, he wouldn't be hot then. I might as well give in, so I can get to the part where he breaks my heart and I can move on.

I get my mind back on my job and hitting my marks for the announcements. I'm doing a great job until the end of the second inning when I announce Cross is at bat again. The pitcher, Rhett Clay, is on first and Lucky Lucine is on third, with two out. Chase is first pitch hunting and not his normal ground ball to get on base. I could hear it off the bat. It was clean with a ring to it and I watched it land in the visitors bullpen, easily 415 feet on his home run hit. I want to jump out of my chair and scream out his name, but I maintain myself. He looks up at me when he steps on home plate and gives me a thumbs up. I smile and give him a thumbs up back. I don't know why. I shouldn't be encouraging him like that.

The rest of the game goes quick. Easy plays and nobody getting on base. Chase came up to bat in the fifth inning, but struck out. When he was at bat in the eighth he walked, but nobody brought him home to score. Then in the top of the ninth inning when the Seals were ahead 5-4 with two outs and ready to win this game, the pinch hitter for the opposing team hits one far into the outfield. Chase runs for it and flies through the air, doing everything he can to reach that ball and keep it from touching the ground. He catches it in mid-air, bounces as he lands on the ground, and slides across the grass in the outfield holding the ball up in his glove like a snow cone. Game over. Seals win.

I watch as the team walks off the field and Hannah grabs Chase for her on-field interview. She puts her arm around him, bringing him in closer for the interview and batting her eyes at him. What the hell? She never does that! She's all business. "Chase, that was an amazing catch out there to end the game tonight. You must be superman, flying through the air like that to get the ball."

He chuckles, "I'm no superman, just an outfielder. That's my job and I never want to let my team down."

"Well, you didn't let your team down tonight. Not only did you make that spectacular catch to end the game, but you smacked a ball into the bullpen for a 3-run home run. Not to mention stealing home on that wild pitch early in the game. You brought in 4 of the 5 runs tonight. This game was truly all you!"

"Thanks, but this is a team sport. I rarely get the opportunity to push my teammates home being lead off, so it felt good to hit the homer. But, the guys had to get on base for me to bring them in. Honestly, the wild pitch was an error I took advantage of. Part of this game is knowing when to take advantage of errors."

"It's nice to be reminded of what you're capable of. Great job tonight. We'll be watching for more tomorrow."

"Thanks." He gave her a hug and she lingered, saying something in his ear before he walked off.

What the hell? Is Hannah hitting on him? And he smiled. He liked it! Jerk! I gaze down onto the field and he's standing there looking up at me. I'm supposed to be announcing the final numbers for the game and I'm off my mark. Shit! I quickly get the announcements done and he's gone.

Chase

Mason gets my attention as I walk into the clubhouse, "Nice grab. What was that with Hannah?"

"She noticed Kristina had been watching me and thought it might be helpful if she saw that I was in demand."

I check my messages and there's no response from Kristina. It's a late night, so the team won't be coming over. But, I'm not ready to go home. I turn back to Mason, "What are you doing to tonight?"

"Hanging out and playing video games."

Fun, that'll do. "Are the guys going to your place or what? I want to go."

He smiles at me deviously, "They aren't coming over, but you're welcome to join us. Bring your headphones."

"What?"

"I have a date with Michelle. We're playing video games at her place. She has better gaming equipment."

"Did you just invite me over to Kristina's apartment?"

"Yup." He smiles, knowing exactly what he did.

"Dude, is that going to get you in trouble with Michelle? I don't want to cramp your style."

"Nope. We're still in the getting to know you phase. I'm taking it slow. She'll think it's funny that you're playing video games with us and that it drives Kristina crazy will be a bonus."

"Drives Kristina crazy?"

"Yea man, seriously. That girl wants you, she just won't admit it."

It's nice to know I'm not the only one who thinks so. "I'm in. Should I bring anything?"

"Pick up snacks and you'll be golden with Michelle."

"Done." I'm not sending her another message. I'll show up at her place and I won't be looking for her.

Kristina

I check my phone as I'm leaving the stadium, expecting my twitter to be blown up by Chase, but all I have is texts from Michelle.

> Text from GamerGirlM - This is me giving you notice that Mase will be over tonight.
> Text from GamerGirlM - We have a video game date.
> Text from GamerGirlM - No "romp" in the plan. Perv.
> Text from GamerGirlM - Hope that's acceptable, mother.

I shake my head at myself, unconcerned with Michelle's antics and wondering if he has already forgotten about me. Should I message him? He better not be off somewhere with Hannah! The way she was pulling him close and hugging him, that's not her style. I bet she was propositioning him on the field when she was whispering in his ear! What does she think she's doing? He's mine! Except for one minor thing. He's not mine. I keep telling him to go away. Mason and Michelle both told me he wouldn't wait forever. I should message him. I don't want him with anyone else. I guess I can't have it both ways. No. I need to let him go. It's better this way. No distractions.

The only problem is that I want him and I don't want to let him go. Maybe I want more than I'm willing to admit even to myself.

Tears stream down my face on my drive home. I keep imagining him with Hannah or some other girl. Giving up on me and agreeing to spend time with another girl who's after him because all I did was push him away. I kept telling him no and wanting him to get me out of his system. He shouldn't be with them. He should be with me. He should be kissing me and wrapping his arms around me. He should be spending the night with me. He should be naked with me. I want him. Why does he have to be a player? There's no way.

I sit in my car until I can get myself together enough to hide my tear-stained face. Times like these I'm glad to find an old bottle of water in my car, so I can wash my face and freshen up without anyone knowing the truth. I'm a grown woman and I can control my emotions, I just can't figure out how to have the job I want and the man I want at the same time.

CHAPTER TWELVE

Chase

I walk up to Kristina's door with a pizza, a pack of energy drinks, and a bag of snacks. I knock on the door and Michelle answers, "Hey, Mase said you might come by. Come on in."

"Thanks." I hand her the pizza and snacks.

She turns to Mason, "I like this guy. He can stay."

"I hope I'm not interrupting anything between you and your boyfriend."

"Who said I have a boyfriend?"

"I shouldn't have to, but me," Mason affirms.

"Interesting." She turns back to me, "Are you here to play with us or are you looking for my roommate, because she's not home yet."

"I'm here for the video games, but if your roommate wants to take my attention I won't fight it." The grin on my face tells her everything she needs to know.

"Works for me."

I play video games with the couple and they're serious gamers. It's work to keep up with them.

Kristina walks through the door, talking to Michelle as she walks through the room to her bedroom and doesn't acknowledge my existence. Just as she's about to step into her room, "I brought pizza. It's in the kitchen if you want some."

She hears my voice and stops in her tracks, turning to look at me. "Why are you here?"

"It's nice to see you, too. I'm here to play video games."

Michelle adds in, "He's not very good at it, but what he lacks in skills he makes up for with enthusiasm. You want to join us? We could team up girls against the boys and beat them worse than they've ever been beat."

"Maybe. Can we play the old school Mortal Combat? I want to see how many times I can chop his head off."

"Sounds good, but I'm committed to Wii bowling sometime tonight. Mase thinks it's more of a date game or something," she says making air quotes.

Kristina disappears into her room and comes back in my favorite PJs with the sunglasses on them. She sits down on the floor between Michelle and I, and leans against me comfortably while we play round after round of Mortal Combat. Each round ending with her brutally chopping off my head and sending it rolling across the floor. Kristina is relaxed and happy. Giggling and actually touching me willingly without being mad at me. I put my arm around her to support her better while she sits leaning against me and she accepts it, snuggling into my body. I kiss her cheek and she turns to me smiling, responding with a peck on my lips before she goes back to chopping my head off and watching the blood splatter everywhere.

She puts her hand on my leg and leans in to kiss me, blinking with her big eyes as she presses her lips to mine sweetly and then pulls back away. We communicate silently and I take her in my arms, pulling her across my body and lean down to kiss her. She meets me halfway with her willing lips and wraps her arms around my neck. Where did this come from? This is what I want. I want her and I want her to want me. She tastes so sweet. I'm beginning to wonder if she really tastes like cookies and it's not lip balm. I press my lips to hers open-mouthed, repeatedly. Wanting more of her and trying not to push or be inappropriate in front of her roommate and Mason. She nibbles on my lower lip and sucks on it, releasing a quiet whimper. She pushes me with her fingers exploring my back and shoulders, and her tongue sliding into my mouth for more. She twirls her tongue around mine until I meet her need with mine and she sucks on my tongue. Oh, fuck. This chick. I hold her close to me, not wanting to let her go and she moves her hands to my hair, holding my lips to hers.

Mason comments, "Uh, we're going to change over to play bowling. Maybe you two want to take what you're doing into the other room?"

"We could do what they're doing instead of bowling. It looks like fun." Michelle suggests to him.

Mason continues, "Please go in the other room."

I pull back and search her eyes for direction, she giggles and leans her head on my chest. "My bedroom?"

I stand up with her in my arms and carry her with me to her bedroom. It's not the first time I've been here and I hope it's not the last. I sit on the small loveseat she has in the corner, not wanting to push this faster. I want her, but I'm not ready to go there yet. I need her to know I want her enough. I want to spend the night with her and I need her to know it's for her. I want to hold her and kiss her. I want to feel her against me. Mostly, I just want to be with her. This is new territory for me. It's not hit it and quit it.

I wait to see what she does next and she climbs off my lap to close her bedroom door. She folds the bedding back on her bed and climbs in, holding it open for me, "Do you want to join me?"

I'm not telling her no this time. I smile at her and pull my shirt off. I can't sleep in my jeans. I fight with myself about the level of will power I have and if I can stay with her in my boxer briefs without getting in her. I don't know what will happen tomorrow or where this change in what she wants came from, but I'm not taking a chance on losing it. I can do this, I sit on the edge of her bed and take my jeans off. She reaches for me, touching my bare skin. "Don't get the wrong idea. I'm not pushing you. There's no getting you out of my system." I climb in bed with her and pull her to me. She moves to climb on top of me and I should stop her, but I don't. I run my hands up and down the length of her arms and pull her mouth down to mine. I want to kiss her. I take her hand in mine and lock our fingers, while our mouths meet. There's nothing like her sweet soft lips. I roll her off of me and pull her back against me, so I can wrap my arms around her and hold her against my body. As I pull her back to me, she's silky and smooth and sexy. A little curvy with her ass pushed into my dick. "Sorry, it's not intentional. I can't control how much he wants you." I change to a whisper and my voice gets raspy, "I want you, too. I want to hold you next to me and protect you, so you'll know you're mine. I can do that. I want to do that. It's more important to me than anything else because I want you enough."

She's silent, but I know she's awake. I hold her and kiss the back of her neck. I explore her curves tenderly, my hands lightly gliding along the surface of her skin. "Goodnight, Sweetness." Falling asleep, happily holding her in my arms.

Kristina

His arms around me, holding me. His warm breath at my ear, traveling down my neck. His fresh manly scent. I'm not ready to sleep. I roll toward him, my body pushed to his, front to front. I run my fingers through his hair at his temple and down around his ear, he releases a soft groan. I do it again and pull my fingers all the way through, exploring the muscles in his neck and shoulders. His hands on me flex and his fingers spread. I place my hands on his face and pull his mouth to mine, kissing him sweetly. I draw a line of kisses down his neck and he gets hard against me. I move against him.

I want him, but it can only be sex. I don't know what I'm doing. Ball players are bad for me. Why am I so attracted to him? Why does it feel so good to have his arms around me? Why did I kiss him and bring him to my bedroom? He's not an option. I can't be with him. Can I?

I kiss my way back to his mouth and stop myself. I push against his hard length and his hands move to my hips, stopping my movement. I kiss him again, playfully I lick his lips and touch my tongue to his. I pull back, sucking on his lower lip. I want more. I roll my hips against him again and his hold on my hips tightens. I press my lips to his and he responds, taking control of the kiss and pushing his tongue into my mouth with need. His kiss is claiming and I feel it travel my body, flooding me with warmth. I meet his urgency, stroking and sucking on his tongue. Suddenly, he stops. He pulls back and gazes into my eyes, his more grey than hazel as they shine back at me. He wraps his arms around me tight with his cheek to my forehead and I can feel him relax. His whole body at ease with me in his arms. His strong heartbeat fading to rest and taking me with it.

CHAPTER THIRTEEN

Kristina

I wake up early the next morning in bed alone. I knew it. Stupid ball players! There's no way he stayed all night with me. I roll over and hide the tears that are forming on my pillow, I can't believe I thought he might really want me enough. A minute later there's a body in bed next to me and arms wrapped around me.

I smile internally and roll over, so I can use him as my pillow. My hands exploring his bare chest and abs while he cradles me in the crook of his arm. I gaze into his eyes, leaning forward to kiss his cheek before I burrow into his embrace. I fall back to sleep, not wanting it to end.

We're both startled by someone knocking on my bedroom door and I call out, "Yea? What?"

Mason talks through the door, "Uhhh, is Cross in there?"

"Yes. I'm sleeping," he responds on a grumble and pulls me closer to him.

"About that, we have to be at the stadium in less than an hour and I don't have my truck with me."

"Dude, we have time. Report time is three hours from now," Chase corrects him.

"I have to be there early. So, let's go," there's a nervous tone to Jones' voice. Makes me wonder if he's lying.

"I'm not ready to leave. Get an Uber." Chase focuses on me, tracing my lips with his finger.

His soft, warm touch melting me. I sigh unintentionally.

His eyes light up and he grins as he presses his lips to mine. "How do you taste so sweet?" He says softly and continues to kiss me. He swipes his tongue across my lower lip, then tugs on it and my belly flutters.

"Cross, come on! You owe me one," his tone is almost desperate.

Chase takes a deep breath, "Fine. Grab my keys and I'll meet you at my truck in a few minutes. I'll drop you off on my way home."

"Thanks, man." I hear Jones walking around and keys clanking as the door to my apartment closes.

"I wonder what that's about."

"I don't care what he's got going on. I've got you," Chase kisses me sweetly and brushes my hair out of my face.

I hear myself giggle like a schoolgirl, and it's new to me.

"I like that sound. Mason can wait," he trails off as he claims my lips gently with his.

Oh yes, Mason can wait. Chase can kiss me like this all day and anywhere he wants.

Chase

I finally have Kristina in my arms and wanting me. Fucking, Mason! He's full of shit. He doesn't have to be at the stadium early. He can wait in my truck until I'm ready. Her sweet laugh has me hard again and I already jerked off earlier when I woke up painfully in need. I need to have control. I don't want her thinking this is about getting laid. But, her skin is so smooth and she smells sweet, exactly like how she tastes. The way she's responding, she's giving herself to me. I can do this, I mean not do her. My will power won't let me down. It's okay, hold her and make-out with her. This chick, she fits in my arms perfectly like it's where she belongs. I want more of her. I'm in my head while I'm kissing her and my hands are on their own mission exploring her body. I catch myself with the tips of my fingers slid between her and the elastic waistband of her shorts, and my other hand up her shirt on her bare back. She wants more and I know my limit, any more and I won't be able to stop. I pull my hands back quickly and wrap my arms around her, not giving up her lips.

She whimpers a complaint at me and pulls away, staring into my eyes, "What happened? You don't want to touch me?"

"I'm sorry, I lost control. I want to touch you and so much more."

"What if I want you to lose control?"

I chuckle nervously, "I'm not ready."

"How many girls have you been with! You're not ready?"

"None of them mattered. None of them were you." What am I saying? She's a runner! I'll scare her away.

She looks at me funny, cocking her head to the side like she does when she's thinking, "Okay. I like how you were touching me. You made me relax last night and I never really sleep. Thank you."

I hold her tight against me and she snuggles into my chest, taking my hands and moving them where she wants them. One up her tank top on her bare back and the other at her waist. I move my hand slowly across her back, appreciating her, and I feel her breath hitch at my touch. "You're beautiful."

She gazes into my eyes and smiles. I'm drawn to kiss her. I can't help myself. I'm like a moth to a flame when it comes to seeing her happy, her gorgeous smile. I stop before I kiss her and move my hands to her head, threading my fingers into her hair and holding her where I want her. I kiss the tip of her nose and she giggles. I kiss each of her eyelids. I kiss her temple and drag a line of kisses to her jawline, appreciating every piece of her and tipping her head back ready to taste her neck. It's not time for that yet, so I press my lips to hers. Sucking and nibbling on her sweet lips, our tongues tied together in a seductive dance that's testing the limits on my will power. It's obvious she wants this to go further and she wants it now. I want it now, too.

Michelle's bedroom door slams and she shouts, "He really left!" Followed by an impressive string of creative cuss words, "Son of a mother humping burnt hairy twat waffle! Damn it!" Doors continue to get slammed in the kitchen and she's stomping around loud on purpose. I look to Kristina, "I'm guessing I should go now."

She nods in agreement, "Roommates can suck. But, I need to check on her." She stops and then starts again, gazing at me, "I don't want you to go. We both need to get to work anyway. I'll see you later."

My cheeks warm and I grab her, kissing her silly. I pull my jeans and shirt on, and she follows me to the door, "Thanks for coming over. I had a good time." I grab her again and lift her off the ground to plant a kiss on her. I need her to keep thinking about me.

"You're still here? Gah!" Michelle walks into the room.

"I'm leaving, and good morning to you, too." I turn to my girl and give her a quick peck on the cheek, "See you later, Sweetness."

I didn't get laid and that's a good thing, though I don't think I've ever imagined myself saying those words together. I have more energy than usual as I run down the stairs to my truck and find Mason sleeping.

From @Kristeeeeena - I want another kiss, but don't come back up. Bad idea right now.

From @Kristeeeeena - Just want you to know I still want another kiss ;)

To @Kristeeeeena - Good

To @Kristeeeeena - I'll have some ready for you when I see you.

Kristina

"Why are you smiling like a fool?" Michelle walks into the room irritated, as I'm messaging Chase.

"I'm not." She glares at me. "Whatever, you've been with Mason every second since you met him."

"So, what's the deal? I thought there was a boycott on base-ball players."

Huh, "The deal is that I was enjoying myself, but you and your boy kept blowing the mood with your interruptions and slamming doors. I'm allowed to enjoy myself, right? Boys are allowed in my room, mother?" My words spitting from my mouth before I filter them and not what I intended. "Besides, I think the issue we should be discussing is you? What's got you in a tizzy?" I'm not discussing Chase. "I'm waiting." I stare at her tapping my foot with my arms crossed. "Is he a bad kisser or something? Tiny peen?" In my head, refuses to give it up and get laid? "Spill it! What's the deal?"

"I don't know if he's a bad kisser. His peen is fine. His arms are strong and muscular, awesome wrapped around me."

"I know you've kissed other guys. He's just okay or what?"

Michelle hems and haws around, not wanting to answer my question. "He hasn't kissed me, other than a kiss on the cheek and forehead."

"What? Yet, you know his peen is fine."

"Oh yeah! I felt it against me when he was holding me. I give it an A+ and I haven't seen or touched it."

"You could kiss him."

"Nope. I leaned in to kiss him, made sure he knew I wanted him to kiss me. He hugged me so I couldn't kiss him and did his whisper thing."

"Whisper thing?"

"It doesn't matter. I think it's his own version of mind control. He uses his words. It's so sexy when a guy uses his words." Michelle turns visibly red and I feel like I should spray her down with a hose or something. Well, Mason should use his hose. "I need a distraction. Tell me about Cross."

"He likes me. He's hot. He's a great kisser."

"And?"

"And, what?"

"The sex."

"We didn't do that, but I think I could've got some if my roommate wasn't being obnoxious."

"He stayed all night."

"Yes."

"He slept in your bed with you? He kept his clothes on?"

"Yes and no, he slept in his underwear and they never came off."

"You turned him down because he's a player?"

"No. He didn't even attempt. He kissed me and held me all night. I wanted him to do more."

"This is crazy. Cross stopped at first base and I can't get Mason out of the batter's box! Aren't big league baseball players supposed to be *players?*"

The irony isn't lost on me. But, privately in my head I keep hearing him tell me, "I'm not ready. None of them mattered. None of them were you." There's no way I'm special to him. Is there?

Chase

I knock on my truck window loudly, waking Mason. He unlocks the door and I yell at him as I open it, "Dude! What the fuck? Are you trying to cock block me? Your girl put you up to that shit?"

Mason sits up and swings his head to the right, then the left, popping his neck. He lowers the passenger window and stretches out with his elbow hanging out the window in his now reclined seat. He's trying to ignore me and reaches to change the station on my radio, but I smack his hand away and point to the decal on my dash that says, "Driver picks the music, shotgun shuts his cakehole."

"What happened in the girls' apartment?" I ask.

"You won't understand. I had to get out of there."

"Why? I thought you dig Michelle. She seems like a cool chick."

"I think Michelle's great. I want to spend time with her and get to know her. I don't want to be led by my dick."

"Okay, what's the problem?"

"It's your fault. She's been fine with me being sweet to her, holding her hand, whispering in her ear, spending time with her. Then you go having a make-out session in front of us and carry Kristina off to her bedroom, shutting the door behind you."

"We were kissing."

"Kissing leads to other stuff."

"You haven't kissed her yet?"

He turns away and doesn't even look at me.

"Dude, you need to kiss her. You need to find out what it feels like to kiss her."

"No, I don't. It won't change how I feel about her. She's perfect for me in every way."

I lean over my steering wheel and turn toward him, "You spent the night with her on my couch and never kissed her?"

"Oh, I've kissed her, but only a peck here and there." Mason continues talking to the window, "I can't be one of those guys that fucks everything with two legs, that's not me. No offense."

"None taken, and for the record I only fucked the ones that were looking to fuck. I don't lead chicks on and I don't break hearts."

"Good to know. Michelle has been worried about that."

"I don't understand how it's okay to spend the night in her bed, but not kiss her."

"I slept on the couch. I know we were on your couch together. I couldn't help myself. You weren't there to see it. I was grinning at her and we were making eye contact, she giggled and kept sitting next to me while we were playing games. She even brushed against me when we were goofing around. She had slipped her shoes off and was sitting cross-legged, and it was her turn to play. Man, she was beating me at my game and I was loving it. I reached over and broke her concentration, tickling the bottom of her foot. She squealed and hopped up real quick, dancing around like she thought a bug was crawling on her. I was interested before, but something about her reaction sealed the deal for me. It also got the attention of Stray, who suddenly had a Southern accent and was calling her darlin'. Cain stood up and took her hand, asking her if she was okay and offering to get her anything she wanted. And, Clay flashed his toothy smile at her and offered to let her sit in his lap, so he could defend her from creepy crawlies. Corey just sat there laughing at the whole thing and I had to do something. I grabbed her and took her down on the couch with me, kicked Stray off the couch and started whispering in her ear. I think she liked it because she rolled toward me in my arms and burrowed into my chest. It felt right, but I shouldn't have done that."

"Get over yourself and kiss her already."

"She wants me to. I want to date her and I've never been good at knowing when to stop. I'm kind of an all or nothing guy."

"You can kiss her and hold her without fucking her. That's what I did last night."

"It'll be better if I wait."

"Dude, she's going to think she's friend zoned."

"She wanted to make-out like you were doing last night, and

got mad when I wouldn't. So far, my whisper has kept her attention."

"What kind of magic are you saying to her?"

"I tell her nice things. Nothing magic, just the truth."

"She was pissed that you were gone this morning. Interrupted me for the second time this morning. Cock blocker number two." The thought strikes me and I'm thankful for the interruption, my will power was losing this morning.

"Michelle will be fine," Mason nods his head and grins with confidence.

Since I'm already at the stadium dropping off Mason, I decide to stay and get a good workout in.

Kristina

As I wander into the stadium, all I can think about is last night. He actually stayed the whole night with me. He didn't expect anything. I don't think I've ever slept that well. His kiss, his hands, his body, he makes me want more. I pushed against his hard cock and he stopped me. He's not ready. It was the stupidest thing I've ever heard. He's basically been fucking every woman who wants him for years. But, he's not ready for me? I remember his words. "None of them mattered. None of them were you." My body tingled at his words. His honest and sincere tone leaving no room to doubt him. He wants me enough.

I want to find him and spend some quality time together in a private corner of the stadium. I know the stadium inside and out. There are plenty of places for some private time. I wouldn't get naked here, but I'm up for a serious make-out session.

Maybe he could finally get to second base. I daydream about Chase holding me up against a wall in a dark room, covering me in warm open-mouthed kisses from my lips, down my neck. My legs wrapped around him and my heat rubbing against his hard length. His warm breath on my neck as he whispers in my ear, telling me what he wants to do to me and telling me how I make him lose control. Thanking me for giving us a chance because he knows we're right together.

Unfortunately, I'm the only intern that's not out sick today and I get to do everyone's job. It's going to be a long one. No time for fun. It's a challenge I'm up to and a reminder to stay focused on my goal.

CHAPTER FOURTEEN

Chase

It's almost game time. I haven't seen Kristina at the stadium yet today and there's a dude announcing.

To @Kristeeeeena - I had a great time with you last night. Can I see you tonight?
To @Kristeeeeena - I was hoping to hear you announcing today.
From @Kristeeeeena - Sorry. Crazy busy.
From @Kristeeeeena - Probably working late.
From @Kristeeeeena - See you soon! :) Go win!

I'll take it. At least she's not telling me to go away.

I walk up the steps from the clubhouse to the dug out and Mason grabs me to warm-up. I survey the scene as we walk out to the field. Seno warming up our pitcher. Sherry getting settled behind home plate. Mason starts in, "I got Michelle a ticket and she didn't come to the game."

"Dude, she has a life and it's not going to stop because she met you. She was pissed at you this morning."

"She'll be fine." He turns away from me and runs to the field doing sprints. He doesn't have my speed and I run after him, challenging him to keep up. He meets me back at the foul line and our teammates egg us on to race, Cain and Brandt joining the contest.

My speed is what I'm known for. I beat them all easily and hear yelling from the stands, "Woooowooo! Go Cross!"

I turn to find Kristina standing at the first base wall, clapping with a huge smile on her face. It's much better than yelling at me and cussing me out. She tilts her head to the side and waves me over. I can't control my smile, "Hey, Sweetness."

She goes up on her tiptoes and whispers in my ear, "I only have a quick break, but I chose to spend it on you." She kisses my cheek and turns around to run back to work, "I'll be too late for anything tonight. Go win!" And she's gone out of sight, but it makes me happy. She came looking for me and didn't have to be pissed to do it.

Chase

It's the fourth inning and I'm sitting in the dugout, Seno pulls my cap off and gets in my face, "Are you in there?"

"Dude. What?"

"You tell me. What're you doing because it's not playing baseball."

I have no clue what he's talking about and don't respond.

"You've missed two opportunities to steal. You were in the wrong place to catch a pop fly. You could've had a double and stopped on first. Where's your brain?" He shakes his head, "Did you fuck that chick yet?"

"No. I spent the night at her place last night. Nothing kinky, she wanted it though."

"Stop thinking about your dick and play the game."

Mason chuckles and Seno turns to him, "You, too. What's with missing that ball up the middle? You could've out run that throw to first." Seno shakes his head, "Grow up and play. We are winning this season. Rookies." He walks away leaving me and Mason nodding at each other.

Top of the 5th inning, we are down by two. Running out onto the field and Seno yells at us, "Focus!"

Kranston is on fire with 7 strike outs and he deserves better support. I smack Mason on my way by him, "Let's do this!" I focus on the game. We want to win.

Kranston strikes out the first two at bat. The third hitter pops it up short to Left Center Field. I run for it and Mason is backing up to get it. I call him off and make the catch. I throw the ball into the stands on my way to the dug out and get a high-five from Mason. I hear Seno yell, "That's it, more of that."

Bottom of the 5th inning, Kranston is leading off and gets a base hit. Mason and I keep each other focused as he steps into the on deck circle and I walk toward the batter's box to "I Want to Hold Your Hand." I can't help but think of her and then I hear the cheers. It's not just Sherry and the stadium crowd. I turn to look and Kristina's there with Sherry, cheering at the top of her lungs, "Let's go, Chase! Wooooooowooo!" It means everything to me. She's here for me. I love it when Sherry cheers for me, but now I get it. Nothing's the same as your girl there supporting you and wearing your number. I blow her a kiss and her bright smile empowers me. "Knock it, Chase!"

I need to get on base and I know better than to crush it

trying for a homer. The first pitch is the one I always watch for, my favorite location and I smack it clean and hard. My bat stays intact and I swing through. It feels good and before I can look up to see it sail twenty feet over the Center Field wall, the stadium is going crazy. I run the bases, pushing Kranston around to home and all I can hear is Kristina, "Woooowooo! Yeah, baby!" I step on home plate and point at her mouthing "all you" to her. Game is tied at two.

Mason gets a single. Martin hits into a fielder's choice, safe on first and Mason's out at second. Martin steals second and Seno hits a double driving him in. Cain walks. Lucky hits into a double play and the score is 3-2 Seals as we go to the 6th inning.

In the seventh inning I hit a double and Martin knocks me in. Our pitching held the opposing team to two and the final score was 5-2 Seals.

I went to the net behind home plate after the game looking for Kristina, but she was gone. Sherry grins at me knowingly, "She could only stay for her lunch break." I'll take it.

Kristina

My job as the intern, gofer, do everything that nobody wants to do and cover everyone that's out sick has been everything I hoped. Until the bottom of the eighth inning when, Hannah, the scheduled on-field reporter blew chunks all over the press box. I know how to do the task, it's just—well, it involves a camera and I don't like to be on camera. I prefer to be behind a microphone somewhere nobody can see me. My specialty is radio broadcasting and announcing. I'm not an on-camera personality.

They didn't give me a choice and I need to do whatever I can to make this a permanent gig. I'm not dressed for this and I have hat hair from wearing my Seals cap with Chase's number on it. Apparently, I'm the same size as Hannah and somehow she managed not to get puke on her wardrobe for today. I change into the short, curve hugging, hot pink dress and look at the shoes I'm supposed to wear with it. Luckily, we don't wear the same size shoes and they allow me to wear the 3" espadrilles I'd left in my car when I opted for flip flops. I'd kill myself in those 4" spiked platform heels on the field. I'm bombarded by the hair and make-up people, they need to learn the term "personal space" and get out of mine. I understand that they have to be close to apply make up and fix my hair, but I didn't give anyone permission to adjust my breasts—which is apparently a thing and I was wearing the wrong bra, so now I've been taped up into place and I'm popping out the top of the dress. At least I know I can get Chase to do an interview with me and he'll make someone else interview with me, too. Fuck! Chase is going to see me like this. This isn't me. I look in the mirror and they've magically made me camera-ready without hat hair. In fact, I look fabulous. Not my style at all and completely uncomfortable in the dress, but fabulous nonetheless. I bet he doesn't even recognize me.

To @GamerGirlM - They're making me go on camera.

To @GamerGirlM - Don't tell anybody.

To @GamerGirlM - Maybe they won't recognize me.

To @GamerGirlM - Yes, it's that bad.

From @GamerGirlM - Don't worry. You got this.

From @GamerGirlM - It's not what you want, but you've been trained for it!

From @GamerGirlM - What position?

To @GamerGirlM - On-Field Reporter

From @GamerGirlM - Oh Shit! With our guys?

From @GamerGirlM - Forget that.

From @GamerGirlM - Show them you're better than Hannah.

To @GamerGirlM - I don't want this job!

From @GamerGirlM - Just do it! Try it! You might like it!

To @GamerGirlM - I'm wearing hot pink and its short and snug.

From @GamerGirlM - LOL If you're good, they'll get you appropriate wardrobe.

She's got to be kidding me with this. She's never steered me wrong when it came to the professional or education world before. I don't have time to question it. Michelle said it, "Just do it!" They shove the earplug in my ear and the booth starts talking to me. It's already the top of the 9th and it doesn't look like there will be a bottom of the 9th. Unless something crazy happens, they want me to interview Cross and Kranston or Martin. Seno as a final option. They've got the stats for the game ready and will feed me the details I need for each interview.

I walk out to the field and watch the last out of the game, a pop fly caught by Chase at the wall in Center Field. The crew leads me to the area in front of the dug out and I'm supposed to grab the players as they come in from the field. I focus on Chase and watch as he runs in and goes straight to the net behind home plate. What's he doing? I need him over here. I stand watching for him to walk toward me. Honestly, I want to see the expression on his face when he realizes it's me. Kranston is already gone to the club house. I grab Martin, "Can we do a quick interview?"

He looks me up and down, "What's your name, sweetheart?"

"My name is Kristina. I'm covering for Hannah. I seem to be covering for everyone this season."

"No problem."

"Thanks. Let's get it done. I need to get Cross before he goes in the locker room, too."

"Wait, you're the chick Chase has been talking about. I saw you kiss him at the wall."

"Yes, well, either way I need to do the interview. He doesn't know I'm doing the on-field interviews tonight. I didn't know until thirty minutes ago."

Martin laughs, "This is going to be fun. Let's do it."

I lead Kris Martin to the camera and I'm getting nothing from the control booth. I know my baseball. I can wing it. "Kris, you did some great hitting tonight and that golden glove of yours was flashing at first base. What do you do to maintain your superior skills on the diamond?"

Kris blushes, "Thanks, Kristina. I try to stay focused on the game and sacrifice most of my personal life during the season. I know I'll only get to play for a short time and I want to be the best I can be for as long as possible."

"It's been noted that you're hitting and fielding better this year than you have in years past. The sports writers have even written articles about how it's your year. Are you doing something different to achieve the higher stats across the board?"

He grins and I know he's not going to give me the real answer, "I've felt my strength and confidence grow consistently over the last few years. I think I'm finally hitting my stride and I'm not stopping here. Having said that, this team makes all the difference. Without a leader like Seno, we wouldn't be where we are now as a team and this season we are a family."

"Thank you so much for your time. Good luck on the road trip!"

Kris smiles and shakes his head as he walks off. Then he looks up at Cross, "Cross, on field reporter wants you." He chuckles, "And she's hot." He walks down the steps into the dug out and stands there watching.

Chase looks at me and does a double-take as his face lights up. He walks toward me quickly. "Hey, Sweetness." His eyes land on my breasts and he stops talking.

"Hey. Ummm, sorry to spring this on you like this. I didn't know I was doing this until last inning. This isn't even my dress." I lean closer to him, "I'd never wear this dress."

"You're gorgeous in it, but it's not you." He leans in and whispers in my ear, "You're beautiful no matter what. I especially like it when you're wearing my number or those PJs with the sunglasses on them."

I know I'm turning red. I'm not supposed to be interviewing players, especially not players that know what I look like in my PJs! "I need to get through this interview with you, okay?"

"Anything for you, Sweetness."

"I'm going to need you not to call me Sweetness during the interview."

"I can do that."

The cameraman nods and we're ready to go, "Chase Cross,

you had some great plays today. But, it seemed to start out slow for you. What do you contribute the significant change to the second half of your game to today?"

He gazes directly into my eyes and I know it has something to do with me, "I feed off the crowd and they were cheering louder during the second half of the game. Also, our team captain gave the rookies a pep talk and that made a huge difference."

"You hit a home run that flew at least twenty feet over the Center Field wall. That's not something we normally see from you. Have you been concentrating on your hitting?"

"My job in the leadoff spot is to get on base, not get out hitting a pop fly that comes up short. I have the speed, so I usually keep the ball on the ground. Sometimes, like today, I get a pitch I can't pass up. Baseball is a team sport, you have to work together to generate runs."

"Good job today. Thank you for taking the time to do this interview." The camera is finally off.

Chase pulls me to him, "That home run was all you. You make me stronger and I want to impress you. The first half of the game I was somewhere with you, not on the field. And, that dress? It makes me want to take you out of it. I know it's late, come to my house tonight?"

"I can't. I'll be here at least another three hours. Too many people out ill today."

He whispers in my ear, "You wanted me this morning. I wanted you. I still want you. I'm not after sex, I just want you with me. It felt right to hold you all night. I want to hold you every night."

I smile at him unable to put the words I want together.

"You did a great job with the interview. Can you do one thing for me?"

"What?"

"Change out of that dress before I have competition." He starts off into the clubhouse.

"Yeah, I can do that. Chase?"

He turns back, "Yeah?"

"Nobody can compete with you."

He gets a big grin and blows me a kiss before he disappears into the club house.

I made it through the interviews, now to get the rest of my work done.

From @GamerGirlM - Great job!

From @GamerGirlM - I saved the interviews, so you have them for your portfolio.

From @GamerGirlM - Also, I'd like to dissect the interaction between you and Chase.

To @GamerGirlM - Thank you.

To @GamerGirlM - It wasn't as bad as I thought it'd be.

To @GamerGirlM - Let's not and say we did.

To @GamerGirlM - Late night. See you around 2am or later.

From @GamerGirlM - Are you going to Chase's?

To @GamerGirlM - I'm working.

To @GamerGirlM - Will Mason be there when I get home?

From @GamerGirlM - No. I put him on a time out. He doesn't know.

To @GamerGirlM - Why? Still mad he left?

From @GamerGirlM - I need time to decide if I want a boyfriend or not.

From @GamerGirlM - He said he's my boyfriend, but he never asked me if I wanted that and he still hasn't kissed me.

To @GamerGirlM - Makes sense. Why commit to the guy that won't even kiss you?

From @GamerGirlM - That is the question I'm trying to answer.

From @GamerGirlM - You should know I think Chase is a keeper.

From @GamerGirlM - Bye!

CHAPTER FIFTEEN

Chase

> To @Kristeeeeena - You can come over any time.
> To @Kristeeeeena - Doesn't matter how late it is.
> From @Kristeeeeena - It's 2am and I'm still at the stadium working.
> To @ Kristeeeeena - Can I help?
> From @Kristeeeeena - No. I just need to get done.

I want her here with me. I want to hold her. I want to kiss her. It's late and the team leaves early in the morning. I need sleep.

Chase

My alarm goes off early and I wish she were here with me. I don't have much extra time this morning. The team is leaving early and flying out to play three games against Washington.

To @Kristeeeeena - Good morning, Sweetness.
To @Kristeeeeena - I'm at the stadium. Are you here?

Nothing. I wander around a bit and check with Carter. She's not here. She's off today.

To @Kristeeeeena - Wish you were here. See you in a few days.

———

Chase

I take my phone out of airplane mode when we land in Washington and it goes crazy.

From @Kristeeeeena - Wish I was there to see you this morning.

From @Kristeeeeena - Phone was dead at the end of my work day and I was tired.

From @Kristeeeeena - Happy to have a day off.

From @Kristeeeeena - Win for me!

To @Kristeeeeena - Wish I was there to spend the day with you.

To @Kristeeeeena - I'm saving up kisses for you.

From @Kristeeeeena - :) :) :)

To @Kristeeeeena - Will you go out with me when I get back?

To @Kristeeeeena - Can I have your phone number?

From @Kristeeeeena - I told you I don't give boys my number.

To @Kristeeeeena - I'm a man, not a boy.

From @Kristeeeeena - That is very true. I don't give men my number either.

Chase

The team has batting practice on the field and I find myself leaning on the backstop between Mason and Seno.

"You rooks got your shit together today?" Seno asks as he stares at Brandt taking swings.

"The chick won't give me her number and ignores me when I ask her out," I say trying to focus on the game.

"Michelle is 'busy' and her responses are all one or two words. She'll be fine," Mason adds his current standing.

Seno releases a sigh and scratches the back of his head. He

looks at me, "You need to keep her thinking about you and don't message her too much. You don't want to look needy." He looks down and shakes his head, then turns to Mason, "What did you do to piss her off?"

I laugh, "I think it's what he didn't do."

"Shut up," Mason snarls at me.

"I don't know what the fuck you did or didn't do. I do know you pissed her off and I don't care if it's your fault or not. Send her flowers. You can make it right when you get home." Seno gives each of us a questioning look, "Anything else?" He waits, but neither of us respond. "Good. Remember, women like winners not losers. My queen likes to see her team win, let's show these women what we've got."

We each take our turn at bat. Seno's on point and he has been all season, he's on a mission. I hit a couple grounders because I know that's what I'm supposed to do and then I let it rip knocking a few in a row out of the park. It feels good to smash the ball, freeing. Mason swings and misses the first two pitches, then hits a couple to the outfield and a grounder. He needs to get his head straight

"Dude, call her and use your magic whisper."

Mason blushes, "Naw, she'll be fine."

CHAPTER SIXTEEN

Kristina

"Are you watching the game today?" Michelle asks.

"I have the day off. No baseball."

"Really? We could watch the guys."

"I thought Mason's on a timeout?"

"He is, but that doesn't mean I have to be. I can watch him and he'll never know."

"Fine, I'm in."

We need a girls' night. It's almost game time. Michelle orders a pizza. I turn the television on and they're announcing the team.

"Look at all of them in the dug out, it's hottie heaven!" The camera pans, "Our guys are sitting together. Woah! Did you see Cross look into the camera and smile? He's so hot!" Michelle exclaims and I wonder if she's been drinking.

"You have your own player to drool over."

"Whatever. I don't know why you don't claim Chase and keep him."

I've been wondering the same thing myself. I know baseball players are bad for me, but when we were together he made me want him. "His eyes change color and give him away, gorgeous light green hazel to a shiny grey." I remember him in my bed, gazing at me with those eyes and holding me all night. "I don't know how Mason can spend so much time with you and stay the night holding you without kissing you."

"He only held me all night on Chase's couch."

"He stayed over night before last."

"On the couch."

"And the other night you two were in your room."

"He slept on the floor." The doorbell buzzes and Michelle gets up to get the pizza, "I don't get it. I don't know why he had to leave early." She opens the door to a large mixed bouquet of pink and yellow flowers.

"I'm looking for Michelle?"

"That's me."

"These are for you. Beautiful flowers for a beautiful girl. Have a good evening," and he walks off down the hallway. She turns around, her face glowing as she admires her flowers. She takes the card and walks toward me.

"Those are beautiful, who are they from?"

Michelle glares at me, then her expression changes and she opens the card quickly, "I think we know who they're from." She points at Mason on the TV and he hits a home run, bringing in Cross in the top of the first inning. I totally missed Chase getting on base.

"What's the card say?"

"The card says, 'Please be patient with me, JJ,' and it has a heart on it." She immediately picks up her phone and I know she's sending Mason a message.

I sit back and watch the game while my roommate is in La-La Land.

The doorbell buzzes again and Michelle gets up to get the pizza, she opens the door to another delivery guy, "I'm looking for Kristina?"

She calls out to me, "Um, it's for you."

I run over to the door, "I'm Kristina." He hands me a crystal vase filled with two-dozen long stemmed delicate pale pink roses. "Thank you." Warmth hits my cheeks and I realize I'm as bad as my roommate. I breathe in the fragrant scent of the roses and open the little card, it says "Sweetness: You are more beautiful than any flower. I'm thinking about you—Chase," and the card has a stuffed bear holding a heart on it.

To @RookCross - Thank you for the flowers.
To @RookCross - They are gorgeous (and better than Michelle's).
To @RookCross - Message me later :)

The pizza finally gets delivered and we sit happily watching our players on the field.

Chase

The game started out pretty well. I did my job and got on base. Mason hit a dinger and brought me home. Nobody has scored since. I'm standing in the outfield in the bottom of the eighth inning and the roof is open. It's a clear night and I look at the dark speckled sky wondering what she's doing. I hear the pop of a bat and a ball is heading my way. I run for it and make a diving grab. I wouldn't have needed to dive if I was paying attention. Focus, Chase. She'll be there after the game. Seno is up out of his crouch watching me, he shakes his head and gives me a thumbs up. He knows I'm distracted.

Bottom of the ninth, still 2-0 Seals. Seattle has runners at the corners with one out. They hit a sac fly that comes directly to me and the runner on third scores. I throw the ball to the infield quickly and catch the runner from first trying to advance. Mason gets the ball and tags him out as he slides into second base. Final score 2-1 Seals.

Chase

I'm finally checked into my room for the night and have time to relax. I haven't eaten and all I can think about is her. I check my phone and see that she messaged me when she got the flowers I sent. I have a reason to respond.

To @Kristeeeeena - Hey Sweetness.

From @Kristeeeeena - Hi :)

To @Kristeeeeena - Do you want to talk?

From @Kristeeeeena - I'm not giving you my number.

To @Kristeeeeena - I know. I meant chat.

From @Kristeeeeena - Oh. Sure.

From @Kristeeeeena - Nice win.

To @Kristeeeeena - Thanks. The game felt long.

To @Kristeeeeena - I've been thinking about you.

From @Kristeeeeena - What were you thinking?

To @Kristeeeeena - I like the way you sit with me playing Mortal Combat while you're chopping my head off.

To @Kristeeeeena - I like holding you all night.

To @Kristeeeeena - I like tasting your lips. You taste like cookies.

From @Kristeeeeena - *blush*

To @Kristeeeeena - Will you have kisses for me when I get back?

My phone rings and it's a blocked number, "Hello?"

I hear the sweetest voice ever, "I've got kisses waiting for you."

I want to melt, but it's interrupted by Michelle in the background, "Seriously?"

I hear a slight scuffle and Kristina tells her, "Go call your boyfriend, if you can call him that. Don't you have to get to first base before he can be your boyfriend? Goodnight!" A door slams and she's back to me, "Sorry, peanut gallery."

"No worries, so are we alone in your bedroom again?"

"Yea," she giggles. "I liked having you in my bed."

"Maybe we can do that again?"

"Maybe somewhere without my roommate, somewhere with no interruptions."

"You're always welcome at my place. I hoped you would show up at my place last night."

"One thing at a time."

I chuckle, "I'm pretty sure you wanted my thing when I stayed at your place. Seems like dating comes first in the timeline."

Her voice gets low, "I know better. You're a baseball player. You fuck. You don't date."

I can't deny my past, she was there, "You're right, that's what I did in the past. That's not me anymore. You make me want more."

"How long until you go back to fucking?"

"I'm not going back to that. I want one special chick." I take a deep breath and feel my words in my stomach, "I want you."

"You're crazy."

"Tell me what you want. Do you want me?" I immediately wish I didn't ask. I don't want the answer and I don't want to be pushing her.

"I want to kiss you again. I want to know why you're not ready with me."

"I don't know what I'm doing with you. I want to make sure I'm doing it right. The only chicks I've been with since high school wanted one thing and got it. None of them wanted me, they wanted a player."

"What if I want the one thing?"

I chuckle, "I know you want the one thing, but your kiss and touch tell me you want more. I have to want you enough."

Her tone changes and she starts talking faster, "I have work in the morning. Goodnight."

She hangs up before I can respond.

To @Kristeeeeena - Did I say something wrong?
To @Kristeeeeena - I'm sorry if I did. I have to learn how to do this.
To @Kristeeeeena - Can we message tomorrow?
From @Kristeeeeena - Yes
To @Kristeeeeena - I wish I could hold you and kiss you goodnight.
From @Kristeeeeena - That sounds nice. Goodnight :)

I didn't lose her completely. I'm surprised she called me.

CHAPTER SEVENTEEN

Kristina

I should've worked yesterday. It would've been easier than making up for it today. Nobody prepped today's broadcast and I have a list of things that I need to do before I do live stats research during tonight's game.

From @RookCross - Good Morning, Sweetness :)
To @RookCross - You got the morning part right.
To @RookCross - Busy.
From @RookCross - Remember you're beautiful. I'll be home tomorrow night.

Chase

It's raining today. The roof is closed. My girl is busy and I won't be distracted by the night sky. The rain seems to have set the tone, dreary, gray, and cold. I take advantage of the closed roof and run the warning track with Seno. It requires no talking, we just run. We don't stay at the same pace, he doesn't have my speed, and I need to open up the throttle. I run a couple laps with Seno to get warmed up and then I stretch out my pace, finally increasing my speed.

My brain closes down when I'm running, clears everything out. Today I'm daydreaming. I'm holding Kristina on the beach when a storm hits. Water falling like buckets dumping from the sky. We're instantly soaked and cold. Her long dark hair dripping. Raindrops on her face and hanging onto her eyelashes. Her warm eyes looking up at me, searching mine with no concern for the rain. My wet hair falls into my face and she reaches for it, grazing my face and softly tucking it behind my ear. I grab her wrist and kiss it tenderly. She goes up on her tiptoes to kiss me and wraps her arms around my neck, running her fingers through the ends of my wet hair. Her sweet full lips worshiping mine until she drags her teeth across my lower lip, tugging on it. I lift her to me and she wraps herself around me instinctually. Our clothes sticking together and wet hair in our eyes. Thunder crashes loudly and I can see flashes from the lightning through my closed eyelids. Her body shakes and I tell her it's only thunder, but she's shaking for me. She wants me. I slide her down my body and take her hand, quickly leading her across the beach to my bungalow. We step inside and I pull my wet shirt off, tossing it to the floor. I gaze into her eyes and feel how hooded mine are. I reach for the bottom hem of her shirt and pull it off over her head, dropping it to the floor. She's gorgeous standing in front of me, wearing only shorts and a bra. Fresh from the rain and cool to the touch. I pull her against me and press my lips to hers, my hands splayed across her back. She reaches around my waist and slides her hands into my shorts, gently squeezing my ass. I move my hands up her sides and cup her tits. She kisses me open-mouthed as she drags her hands up to my hair and holds my mouth to hers. I move my hands to her neck, holding her and kissing her. She unbuttons her shorts and drops them to the floor, puddling at her feet. She unties my shorts and slides her fingers between me and the waistband. I push them off and take her hand in mine, wrapping her fingers around my dick that's hard for her. Her breath catches audibly and I pick her up, feeling her skin against mine. I kiss her with need, lifting her higher so I can bite and suck at her collarbone. She releases a moan and I take her to my bed. I'm hot, and heavy with desire. Everything is hazy. I've wanted her, needed her for so long and I finally have her. I want to love her and make her cry out my name. The haze takes over and everything is just happening. We're one, and it's how it's meant to be.

"Cross! Time for BP." I'm startled and I still don't know what it's like to have her. I'm dripping sweat. I'm also hard, I'll have to handle that.

To @Kristeeeeena - Been thinking about you. Hope your
day got better.

Chase

Nobody had said the word streak out loud, but when we saw the lineup for today we knew it was over. Stray catching instead of Seno. Mason is day to day, apparently he got cut on the cleats when he was tagging the player out at second at the end of the game yesterday. New guy George Hart is in the lineup covering shortstop for Mason. And, Mark Rock is covering me in Center Field with Bubbles in Right. We haven't won a game with Bubbles in the starting lineup all season. Seno told us that Skip was right, we all needed a day off and not to push. He'll put us in to play if he needs to. We're confident we'll be back to winning tomorrow.

Watching the game from the dug out is interesting. One, it reminds you what you're doing and refreshes your perspective. Two, veteran players do some crazy shit in the dug out. You'd think it would be the rookies, but it's not. The veterans have spent so many hours in the dug out that they have games to play. Everything from an old school hot foot to throwing seeds and shells at their teammates.

We lost 3-1.

I go out to eat with Mason and go back to my room. No messages from Kristina. I turn up the volume on my phone in case she calls and turn in early.

CHAPTER EIGHTEEN

Chase

To @Kristeeeeena - Good Morning, Sweetness...early game today, see you tonight!

The lineup is back to normal and we're ready to play. They taped up Mason's hand, he's even good to go. The team is amped up, ready to go home and face Florida. We needed the day off. Time to beat Washington.

I get a four pitch leadoff walk to start the game and take my base. Mason hits a ground ruled double on the first pitch, he's becoming a double making machine. He could be a middle of the lineup hitter. Martin hits a double bringing us home, score 2-0 Seals and Washington has pitchers up warming in their bullpen. Seno works the pitch count up and draws a walk. Lucky Lucine is feisty today. He's communicating with Skip and the runners, and he's all smiles—a play is on. He's crowding the plate and almost dancing in the batter's box while he waits for the pitch. I look at Seno and Martin, both trying to keep their game face on. The pitcher buries a slider in the dirt and it gets away from the catcher, both runners advance on the passed ball and Lucky keeps dancing. Lucine gets hit by the pitch and the bases are loaded with Seals. Brandt comes up to bat and skies one to right field on the first pitch. His first grand slam in the Bigs. 6-0 Seals with no outs. Washington changes pitchers, and strikes out the next three Seals.

I'm leading off again in the second inning, which doesn't happen often, and work the pitch count full. I hit a grounder up the third base line and leg out the throw, safe at first. Mason pops up on the fourth pitch and I make it a sac fly, getting to second base safely. Martin strikes out on five pitches. Seno crushes a homer to the parking lot. Lucky choppers one up the center and gets tagged out at second. 8-0 Seals.

Washington responds in the bottom of the second by making me cover every inch of Center Field. Every hit is in my zone and I don't let the ball touch the ground. We get on base, but nobody scores in the third, fourth, and fifth innings. I'm jumping at the wall, sliding across the field and diving to get the outs. I make it a rule not to show injuries or pain. I don't want to be pulled from the game.

Skip makes me part of the double switch in the middle of the sixth inning and I make my case, "I've got Center covered. Leave me in. I'm a dog playing fetch today."

He looks me up and down, "You're scraped up, bloody, dirty, and have more holes in your uni than I've ever seen in all my years as coach here. See first aid and get cleaned up. You're done for the day."

"Yes, sir." I storm off to the club house and indulge myself with a long hot shower before the rest of the team gets there. The medic is waiting for me when I come out of the shower, ready to disinfect and bandage up my battle damage. I played hard today and it feels good.

Kristina

I feed the lineup change to the broadcasters and ask for more info when I see the double switch taking Chase out of a game that he's been the star in. There's no details, just a double switch at this point.

> To @RookCross - Pulled you out on a double-switch?
> To @RookCross - Are you okay?

I go back and scan through highlights from the last few innings. He's made some unbelievable plays and has some serious hustle, but his uniform is getting more blood soaked as the game goes on.

> To @RookCross - Chase?

Chase

I'm putting my phone in airplane mode when I see I've missed a call from a blocked number. There's no voicemail. I check my twitter and see the messages from Kristina with no time to respond.

> To @Kristeeeeena - Planes taking off. I'm fine.

Kristina

Why isn't he responding? He was playing his position better than anyone else in the league. He must be hurt or they wouldn't have pulled him. I go back to the feed searching for details. Why haven't they said anything? How hard would it be to give a quick update? The game is finally over and I get a break from assisting the broadcasters. I resort to a bathroom stall and social media. I need to know what happened. He always tweets, nothing. Nothing anywhere. I can't do this. I go to my cubicle and replay the game on fast forward searching for something, anything that will tell me what happened. He's got holes in his uniform at the knees and along his thigh near his hip. His pants are bloodstained at the knees and he's bled enough for it to drip down his leg. His forearm is raw. No matter his condition or injury, his expression is determined.

I notice the team is on their way home and watch the coach's post-game presser hoping one of the reporters asked about Chase. Finally, something! Nothing about any injury, only praise for how hard he plays and a joke about the coach not liking the holes in his uniform, but he did give confirmation that we will be seeing Cross in the lineup for the next game.

My whole body relaxes and tears stream down my face uncontrollably. I can breathe again. I stop and gather myself. I can't be this person. Fucking baseball players! Why did he do this to me?

Chase

The plane lands and I turn off airplane mode to find my message to Kristina didn't go through. It sends and I message her again.

> To @Kristeeeeena - Sent that message before we took off and it didn't go through.
> To @Kristeeeeena - Just landed in San Diego.
> To @Kristeeeeena - I'll be at the stadium soon. Are you there?

I'm suddenly excited, I know she's working today. I'll get to see her soon.

I drop my stuff off in my locker and wander around a bit, hoping to run into Kristina.

Carter pulls me into his office, "I saw you looking all lost puppy dog and checked to see where she is today. She went home early. She left an hour ago."

"I don't get this chick. Thanks."

> To @Kristeeeeena - Are you okay?
> To @Kristeeeeena - Did I do something wrong?
> From @Kristeeeeena - Please leave me alone.

I hear Seno in my head, "Keep her thinking about you and don't message her too much." I go home and attempt to get my laundry done.

> Text from Mason - Video games at your place?
> Text to Mason - Sure. Bring pizza.

The pizza is gone and Mason's phone has been blowing up. I've only got two messages, and they're both unexpected.

Text from Chip - We miss you.
Text from Dale - Want to play?

Mason stretches and stands up, "Well, time for me to go. See you tomorrow."

"Dude, we're in the middle of a game."

"I'm tired," he fake yawns and laughs.

"Michelle?"

"Yeah."

"At least one of us can have some fun."

"Don't worry. I won't. Sticking to the good boy plan."

"Dude, you gotta do something. At least tell her what you're waiting for."

"I'm thinking about it. Maybe I can sleep in her bed, but on top of the blankets. Bye." He trots out the door to see his woman and all I've got is an invitation for sex with the twins. I never thought that would be a bad thing.

I'm going to bed before I make a bad choice.

To @Kristeeeeena - Goodnight

CHAPTER NINETEEN

Chase

I get to the stadium early, hoping to run into Kristina since she hasn't responded to my messages. I walk into Carter's office and he never even looks up, "She's PA Announcer again today. It's retro day and I already have a cap made for her."

"Perfect. Is there anything new and obnoxious in the team store to deliver with the cap?"

"Are you trying to piss her off?" He asks sarcastically.

"Yes."

"Whatever you want, man. How about a ragdoll Cross?"

"Are you fucking kidding me right now? They have those?"

"Oh yeah, they made ragdolls of you, Mason, and Martin."

"Take her that, too. The bigger the better." I grin, happy with myself and knowing I'll be kissing her at the first base wall before the game. "Thanks."

Chase

Michelle is back behind home plate with Sherry. It looks like Mason has hooked her up with retro gear. I wonder what he did to get back in good graces. No sign of Kristina. There's only a few minutes left before the announcements start. Where is she?

Kristina

What doesn't he understand? I told him to leave me alone. I've told him not to send things to the control booth, but he still does that too! I should throw the doll into the stands! Right out the control booth window! Or, maybe, hang it by a noose and let it dangle there for the whole game. Maybe that would get my point across. The ragdoll really does look like him, it even has muscles in the same places, the same hair. Damn it! I put the cap on backwards and get to announcing.

I see him look up to the booth and smile as I announce him and "I Want to Hold Your Hand" plays. He's irritating. I turn to the sound operator, "Would it be possible to change his walk-up for his next at bat?"

"Yes, but I need a written request."

I write a note and hand it to her, "Will that work?"

"No problem. This should be fun."

Chase is walking to first and I keep up with my announcing on queue. I hear Michelle yelling for Mason as he walks up to bat and decide, why not? I write a note requesting to change Mason's song, too. I know I shouldn't, but I'm done with the players. Mason hits a double and I try to focus on my task at hand.

Bottom of the third inning, I announce Cross and "I Don't Like You" by the Wrecks plays as his walk-up song. I watch as he stops halfway to the plate and swings his bat wildly. He hits a home run on the first pitch, knocking in today's starting pitcher, Corey Grace. I obviously don't affect his game.

Chase

Did she really change my walk-up song? She won't message me. She won't give me her phone number. She didn't find me at the wall and kiss me. "I Don't Like You," she's full of shit! I step on home plate and Mason shakes his head at me. She announces him and "Kiss Me" by Sixpence None the Richer plays.

He turns to me and mouths, "What the fuck?" I see him look at Michelle and she shrugs, but likes the idea. She makes kissy lips at him and laughs.

I yell into the clubhouse, "Carter!"

He pops his head into the dug out, "What do you need?"

"Change my walk-up song to," I stop and think for a minute and write it down. I hand him the note.

"No problem."

"Wait. Change Mason's, too. Make his," I add to the note.

"He's okay with that?"

"Um, yeah." What the fuck? Why not?

Carter nods and disappears.

Seno glares at me, "Are you causing trouble?"

"Just having some fun, I figure it can't hurt. It's making her think about me." I'm surprised to hear the happy tone in my voice and realize it's because of her. I'm happy simply thinking about her or playing with her.

Seno shakes his head and I enjoy the game, waiting for the next move.

Kristina

Bottom of the 6th, I announce Chase again and his walk-up song changed to "My Favorite Liar" by The Wrecks. Are you kidding me! He doesn't believe me. Cocky bastard! Of course, all the women like him. He's not giving up on me and I'm trying to push him away. I almost miss my mark to announce Mason because I'm in my head. I look up and see that Chase got a double while I hear "The Last of the Real Ones" by Fall Out Boy play. I wonder which of them changed the song. I do like the sentiment, they are real. I immediately write a note and hand it to the sound operator.

She laughs, "You all are keeping me busy tonight."

Chase

Sitting with Mason in the dug out, "Did she change it again? How'd it get to Fall Out Boy?"

"I did it that time. Why not, right?"

"Good choice." He shakes his head in a way that tells me it's okay this time, but don't do it again. I'm cool with that.

It's a low scoring game and we aren't getting many at bats.

Mason and I will both get an at bat in the 9th if the other team scores, possibly the eighth if we score.

The score is 3-0 Seals in the bottom of the eighth and we're up at bat. I'm anxious to see if my walk-up song changes again. Swinging the bat in the on deck circle and she announces me, her voice sounding clear and almost chuckling. "Sunglasses at Night" blares through the sound system and I can't help but smile at the imagery it conjures in my head. All I can do is see her in those PJs. Fuck! I get hard walking to the plate. I bend over at the plate and rub dirt on my hands to buy me a minute and glance up at her, wondering if she knows what she's done. I do my best to concentrate on the ball, even asking for a time out and stepping out of the box to focus.

Seno yells from the dug out, "Get your head on straight!"

I see the ball in the pitcher's hand and try to slow everything down. It's straight up the pipe in the middle of the strike zone and doesn't look like it has any wiggle to it. Hoping for a walk, but I have to hit this. There's a crack off my bat and the ball is flying to Left Field. I drop my bat in pieces and run, hoping the ball won't get caught. The fielder couldn't get to it in time and on any other at bat I would've made this a double, tonight I'm happy to be safe at first and not sliding into the base.

Kristina announces Mason and "1950" by King Princess plays. She's on a roll! Mason looks irritated, but Michelle yells out that she loves that song and he's happy again. She'll get everything she wants from him. I can see it now. But, it's on his time schedule. I kind of respect that. I'd still be hitting it.

I hope for a walk or a home run, anything that keeps me from having to run fast. He choppers it up the diamond and I need full speed. Middle infielders miss the ball and the Center-fielder is running in to back them up. I'm already on my way to third and need my speed. I don't want to slide. I have to slide. I make it to third base safely, even keeping all my good bits intact. Mason's safe at first. Martin hits a home run and I run across home straight to the dug out.

Seno's laughing at me, "Hard problem to have. I think she won that battle." She absolutely did, but I'll never admit it out loud.

Top of the ninth, Seals are ahead 6-1 and Skip pulls me for the double switch. Thank you for small favors because this hard-on won't go away. I head into the clubhouse, showering at attention and lean my forehead on my arm against the wall allowing the water to fall over me. I close my eyes and imagine us in the rain together naked, pushing into her heat with her lips at my neck. It's all it takes to relieve the pressure. I need this chick.

Kristina

Home games are better. I have access and verified he isn't hurt in seconds. Not that I care. Fuck. I care.

Chase

She still hasn't messaged me. I don't want to message her too much, but…

To @Kristeeeeena - I'm home for the night. You're always welcome to join me. Your terms.
From @Kristeeeeena - Okay
To @Kristeeeeena - Goodnight, Sweetness.

None of this changes the way I feel about her. I want her with me. I want her in my bed. I want my lips on hers. I know she wants me, too. I don't know why she keeps fighting it.

Kristina

I'm tossing and turning. In my bed. Alone. I don't have to be. I could be with Chase. I sleep when I'm with him. Maybe I should call him and have him over? I need sleep. Or, I could go to his place. He did invite me. He keeps inviting me. I love his arms around me. He gives me the protection I'm missing. It's more than comfort and feeling safe. It's not fair to use him like that. I can't keep him. I haven't cried and worried this much, well, ever. It's too much for me. I need to focus on my goal and get the gig I'm working for. No, there will be no baseball players for me.

What if I can have a baseball player? What if, hypothetically, I want one? What if I eliminate the whole ball player boycott? Is it a possibility? If not, I want a night with him. I want to know what it could've been like. If I regret it later, I want to know I did it and have the memory.

I pick up my phone, hoping there might be a new message from him. Of course there's not. It's 2am. I need to let it go.

CHAPTER TWENTY

Chase

Saturday's game was a total blow out. Seals lost 9-0. Skip instituted a new rule: No changing your walk-up song mid-game. I changed it to "Head Games" by Foreigner before the game started. I may not have won the game, but I made the final play.

Sunday's game is early and Monday is an off day. We all need it. We need a few off days, but that's not an option in the life of a professional baseball player. No BP and if we win, party at my place. I already restocked the party supplies. We always win on Sunday. Sunday is Run Day.

Fielding isn't looking good today, but the Sunday Run Day rule is holding true. Everyone on the starting lineup has a hit in the first two innings. I want the game over. I need a break and a couple days at my beach bungalow will be perfect.

Top of the 6th inning and the score is already 10-1 Seals. Skip pulls the key players and puts in the second stringers, they need playing time and we need a break. Final score 12- 5 Seals.

To @Kristeeeeena - Team will be celebrating at my house.

To @Kristeeeeena - Hope you can join us.

To @Kristeeeeena - I'm going surfing in the morning if you want to stay over.

To @Kristeeeeena - No pressure. Whatever you want.

To @Kristeeeeena - I wish you'd talk to me or at least respond.

To @Kristeeeeena - Please, Sweetness.

I look and realize I've messaged her like a stalker again. I shove my phone in my pocket and go home.

Kristina

I've tried to stay away. He's my weakness. Sweetness. Every time he calls me that it goes straight to my heart and flutters down to my belly. He doesn't know that. Nobody does.

I've been hiding out a bit, trying to get my head straight and not do anything stupid. The problem is that quiet time can reveal the truth. It's not my head that's the problem, it's my heart. My head knows what I want to do and focuses on the goal, but it has nothing to do with what my heart wants. This time, my heart might be winning.

I worked as long as I could after the game, an intentional distraction. I leave the stadium on auto-pilot and go home. I can't get him out of my head, and maybe I don't want to. I walk into my empty apartment and texts pop through.

Text from GamerGirlM - I'm with Mase at Chase's.

Text from GamerGirlM - You should be here, too.

Text from GamerGirlM - No response required.

Text from GameGirlM - You know you want to.

Text from GamerGirlM - Do it already!

I toss my PJs, swimsuit, and clothes in my overnight bag. I'm going surfing with Chase in the morning.

I get to Chase's and walk in without being noticed. The team and guests are all outside on the beach, and who can blame them? It's the perfect day for it. Nerves hit me and I'm exhausted. I place my bag in the corner of his bedroom with intentions of going to find Michelle, but his bed is so inviting. It's a cloud of soft fluffy blankets. I run my fingers along his bed and imagine him sleeping there. His masculine scent overtakes my senses. I sit on the edge of his bed and lean back on his pillows. It's perfect. I sink in and it's so comfortable. I'm so tired. Maybe, just a quick nap…

Chase

The team is over to celebrate again, but my bungalow has turned more into a space that everyone can use. The permanent team bonfire. I'm okay with that, the team is family and I like having them around. It seems I'd be here alone without them.

The waves are coming in larger than normal and nobody here needs me, time to surf.

I go in my bedroom to change and hit the waves. I find an overnight bag in the corner of my room and look around. Someone's in my bed, sunk down into the mattress and buried under my comforter. I can only see their outline as they sleep in my bed and it's defined as the Stay Puft Marshmallow Man. I hear a sweet little noise and my body goes on high alert. Kristina's in my bed and she brought her overnight bag. I didn't even know she was here. I need to recap this. The woman I want is in my bed and brought what she needs to stay the night, but I can't have her because she won't date me. So, I can't have her phone number and she refuses to date me, but she's sleeping in my bed and seems to like to kiss me. At least she used to like to kiss me. And, she's planning on staying the night with me? How's this going to work? I guess I can sleep in the same bed with her and hold her again. It does sound nice to have her in my bed with me all night. Spending the night with her was, I don't know—special. She made it challenging to keep it in my pants. We both wanted more. Or, I could sleep on the couch, but it may be occupied again. Seems like one of the rookies is on my couch most nights. Feels like I'm set up for failure. I can't pick up where we left off. I need her to know that I still want her enough. Besides, I'm leaving for a road trip in two days. I can't be with her and then leave. I want to spend more time with her. What are the Las Vegas odds on me sleeping with her and not *sleeping* with her? Sounds like something I'd put money on and I know which way I'd bet. I don't think those odds are in my favor. I hope she's not still trying to get me to fuck her out of my system. I need Sherry.

I go to the bonfire to find Sherry cuddled up with Seno, and sit next to them. "What do you want?" Fairly rude reception from Seno, especially considering they're at my house. No idea what I interrupted.

Quietly, I share my situation and wait for advice.

"What do you want to do?" Sherry asks.

"That's not a fair question. I've wanted her for months. It's the first time she's been in my bed and she's there alone, she chose to sleep in my bed and didn't even say anything. I'm supposed to take her to my bed, not find her there sleeping. She still won't give me her fucking phone number, but she'll walk into my place and make herself at home in my room? She brought her stuff, she's planning on staying over."

"Do you want her here?" Sherry questions.

"Yes."

"You need to find out what she wants."

"Fine. But, what if she wants me to fuck her out of my system? That's what she wanted when she tried to get me into her bed the first time. I don't want her to feel like that. I'm not using her. It could be awkward if she thinks I'm turning her down again. What she wants seems to change."

"Are you ready to have sex with her? Really?"

"Not until she goes out with me. I need her to know she's special and that I want her enough."

"So, tell her you really want her, but you aren't ready yet. She should respect that."

"Are we talking about the same confusing chick? She doesn't always make sense or do the logical thing."

Seno adds, "Sometimes rules are meant to be broken," as he holds Sherry tighter. "You have to do what's right for you. Everybody's different. Maybe she doesn't like to go out. Fuck, maybe she has a boyfriend."

"Do I leave her alone in my bed until later or let her know I know she's here or climb in bed with her? Never mind. I know what to do."

"Good luck," I get from both of them as I walk back in the house and into my room.

Chase

I carefully sit on the edge of my bed and roll over on top of the comforter, trying to find exactly where she's buried. I pull the blankets down to reveal her face and I'm driven to snuggle up against her. I put my arm around where I think she is and kiss her cheek sweetly. She's not fighting me, pushing me away, or trying to get me to fuck her. I want to climb in under the blankets with her and kiss her. I want to feel her warm body next to mine. I want to push my dick into her and feel her tight around me. I think the blanket barrier is a good idea for now and I probably shouldn't drink tonight. She looks so sweet and beautiful. Something about her being in my bed makes her feel like she's mine and gives me permission to kiss her. I press my lips to hers softly and feel a magnetic pull between us, pushing me to take more than one soft, innocent kiss. I want her badly, but I can't go there. Kissing her, well I have to—I need to. I press my lips to hers repeatedly with her between my arms and she kisses me back without opening her eyes. I nibble at her lower lip and she opens her mouth for me on a sweet moan. I slide my tongue across her lips and against her tongue, needing her kiss, needing to taste her and wanting more. She moves, pulling her arms out from under the blankets and pushes me away. She opens her eyes and looks at me differently. Without saying a word, she reaches her arms around me and pulls me back to her, kissing me senseless. Fuck me. I want to know why she's in my bed. I want to know what she wants. I want to know if she's really staying with me tonight. And damn Seno, now I want to know if she has a boyfriend and if she does, he has to go. Kristina's mine now. All I can do is feel her lips on mine and her arms holding me to her. She drags her teeth over my lower lip and sucks on it lightly while she pulls away from me.

She stops and gazes into my eyes, "Hi," is all she says and her voice is different. Sleepy maybe and sweet. Like she's let her guard down.

"Hi," I don't want to disturb the mood. I love that she's being so sweet.

She smiles, "I brought my overnight bag, so I can stay with you tonight and maybe go surfing in the morning."

That counts as a date. I'm not asking if she will go out with me anymore. I'm asking her to do specific things with me, like going surfing or maybe going out to eat. I love the sound of her voice saying, "stay with you." I'm feeling lucky and want to ask for her phone number, but I think better of it. I leave on a road trip Tuesday morning. I'm not having sex with her until I get back. I'm not starting something and then leaving her the next day, that can't happen. I'm suddenly slammed with the realization that I've never had a woman in my bed at my bungalow. It feels so right. Foreigner takes over ear worming me with their love songs and I must be going crazy. Does she feel it, too?

My body is humming happily, "I'm so happy that you did." I want in her so bad right now, the head on my shoulders is spinning and the one below my waist is throbbing. I need to stay in control. I bite and suck at her soft lips, and I feel her body moving underneath me. This blanket barrier needs to go, I need to touch her. Stop! I gather the calmest voice that I can, "Kristina, do you have another guy, a boyfriend?" It sounds so childish, but Seno said it and now I have to know.

She looks at me with big eyes, "I wouldn't be here if I did. I've never cheated and I never will."

I smile, "So, I'm your only guy right now."

"I'm not dating anybody right now."

"What do you call what we're doing?"

Kristina smiles, "Kissing in your bed." She giggles knowing that isn't what I asked.

"There will be no other chicks in my bed and I won't kiss any other chicks, unless you tell me we're done." I look into her eyes, wanting her to know how much she means to me. "Just you, Kristina." I take a deep breath. "Please tell me you want me and only me." I'm in uncharted territory. I haven't had any type of exclusive relationship since junior high. I haven't wanted one. But, Kristina—she's different and I want to be with her even if it's only kissing.

"I can't. I don't want you. You drive me crazy and freak me out. The one thing I've wanted to do is be in the control booth at the stadium and I get the chance at the PA Announcer, the ultimate gig—I totally fucked up and I wouldn't have if it wasn't for you. I couldn't help it! Then the afterthought about how often you're at bat and at risk, left me shook. No, I can't want you because you screw me up. You and your sending me flowers with sweet notes, caps with your name and number on them, you looking up and smiling at me in the control booth, you blowing me kisses and, seriously, changing your walk up song? I keep telling you no and I haven't even given you my phone number! Yet, you don't stop. No, I don't want you. I can't want you."

My heart sinks, but it doesn't make any sense, "Then why are you here? Why do you keep kissing me? Why are you fucking with me?" I stare at her and wait for an answer.

Kristina lets out a deep sigh, "That whole rant I just spat out at you doesn't matter. I can't stop thinking about you. I can't pass up a chance to kiss you. I don't want you. I have to have you, be near you, and it doesn't matter how much more sense it makes to walk away because I'll give everything else up before you."

All of a sudden the barrier and my dick, neither one of them matter. She's as messed up as I am. I get up and lock my bedroom door. I pull my T-shirt off and climb into my bed under the blankets wearing only my board shorts, reaching for her and holding her to me. I nuzzle my face into her hair, "I know. It's scary for me, too." It's amazing to have her in my arms. I can feel her breathing and her heart beating. I hold her curled into my chest and her warm breath caresses my skin. She entangles her bare legs with mine and I realize I don't even know what she's wearing. It feels like a silky little top and short shorts, probably pajamas again. It doesn't matter. All that matters is that I have her in my arms and I'm going to keep it this way for as long as I can. The team will pick up and lock up on their way out, they'll get it. I don't know if I should talk to her or just hold her. It's not about sex. Kristina touches my chest, delicately exploring from my collarbone to my pecs to my abs. Slowly moving lower and closer to things I'm not sure we're ready for. I grab her hand before she can get to my shorts. "Kristina, I," I groan at the words I'm going to say, "I leave Tuesday morning for a road trip. I don't want to have sex with you and then be gone for days. I want to be here with you and know we can be together for days, spend our nights together and spoil you." My voice goes raspy, "I want to push into you while you're kissing me and I know I shouldn't say that because it sounds like I want sex, but I want you. I don't want us to just be sex. I want you to know how much I want you and believe that I want you enough."

"Chase, show me how much you want me. Take me."

"Kristina, it's not a good idea. We need to spend time together. We need to get to know each other." She presses her lips to my neck and, "Anything you want. I'll give you anything you want." She climbs on top of me, her body laying on top of mine while she continues to kiss, lick and suck at my neck. Her breasts squish into my chest and her hands are in my hair. I can't control myself and I don't want to wait any longer. I know I should, but I tell myself this is one of those times that rules are meant to be broken. I slide her shorts down over her hips and touch her bare skin, I feel her breath hitch. I run my hands up her sides and pull her top off over her head. I have her naked, lying on me in my bed. She had no objections to me taking her clothes off. Her skin is soft and silky all over. I keep touching her, caressing her. I move my hands to her tits and take one of them in each hand, squeezing them gently and kissing them where they come together. I give each of them attention, licking, kissing and sucking at her nipples. Her reaction is crazy. I can feel her whole body needing me, wanting me. She said she doesn't want me, but it's a lie. She wants to protect herself and there's no protection from this. I move my hands down her body, simply touching her and getting to know her shape. I wrap my arms around her and pull her mouth up to mine, kissing her with no doubt of what's on my mind while I hold her tightly to me. I pull back, "Tell me to stop. Tell me to stop before I can't stop." My pulse is racing and I'm nervous. I'm never nervous. "Kristina."

"Chase, please, I want to feel you. I need you." She's breathless and her words make me want to please her. "Condom, okay?"

"I'll always protect you, I've got you." I kiss her neck and roll us over so she's naked underneath me. She reaches for my shorts and unties them, gesturing for me to get rid of them. I do as she asks, stripping bare and grabbing a condom from my nightstand. I hit the remote on the stereo, turning up the music in the house. Foreigner is playing "Feels like the First Time" and my nerves feel the same way. What if I'm not what she wants? What if I'm not any good? I lean on my arm and press my lips to hers tenderly, I want her and I don't want to just fuck her. I want to take care of her and please her. I move my free hand down between her legs, feeling how hot and wet she is. Fuck me, I need in. I need to feel her wrapped around me. I rip open the foil wrapper with one hand and my teeth, and roll the condom on. I rub my tip against her opening, she's tight and I can feel her nerves, "We can still stop. I don't want to push you."

"Please, Chase. I want this." She goes back to kissing my neck and it's my downfall. I slide my finger inside her, sliding it in and out of her wet heat. "Oh."

"Don't worry. I'll take care of you. That's my finger. I promise I won't hurt you." I want her to relax and she's too wound up. I understand, I could hammer nails with my dick right now. I slide in a second finger and she cries out. I can't do this. I'm too big for her. I'll hurt her. I kiss my way down to her sex and lick her clit while I stroke her with my fingers, flicking at it with my tongue and then sucking. I slide down further, pulling my fingers out and burying my face. Licking and sucking at her folds, she reaches for my head and runs her fingers through my hair while she feels me at her center. I feel her pulse quickening.

"Chase, please. I want all of you the first time."

I slide my finger back in and keep stroking her. "I want you to have me. God, I want in you. But, I'll hurt you."

"Please, all of you, now. I want you, okay. I want you!"

"I really do want you," I'm hard and needy. I press my lips to hers and she whimpers with need. Her sweet whimper. She rolls her hips and my hard dick feels her heat firsthand. I know it will hurt her, but she wants it anyway. I wrap my arms around her tightly, holding her against me while we kiss and push into her a little further with each stroke. I don't let her go and I keep it slow, giving her everything I can on each stroke. Feeling her so tight around me, "Oh, Kristina. We'll make it better, I promise."

"Chase, please don't hold back. I want all of you. Give me all of you." She says breathlessly.

I pull out and look at her lying there in my bed, asking me for more.

"Please, Chase, please." And I just want back inside her. I've waited for her for so long and she feels so good around me. I can't help myself and I slam all the way into her a couple times, "Chase! Oh! Chase!" She screams out my name and I push all the way in until our bodies are mashed together. I look at our connection and see how tight she is around me, knowing how hard I am and how much of me is buried inside her. How I slammed into that tight hole and made myself fit because she wants all of me. Fuck she feels amazing and she wants all of me.

"Kristina, tell me its good for you. Tell me you feel it, too." I stroke in and out of her slowly as I lean in and kiss her, claiming her mouth as my own, and in my heart claiming her as mine. She whimpers and cries out with every pass. "Tell me your mine. Tell me what you want. I'll make it happen. Anything and everything for you." Fuck! I'm losing it! The feel of our bodies together, my skin burns everywhere she touches me, like she leaves a trail of flames in her path. I want more of her. I whisper in her ear, "Does it feel okay? I need to know I'm not hurting you. I never want to hurt you."

She turns to face me smiling, "It's perfect, Chase. You're perfect." Her sweet soft voice cuts straight through me. Fuck me. "You don't have to be careful with me. Show me you want me."

She's killing me. I'm already thinking about baseball to keep from firing off. I kiss her, claiming her completely and taking control of everything, while I keep moving inside her, pulling out and then pushing back in repeatedly and slowly. I feel her arch in pleasure underneath me and I start to move faster. "Oh, Kristina." I need her to finish first. Finishing first is not an option for me. I sit back on my knees and lift her right leg in the air, kissing her ankle and leg, while I keep moving harder and faster. Her leg resting against my shoulder, I reach under her and grab her ass, pulling her closer to me. I hear her crying out my name and it's like magic. Her cry turns to a squeal when I feel her tighten up around me and she's pulling me with her, I couldn't stop if I wanted to and I don't want to. She feels amazing as I pound into her hard, pushing her orgasm and being overcome by mine. I feel like I'm going to explode like never before while her body continues to squeeze me.

"Oh, Chase! Chase! Oh! Fucking amazing, oh my..." She trails off and grabs me, pulling me down to her and making me stop moving. But, that's all it takes and I'm done. She kisses me, then stops and gazes up at me doe eyed. I'm not quite with her yet, I feel like I'm coming forever and keep moving as much as I can as I finish. I move to pull out and she stops me. "No, just stay here and kiss me. I want more of you, Chase." I smile and she continues, "Do you still want me or..."

I cut her off, "I told you it isn't possible to fuck you out of my system. It's not like that, Kristina. Of course I still want you. I want you more than I did before and I didn't think that was possible." Listen to me! Fuck! Can I really only have one chick? Fuck me. Yes. I press my lips to hers and I'm still hard, ready for more. Her lips are inviting and she's full of desire. I start to move inside her, but she stops me.

"I'm not ready yet."

"It's okay. I thought you wanted more. We don't need to do anything."

"I do. It's just, uh, you're big and I'm not prepared."

"I'm happy to hold you all night. I want you here with me." I smile at her. I pull out of her slowly and go handle some quick business in the bathroom. I return to find her dressed and putting her shoes on. I don't understand. "Where are you going?"

"Well, I thought I should go home."

"No." I walk over to her and put my arms around her, still naked. "You're staying with me tonight."

"We already…"

I cut her off, "No. I'm not playing this game with you any more. I know you want to be with me and you know I want to be with you. You have a choice: Get back in my bed with me right now or join the party with me and I'll hold you out by the bonfire. No more running scared."

She stares at me and doesn't speak.

"Are you just in this for sex? Did you just use me?" The words come out a little loud and more harshly than I'd intended. I guess it could be true. I did find her in my bed. She could've been waiting for me and hoping to get laid. Fuck! I gave her what she wanted and now she's out. This is why Seno said to date first, I need to know if they want me or a ball player. Now I'm angry. I've been waiting for her. I wanted her and no other chick. Fuck! "Kristina! You better say something quick." I'm pacing around my room while my head spins and I'm not letting her leave my room no matter what she says. I know the truth and this is bullshit.

She looks at me blankly and disturbed by my tone.

"You told me you wanted me to keep kissing you and now

you're up and dressed? Ready to leave? Tell me you didn't use me."

"I'm not using you. I'm embarrassed." She says quietly.

"You have no reason to be. You're staying with me."

"Okay."

"Good." I walk to her and make her decision for her. I unbutton her shorts and push them down until they fall to her feet. I pull her top off over her head and toss it on the floor. I take in the view of her in matching jade lace panties and bra. She's hot. Slender, but not skinny and curvy in all the right places. I pick her up, bringing her tits to my mouth, "Wrap your legs around me and hold on, I'm taking you back to bed." She wraps her legs around me and holds onto my head, playing with my hair. I lick and suck at her tits through her lace bra and she shudders. I sit on the edge of my bed and lay back with her in my arms. My dick is still hard and reaching for her.

She slides down my body wanting to find my mouth and bumps into my waiting hard-on. She reaches back and puts her hand around me, feeling me. Her touch sends more of that electricity through my body.

"Sorry, he can be rude." I laugh.

"Don't be sorry. Feels like he wants me."

"He definitely does. So do I, but I want more than him."

She giggles at me and slides down a little further, like she's going for my neck. She reaches behind her again and strokes my hard length, obviously liking the feel of it. In a second she's guided him in and slides onto me. She slides back and forth a few times.

"Kristina, you can't do…" But, I lose all ability to think and speak when she sits up and rides me like a cowgirl. Grinding against me while she's mounted on my hard dick. She's so hot and wet, and I can actually feel everything. Fuck me, fuck me, fuck me! I need to get her off of me, but she feels so good. "Kristina?"

"Yeah," She responds out of breath.

"No condom." I don't want to stop either, but we can't do this.

"Yeah, okay." What the fuck?

"Um, not okay."

"Feels good."

"I know, it's way better. But, we need a condom." Two months ago I didn't even know who I had in my bed and if I had sex, now I'm the voice of reason? This chick. I say things to her and I mean them. I told her I'd protect her.

"Just a little more, please." Her eyes are closed and her skin is turning red and blotchy.

"No, no more. You're going to make me come."

"No, I'll come and then I'll stop."

She doesn't seem to get it, "Kristina, are you trying to get knocked up by a ball player?"

"You feel good. I need you, Chase."

Fuck me. Baseball. Baseball. Baseball. What's worse, Basketball. Basketball. Men's stinky locker room. Dumpsters. Baseball. Baseball. Baseball. I need a plan here. That's it, get her off quick and get her off me before I blow. I press up into her and she cries out. She's close. I reach for our connection and it's crazy how solid I am right now. Don't get distracted from the mission. I reach for her clit and touch it lightly, circling around it softly and adding more pressure, then I press it and I feel her get wetter. "Kristina, listen to me." She nods. "You're fucking amazing. You make me so hard that I don't know how you and your tight little hole are doing this right now. I'm huge and up in you. I don't know if you looked, but I'm eight inches long or so and right now, you've got me at max. I couldn't be stretched any harder. I'm at least two inches thick and a while ago you could barely take my finger. Do you feel that?" I press up into her again and again and again.

"Yes," her voice shakes.

"Come for me. Feel how hard and hot our connection is. Come for me." I should pull out because I'm out of control, but I'm as bad as she is. "Kristina. Kristina. Kristina. Oh, fuck me! Fuck me!" I'm on the far edge and no better, but she starts to come and I can feel everything—Fuck, no condom. Baseball. Baseball. Baseball. Maybe I can bring it back in. I can have control. I can have control.

"Chase! I'm yours. I'm yours. Oh, God, I'm yours." She collapses on my chest and I pull out of her as quickly as possible. What was I thinking? Her wetness is all over me and I'm coming like a fucking hose in two strokes. This is crazy. I feel her heart beating against my chest and she's not moving.

"Sweetness, are you okay?"

"I'm better than okay. Sorry."

"Don't be sorry. Tell me your mine again." I'm such a fucking chick.

"I'm yours, Chase. I'm yours." Her voice is so sincere and sweet that my heart leaps in my chest.

I kiss her on the cheek, "No other dudes? Only me? And, you'll be my girl?"

She smiles giddily, "No other guys. Only you. Nobody compares to you. I'm already your girl." She laughs, "Does that mean you're my boyfriend?"

I hadn't thought about it but, "Yes. You're the only chick in my life." It makes me happy to say it. "Put some sweats on." She glares at me funny, "Work with me here." I pull on sweatpants and a zippered hoodie. I watch as she pulls leggings out of her bag and a T-shirt. "Hold on." I toss her a Seals pullover hoodie that will be huge on her and keep her warm. She pulls on her leggings and my hoodie, looking fucking sexy in my hoodie that fits her more like a dress. I grab my extra blanket and hand it to Kristina. I take her hand and lead her out of the bedroom to the bonfire. There's nobody left in the house and it's been cleaned up, no gamers left, and nobody passed out on my couch. I snag what's left of the food from the patio table and a couple bottles of water from the ice chest. We find the Senos, and Mason and Michelle both coupled up, wrapped together in blankets at the bonfire.

"Is everybody else gone?" I ask.

"Yea, everything is taken care of. Just us left enjoying the bonfire." Sherry offers the answer and smiles as she witnesses Kristina and I together.

I sit down on the sand and take the blanket from Kristina. I wrap the blanket around my back and pull her down to my lap. We snack on the leftovers and snuggle together with the blanket around us. I pull the blanket over our heads and find her lips with mine, simply brushing my lips against hers and I feel her smile. I whisper to her, "Will you stay with me until I leave Tuesday morning?"

"I'd love to. I might get called in to work tomorrow and I need to go home and get clothes before I have to work Tuesday morning. Okay?"

"I can work with that. Can I have your phone number now?" I still hesitate to ask, but I'm feeling confident.

"Yes. I'll put it in your phone when we go back in." I place my hands on her face and bring her lips to mine. I kiss her possessively, open mouthed and claiming. She's mine.

We sit together at the bonfire as it crackles and pops. It's starting to die down and we aren't adding to the fuel, it's getting late. The embers around the edge are glowing hot orange and the fire is still burning three or four feet high in the center. Sparks fly off into the night sky and the fire has a life of it's own. The flames are more yellow than orange, but it's still providing us with warmth on the beach and cutting the chilly breeze. I sit and stare into the flames while I hold Kristina. I've never noticed the depth of the flames and how they dance, a sexy seduction as the flames join each other and become one.

Mason and Michelle get up and leave with a wave. He has his arm around her and she's wearing his cap. Kristina's starting to get cold and the fire is fading. I pull the blanket around us tight to keep the air out and hold her, snuggling together. This is new for me and I like it. It's a new comfortable feeling that I've never experienced before and I'm happy. Seno gets up and puts his blanket around Sherry's shoulders. He holds his hand out to her and helps her up awkwardly. She's noticeably more pregnant every time I see her and that makes me happy that we've been winning because I know there's a very good chance that Seno will start to lose it when Sherry isn't traveling with him. Since he met her, he hasn't been the same when she isn't there with him. I'm hoping it will be different. I'm sure she wants to be with him. Seno smiles and gives me a high five, "Buy extra condoms and snacks. For you, probably cookies and don't ask Sherry, it's too much for her right now, unless you want to come over and do all the work. She needs to sit and relax, the kid is strong and keeps kicking, keeping her up at night. Remember to hydrate and be ready on game days." He walks away holding Sherry's hand and I realize his grumpiness lately is worry and I understand better than I did before.

"Sweetness, are you ready to go in for the night?" She nods and gets up, somehow managing to stay in the blanket. I wrap her in it and pick her up, carrying her into the house and kissing her. She holds on with her arms around my neck and doesn't complain. I take her to my bedroom and lay her down on my bed. "Can I get you anything? Snacks? Water? Me?" I chuckle and toss her my phone, so she'll add her number.

"I'd like all three, please." I laugh at her response and she makes sure I know she's serious, coming after me and going on tiptoes to kiss me. I put my hands on her waist and hold her there while we kiss, leaning toward never making it to get snacks.

I take her hand and drag her to my kitchen, "Make yourself at home. Take whatever you want." She slides her free hand into my sweats and grasps my dick in her hand. She makes eye contact with me and I can see her heat. She takes her hand from mine and reaches up to kiss me while she unties my sweats and pushes them down, releasing my dick and stroking it. She slides down my body and kneels on her knees in front of me, focused on my dick. She pushes me back against the kitchen counter and kisses my tip. I watch her soft full lips take me in her mouth and suck me in as far as she can, licking my length and dragging her soft lips along my dick. Her sweet lips and her hot, wet mouth on me, driving me crazy. I can't believe she's doing this. "Sweetness, I don't expect you to do that. I, uh, fuck me." She makes me unable to speak and it makes her giggle, adding a vibration to the sucking and licking. All I can think about is getting back inside her. I grab her hand and pull her up to standing, I slide her leggings and panties off at the same time, "Sweetness, you drive me crazy." I unzip my hoodie and pull hers off over her head, holding her bare skin to my bare skin. I lift her up and hold my arms around her tight, kissing her and she wraps her legs around me. I love that. I let her slide down a bit and bump my dick, "I need inside you, Sweetness."

"Yes, please." She gazes into my eyes, searching for something and biting her lower lip. I smile, happy we're in the same place and push my hard dick up into her roughly so I get all the way in. She screams out as I shove into her and holds onto me tight, biting at my collarbone.

"Okay, Kristina?"

"Uh, huh. More. Condom?"

"Don't worry. Under control."

"I trust you." I think is what she says next but she wasn't really talking, it was more trying to remember to breathe as I stroke up into her. I could set up camp when I'm inside her and stay there. She moves her hands to my shoulders and starts to move with me. The heat between us is growing and this is a bad idea.

"Taking you to bed, Sweetness." I carry her into my room and crawl onto my bed, still in her. I lay her down and stroke into her deep and fast a few times.

"Oh, Chase."

"I know, Sweetness. Me, too." She's so warm and soft, it feels right. I take both of her hands in mine and lock our fingers, while I gaze into her eyes and I don't know what I'm looking for. I push into her slowly and deliberately, over and over without taking my eyes off of her. She finally locks eyes with me and I feel it throughout my body, she can see straight into my heart and soul. I'm happy to be in her and I want to stay there as long as I can, but mostly I want to make her feel good. I want her to want me. I want her to need me. I want her to want more. Fuck me, I want more. I need to be thinking about a condom, not wanting more. I pull out quickly and put on a condom before I'm lost any further. I go back to where I was, holding both of her hands and moving slowly. I lean into her ear and kiss her all around it, sucking on her lobe with my warm breath at her ear. My body is on high alert. My heart is running the show and this has never happened to me before. "How did you get so far into my heart?" Please don't break me. She squeezes my hands and then releases them, reaching around my shoulders with her arms and holding me, burying her face in my neck while we move together.

It's never been like this before. I'm so lost and all I can think about is her. What can I do for her? How can I make her feel good? How long can I have her? How do I make her want me? What do I do to make her stay? Does she want me like I want her? Is it all in my head? Fuck! I'm all in my head! I knew I shouldn't have gone there. I knew I needed to wait until after the road trip, at the soonest. I shouldn't have broken the three dates rule, but she was never going to go on a date with me. I don't understand why, I have no clue. What do I know? I know she wouldn't date me. I know she wouldn't give me her phone number. I know she had to kiss me whenever we were in the same place, she couldn't help herself. I know she gets quiet when she's nervous or embarrassed. I know she yells and calls me names when she's mad, even if it doesn't make sense. I know she came into my house and slept in my bed like goldilocks, and didn't say anything, just waited to be found. I know she planned to stay the night and go surfing. I know her lips are soft and full, and she tastes sweet like cookies. I know she'll give everything else up before she gives me up, huh, and ain't that the kicker? She actually told me that. She tried to protect herself. She didn't want to want me or be with me at all—she doesn't have a choice, she has to have me, she needs me. I know one more thing, that's exactly how I feel. I just didn't try to deny that I wanted her. She already knew she was risking her heart and wanted to protect it. She's been in this place before. Shit, she's been hurt before. I don't want her to get hurt again. I won't be that guy. I said I would always protect her and that includes her heart. Right now I need to focus on making her feel good and we can talk later.

The friction and heat between us is building, but I can't wait. I push into her hard and fast. I'm out of control with need. I sit up and grasp my dick at the base, watching as I slide in and out of her, watching her face while she's taking me in. I let go of my dick and slam it all the way back into her, waiting to see her expression change. She cries out and starts to turn red. "Did you like that, Sweetness?"

"Yes."

"Do you want more?"

"Yes." Fuck me.

"Promise to tell me if I hurt you."

"Uh huh," she whimpers. "More, Chase. Please."

I lift her legs up and hook them both with my elbows. I push into her hard a few times and I can see that she likes it as she starts to writhe around underneath me and arches into me. "That's it, Sweetness. There's more coming. I'm going to hold you all night long and keep you safe. I'll always protect you." I keep pushing in and pulling out, over and over. I lean over her and take her legs with me, bending her knees back to her ears and push in as deep as I can get. "Kristina, oh you're so good. You're my good girl." I hear her whimper and pull out, watching her reaction. I slide back into her and pound into her hard, with her bent in half, getting as deep as I can on every pass and with every stroke sending myself closer to oblivion. Her breath is ragged and I don't want to be done yet. I lean in tighter and latch onto her tit, sucking on it and pulling it, not letting it go. I watch her expression change and feel her body tense. I slam into her more and keep at her tit. My orgasm sneaks up on me and I can't stop, my needs take over as I pound into her to completion uncontrollably and I cry out her name,

"What are you doing to me? Oh, Sweetness!" She's right there with me as I fall over the edge and the intensity of her orgasm pulls mine further. Both of us crying out uncontrollably. "Kristina!"

"Chase! Please don't stop! Oh, Chase! Chase! Ohhh!"

"I'm not stopping. I've got you, Sweetness. I'm here." I release her legs and wrap my arms around her. I'm not sure if it's for her or for me, I just know I need to hold her.

Kristina

His arms are wrapped around me tight. He nuzzles into my hair with his lips at my ear and warm breath traveling down my neck. I can't remember a time when I've been so satisfied or desired. He bites my earlobe tenderly and kisses my neck. His body is hot and resting on me, his heartbeat slows and takes me with him. He whispers, "Stay with me, Sweetness." There's no place I'd rather be.

CHAPTER TWENTY-ONE

Chase

I wake up needing to pee and it's way too early. I'm not alone and I'm tired, sleepy, confused. I take stock of the situation. I'm entangled with a chick, mostly lying on top of her with my arms around her and my dick is still in her. The weird thing is that I like it and I'm not trying to figure out how to get away without gnawing my own arm off. Also, I'm in my own bed and I never have chicks here. I relax for a minute and remember the night before, finding Kristina in my bed and then doing my best to keep her there all night long. Oh yeah, fuck me. I must've fell asleep on top of her that last time. I hear her breathing, sweet and asleep. I don't want to wake her, but I kind of have to slide out of her and off of her. Not much chance that I don't wake her up. "Sweetness? I'm not leaving you. Have to take care of business and I'll be right back here to you. I promise, Kristina, I'll hold you all night long just like I said I would. You're my girl." I'm not getting any response, but I can't wait. I carefully slide out of her, making sure not to lose the condom and she whimpers. I get up and take care of business. I grab some water and go back to bed. I fix the blankets and cover us both up. I snuggle up next to her and kiss her cheek. I wrap my arms around her and since she's sleeping, I talk to her quietly, "You're so beautiful, my Sweetness. I promise to keep your heart safe. I won't break your heart. I need you. Please don't break mine." I look at her and watch her sleep until I drift off to sleep.

Kristina

I'm snuggling up to a warm, hard-bodied man and I'm naked. So is he and he's hard everywhere. I touch him gently, lightly tracing his features and exploring his toned muscles. I've had my night with him. No matter what happens, I will always have the memory of our night together. But, I can't imagine leaving him. He has control of me, maybe too much. I like it. I want more. My body hums and I want him. He's sleeping with his arms around me protectively. I think that's the sleep magic, he's protecting me and I trust him to make sure I'm safe. I don't always want to take care of myself. I can, but it's different with Chase. He needs to protect me and I want to let him. I snuggle in tighter and run my fingers through his thick blond hair, brushing it out of his face. I kiss his cheek and it leads me to his strong jaw, on my way to his neck and ear. His hands claim me appreciatively, but I don't think he's awake yet. I giggle at his ear, "Do you still want me here?" I ask, but I know the answer. He wants me here, even if it's just for sex. I kiss his neck open-mouthed and rub against him.

Chase

I wake up to warm soft lips on my neck and Kristina's arms around me. I love it. I've never had this before, but I could get used to it quick. I groan happily, "Good morning, Sweetness." I reach for her and pull her on top of me. She laughs and straddles my abs. I rub her bare thighs and gaze up into her eyes. "You make me happy. I'm glad you stayed with me. I was afraid you'd leave while I was sleeping."

Her eyes change as she stares at me, "I was worried you'd change your mind and I stayed too long."

"No, Sweetness. You're always welcome here and you can stay over with me any night you want. I like you here with me. That's not going to change." I don't have words for what I want her to know. I want her to understand what she means to me, but I don't understand it. I pull her down to me and press my lips to hers while I hold her between my arms and feel her body against mine. She opens her lips for me and I slide my tongue into her mouth, touching hers. I love the way she feels. She feels like mine.

She looks me straight in the eyes, "I won't break your heart, you'll be the one that breaks mine." My heart hurts hearing her words.

"I'll never hurt you. Who hurt you? What happened?" I shouldn't ask, but I kind of want to beat the guy.

"It doesn't matter. I'll always get hurt. I fall for the wrong guys."

"Not this time. I'm the right one for you, Sweetness."

She glares at me like I'm crazy. I understand because I feel the same way, I've lost it. "How can you say that? You can't mean it."

"I just know. You're the only one that makes me feel like this, the only one I want to be here when I wake up in the morning, and the only one I want to be wrapped around when I go to sleep."

"You're full of shit! You're just trying to make me stay and fuck you!"

I tighten my hold on her and run my fingers through her hair. Somebody has really fucked with her. My voice low, "I'll never lie to you. I want you with me, and we don't have to have sex." I hold her eyes with mine before I make my admission, "Kristina, I've never had another girl over to my house. Only you, Sweetness. I don't know what that means. I don't understand any of this. I know I want to be with you." I wait for some type of response, any reaction.

She continues unsure, "What if I want to have sex?"

"Condoms are in the nightstand. I won't complain." I smile and she rolls her eyes at my sarcasm. "How about breakfast and surfing?"

"Those things sound like we'd have to get out of bed."

"True."

"I don't think I'm ready to get out of bed yet."

"Let me hold you and we can go back to sleep."

She reaches for my nightstand to get a condom and turns around, giving me a beautifully curvy rear view while she touches my dick, kisses the tip and puts the condom on me. I've never had a chick put a condom on me and touch me like this. It's always more about fucking me. And fuck, her touch is life changing. She really wants me, needs me. She doesn't just want to fuck a ball player. I squeeze her ass cheeks and get a peek at her sex, she's already wet and I can't help but slide a finger into her to feel her heat. She pulls away from me and turns around, taking my view away. She leans in like she's going to kiss me, and goes straight for my neck. She already knows it's my weakness. She slides back and mounts my dick while she sucks at my neck, "Oh, fuck! Kristina!" She moves on me, sliding her slick heat on and off of my dick. I don't know what she does to me, but I have no control. I move with her, trying to get more of her and she sits up straight, taking me completely. She watches my face while she rides me and I watch her. She moves constantly and starts to bounce on me like I'm her toy, and I happily accept the job—future title, "Kristina's Toy." The way she feels wrapped around me and in control is un-fucking-believable. I put my hands on her waist, guiding her hips and feeling her move on me. I don't understand what she does to me. I feel open and bare to her, like I belong to her and she has control of me—all of me. I'm overcome by emotion and I need to hold her. I pull her down to me and hold her tight in my embrace. I'm breathing heavy and it's not from the sex. She wraps her arms around my neck and cuddles into me, not questioning my actions.

"I'm with you, Chase." She whispers in my ear, "Am I your first? I mean, I know you've had a lot of sex, but like this?" I don't speak. "We're not just sex, baby. There's something. I can feel it and I know you do, too. I don't mean to freak out, it's self-defense. It makes it better when you hold me tight and take control." She stops and takes a deep breath, "I knew it was different for us when we were in Arizona, it scared me and I ran." Her voice is shaky and she keeps her face buried in my neck. "I don't want to get hurt again, but I couldn't stay away from you." I move my hand to her neck and caress her back, cherishing her because it's all I can do. I never want her to get hurt again.

I take control and roll over on top of her. I push into her slowly, feeling her and thinking about her. "Your eyes are beautiful. You feel so soft and silky under my hands. Your lips are full and sweet. I've never been with a chick that makes me feel like you do. You make me feel special, like I'm the only one that can make you feel like this. Like I'm the only man that has made you cry out his name. My dick is at your mercy, I lose control when I'm inside you." I'm lost in her, moving slowly and my heart is beating out of my chest.

"Chase, baby," she puts her hands over my heart, feeling it beat for her.

"Oh, Sweetness. You feel so good. Feel me hard in you, stroking you."

"Yea, Chase. I feel you. There's no way to not feel you. You're huge, baby. You make me feel so full. It's perfect and when you hit that deep spot, you own me."

Fuck me. I need to know when I find that deep spot and I need to find it now. I push all the way into her and she whimpers. I don't want to take her hard, I want... I really am losing it. She's just a chick. I'm leaving tomorrow morning and won't see her for days. Shit! She just gave me her phone number and I don't even know if she gave me her real number. Get out of your head! You know she's real. Take it slow. She's the runner, not you. I reach down between her legs while I move in and out, in and out, her tight heat pulling at me with every stroke. I spread her legs farther and work my way in deeper.

"Oh, Chase! More, baby! Oh!"

I touch her swollen nub and stroke it in time with my dick, moving faster and harder as I watch her climb to the peak.

"Chase! Chase! Oh Chase! Oh baby! Yes!" She cries out and screams out loud as she comes hard around me and pulls me with her unexpectedly. She has control of me and it's crazy.

I hear myself call out her name in ecstasy as I grab onto her and hold her tight. Both of us reaching for the other, needing more contact.

I roll off of her and hold her to me. I need her. I want to take care of her. "I'll be right back, Sweetness." I run to the bath-room, wash my hands and make my way to the kitchen. I look for something to eat, and a tray or something, but I'm not prepared. I pour milk into two mugs and find the last of the baked goods that Sherry left for me, to share with Kristina. Man, I really like this girl if I'm sharing my cookies. I walk back into my bedroom and find Kristina wearing my T-shirt, sitting in the middle of my bed. I smile because I love it. "I don't have breakfast or really anything to eat left in the house. I have milk and the rest of the cookies Sherry left for me. Want some?"

She looks at me wide-eyed and I think she's going to lecture me on breakfast, "Bring it over here! I love cookies and milk." Totally my girl. "Sherry made these?"

"Sherry bakes a ton, but not so much right now. She had some stuff frozen, so she could have it ready for me throughout the season. This is the end of it. It's too much for her right now."

"Why does she bake for you?"

"She likes to bake. Seno is my buddy. I was Best Man at their wedding and I kind of introduced them. She takes care of me like my baked goods dealer." I laugh. "Baking is relaxing for her and a hobby. Somebody has to eat it."

"These are delicious."

"She's a great baker. I love her chocolate chip cookie bars and her brownies. Those are the best. She makes all kinds of stuff. Everything is good."

There are so many things I want to talk to her about. I don't know where to start and I don't want to overwhelm her, but I don't want her to freak out. I hear my phone and grab it to see who's looking for me.

Text from Seno - Sherry can't travel. Want to share a room for this road trip?

Fuck. He's going to need me this road trip.

Text to Seno - Yes. Is she okay?
Text from Seno - She's fine. It's too hard for her and Dr told her to stay home. No more plane rides.
Text to Seno - Who is taking care of Sherry?
Text from Seno - She will be fine. Trying to get her to go to her Mom, but she insists she can take care of herself. Stubborn.
Text to Seno - What if I can arrange some company for her?
Text from Seno - I would love that, but she needs to relax.

"Kristina, do you bake?" It's not selfish if it helps Sherry, right?

"I wish. I can bake cookies from the pre-made cookie dough." I explain what's going on and Kristina texts Sherry, arranging for baking lessons while the team is away.

Text from Seno - Nice one! I'm not even in trouble for setting her up because I didn't! Thanks, Man.

"Do you work when the team is away?"

"Yes. Most game days and sometimes only half a day. I'm off today, like you." She smiles. "I know the team's schedule. I know you're in San Francisco tomorrow, then Houston, then Chicago, and then you're back home with an off day a week from Thursday. You should be home on Wednesday, I'm guessing."

I look at my phone and notice the text from Kristina, she sent me the kiss emoji. She also took a selfie while she was wearing my hoodie and added it to her contact info in my phone. She looks at me funny while I'm checking it out and takes my phone from me. I grab her and snap a selfie of me kissing her. I set it as my wallpaper and text the photo to her, finding that she changed her contact name to read: Kristina Girl-friend. I absolutely love it and decide to pick on her. "Is that your way of marking your territory?"

She laughs, "Trust me. I mark my territory."

We spend the morning together, lazy on the beach. We don't have enough energy left for surfing. I take her to her place to get clothes and I do some laundry for the road trip. At sunset I take her for a walk on the beach and hold her hand while we kick at the water that tries to reach us. I stand behind her with her in my arms, watching the last minutes of sunlight disappear.

"The sunset is beautiful with all the pinks."

"It's not as beautiful as you, my Sweetness." I turn her to me and kiss her, feeling it all the way to my toes. We're electric together. "You're gorgeous and mine." I smile as I say the words.

We walk back to my bungalow, "Can I take you out tonight?"

"I'm hungry, can we just order delivery? Maybe play video games?" Did my girl say that she'd rather stay in and play video games? She really is perfect.

"Whatever you want, as long as you're staying with me I'm happy." I call in an order of chicken parmesan for two and sit down on the couch with Kristina. I put my arm around her with intent of picking a game, but end up making out with her until the food gets delivered. The evening is comfortable as we eat together, enjoying each other's company on the patio with the lights twinkling around us, and the ocean roaring in the background. We talk about baseball, video games, music, goals, and home. The conversation simply flows and I always have something else I want to ask about her or tell her about. The chill finally chases us inside. We sit on the floor in my living room with our backs against my couch, leaning on each other while we play head to head video games and have a great time laughing, sometimes with each other and other times at each other.

After Kristina used her combo moves to chop my head off and laughed at it rolling around on the screen a handful of times, "Are you ready to go to bed? I have to be at the stadium early."

"You just don't like to lose," She retorts.

"I'm not losing. I'm winning because you're still here." I gaze into her eyes and feel my heart beating. I take her hand in mine, intertwining our fingers and smile. Kristina leans in to give me a sweet kiss on the lips and looks down, blushing and happy. We get up and go to my bedroom, changing clothes and getting ready for bed. "Will you get up early and go to breakfast with me?"

"Maybe," She says, teasing me.

"Maybe!" I repeat back at her as I reach over and pull her to me, tickling her until she's laughing to the point of tears and squealing. She feels so right.

I turn some music on low and The Damnwells start to play "I Will Keep the Bad Things From You." The melodic guitar and vocal tone suits my mood as I take Kristina in my arms, not wanting to let her go. I want to hold her and kiss her and... I'm going to be gone for ten days, I don't want her to forget me. I don't want her to remember me as the dude that kept fucking her. I want her to still want me when I get back. This is crazy. My head is my own worst enemy. It makes me vulnerable. "Kristina, Sweetness, promise me you won't forget me while I'm gone?" No, that's my fucking heart taking over my world. How did I get here? No, I'm not going to complain. I'm happy and feeling things I've never felt before. Scary things I don't understand and I don't know how to process. I want her. I need her. I need her to only want me.

Kristina smiles at me warmly, "Do you really think I could forget about you?"

I stare at her, unable to answer because my heart is in control and hasn't learned how to control my voice yet.

"There's no way I'll ever forget about you, Chase. You're not my first and you may not be my last, but one thing I know for sure is that I don't forget guys I fall for. And, Chase, I'm on the path to falling for you." The gold flecks in her warm green eyes sparkle while they look into mine.

I leave the music playing and turn the lights off. We climb in bed together and I want her near me. I want to hold her. I want to feel her against me. I want to feel her silky hair and smell her scent. I want her to know how I feel about her, without any question. I want to know that she's safe and with me.

I'm wishing that I had stuck to the three dates rule. I'm dreading leaving her in the morning, but it would've happened sooner or later.

Kristina

I wake up cold and lonely. It's dark, with only the shine of moonlight filtered by the draperies lighting the room. I have the blanket curled tightly in my fists and pulled up to my neck. My eyes adjust and I remember where I am. Chase sighs and I realize I'm hanging off the edge of his king sized bed, while he's still where he started the night and resting contentedly. I rarely sleep well, but the nights I've been with him are the best sleep I've ever had. Why am I so far from him? Clinging to the edge and blankets for comfort? He's so far away. I sit up and gaze at him, lying there comfortable and at rest. He's gorgeous and he wants me here with him. I release the blankets and move over to him. He's where I belong. I kiss his cheek sweetly and wrap my arm around his waist as I make his strong chest my pillow. Instinctively, he pulls me closer. I put my feet between his legs and accept him, snuggling against him and fall back asleep effortlessly.

Chase

I wake up in the middle of the night and she's using me as her pillow. She's sleeping and breathing deeply, curled into me with her head on my chest, her legs entangled with mine and her arm possessively across my body. My arm is around her back, holding her to me. She's beautiful. I push her hair out of her face and kiss her forehead, content and satisfied to have her in my arms. I close my eyes and start to drift back to sleep, when I feel her kiss my chest and her hand wrap around my dick. I splay my hand across her back receptively and only half awake.

She makes sweet little noises and pulls herself on top of me, pressing her hands and lips to my chest. She's biting and sucking all over me. I'm hit with deja vu from that first night in Arizona and I know how I got the marks, I remember watching her then as she traveled my body just like she's doing right now. The thought of stopping her is not an option because she feels so good on my body, her hands touching me, her tongue licking me, her mouth sucking on me. The difference now is that I want in her and I know what it's like to be there. I reach for her hips and press her against my hard dick, so she can feel how hard I am and how much I want her. She slides her panties off, reaches for my hard length and guides me inside her without taking a breath. Oh fuck, she fits me better than my baseball glove. I move inside her mindlessly, unable to help myself. I can't stop myself from taking her selfishly. She keeps biting and sucking at my chest, pushing me forward and making me want more. I try to take control, I want her under me, but she stops me and sits up. She starts to ride me, grinding against me and touching herself. I'm watching her every move and it's driving me crazy —the way she takes control, the way she's touching herself. I look at her face, her eyes are closed and her body is relaxed. I push up into her and she cries out, leaning her head back and arching her body. Her eyes open, she finally looks at me and smiles. I don't think she's really awake and I wonder if she knows what she's doing. I know I'm only half awake and, man, this sleepy state I'm in is sexy, hazy, indulgent. I can't help but to keep watching her. She rides me harder and harder, pushing down onto me like she needs more, grinding against me and rubbing her clit. I'm just happy to be part of it and I keep watching her. She moves faster and rubs at her hard nub faster, harder, fiercely, until she suddenly falls apart, screaming out as she comes around me. I was in complete control, now suddenly

I'm ready to explode and not prepared. Damn it! Fuck! I want to come right where I am. I just want to go with it, feeling her around me tighter and tighter. Fuck me! Fuck me! Fuck me! I groan, needy and on the edge.

"Just do it. It feels too good not to." Kristina says in a sweet voice and I know I can't because I told her I'd always protect her. I'm still not sure she's awake.

"No, I have to protect you, Sweetness. You're my girl." I pull out and go for a condom, but I'm too far gone. Kristina watches me grasp my dick and start to stroke it. She leans down and takes me in her mouth, licking and sucking at my hard dick. It's the end of me. I come almost instantly in her hot wet mouth and she doesn't pull back or stop. She sucks and licks at me, like she wants more. Oh, fuck me I'm so done. I watch her and it's so hot to see her finishing me like this. Fuck! I can see her swallowing. She licks me clean before releasing me and all I can think about is her. I couldn't forget her if I tried. No woman has ever treated me the way she does, touched me the way she does.

Kristina lies down next to me and all I can do is look at her. I don't know what to do with myself, I just, she is, I mean, fuck me. I gaze into her eyes, baring everything to her and feeling things that I shouldn't. I pull her to me desperately, claiming her mouth with one kiss and pulling back to see her eyes. I want to know she's in the same place with me and I have no idea what I'm searching for. I roll her underneath me, burying her in my bed sheets and comforter like we're cocooned in our own private cloud. I touch my lips to hers softly and take a deep breath, inhaling her into me while our electricity shocks me through my limbs and stabs me in the heart. I put my hands in her hair, holding her head while I kiss her tenderly. I know I'm naked and on top of her, but I just want to kiss her. I love her lips. I want to cherish her sweet lips and taste her. I try to memorize her lips and the feel of her, her sweetness. I feel her heart beat with mine and I can't breathe. I can't do anything but kiss her like she's the air I need to breathe. I want her for more, and damn it, if I don't want her enough.

CHAPTER TWENTY-TWO

Chase

We wake up when the early alarm goes off, forehead to forehead with arms wrapped around each other and her feet between my legs. "Good morning, Sweetness," I say quietly and realize that even though the day is starting out better than almost every other day I've had in my life, I have to leave her to go on the road in a few hours and I'll be gone for ten days without her lips, her body, her. She rubs against me and snuggles in, not wanting to get up. "Sweetness, if we get up now we have time to get ready and go to breakfast before we go to the stadium."

"I don't want to."

"You don't want to what?"

"Get out of bed."

"I'll get up and get ready, you can stay in bed while I shower."

"No. I don't want you to get up."

"We can't stay in bed all day. I'd love to stay here with you, but it's not an option. You have work this morning, right?"

"Yes." She mumbles something to herself, almost like she's cursing herself out.

"You're going to the stadium with me this morning, right?"

"Yes."

"Sweetness, I don't like that I have to leave you. It's part of being a baseball player. We travel. But, I'll come home to you and I'll think about you while I'm gone. I told you, no other chicks. You're my girl." I brush my thumb across her cheek, "I mean it, Sweetness. It's only you for me." My voice is raspy and sincere.

Kristina smiles at me and her eyes light up, "Can we skip breakfast and stay in bed longer?"

"Whatever you want."

She focuses on me and I can see flames reflected back at me, "I know what I want."

"Yea? Tell me what you want." I want to hear her say it.

She looks around the room, before she finally focuses on me, "I want you to kiss me more, like you did early this morning when I fell back to sleep in your arms." She blinks a couple of times. "I want you on top of me and in control of me. I want the sex to match the kiss."

"You want me to fuck you while I kiss you?"

"I guess, not really. When you kissed me it was different. I don't know, like we were connected and I could feel it." She closes her eyes.

She felt it too.

"I'm sorry. I'm being stupid. Forget it."

I can't let her forget it. She needs to know I felt it, too. I have to know it's the same for her. I have to put it out there. "You mean it felt like electricity was running through your body and we were somewhere alone where nothing else mattered? Just us and we needed each other to breathe?" I'm freaking out inside now that I've said it. What if I'm crazy? What if she has no idea what I'm talking about? What if it's only sex for her? I feel myself start to shake and I sit up, waiting for her response. This is the longest second of my life. Why did I tell her that?

She smiles at me, "I felt like you were sending sparks through my body. Like you were the only thing keeping my heart beating. Like you had whisked me off to a fantasyland that only we could go to." I gaze into her eyes and feel my cheeks get warm. "It didn't feel like something you could do while you were fucking."

I lean back against my headboard. I pull her to me, so she's straddling my legs while I start to kiss her tenderly. Honestly, the way I want to kiss her. The way I can show her how I feel about her. I can feel her melting in my arms. I remember last night and reach for a condom before we have a problem. I get it open and roll it on while I kiss her. I splay my hands on her bare back and hold her while my lips explore hers. I feel her breathing change and ask her, "Do you want more, Sweetness? Do you want me inside you?"

"Yes, baby," Slips from her lips on a sigh.

I lift her up and slide her down on me. She moves slowly, working me into her all the way. She feels crazy good around me. I simply hold her against me and continue kissing her lips gently, tenderly, telling her how I feel without words. I don't know how to show her how I feel with my dick and the rest of my body. Something I've never done. Something I never thought of. It was always chicks that wanted to fuck me. I guess I was a dick to conquer, a notch in their bedpost, a challenge maybe. Another ballplayer to fuck. I don't even understand how I feel. I don't know how to explain it. I feel her and place my hands on her hips, guiding her to slow movements with me. Feeling her body and desires with my hands, and making them happen. My body floods with warmth and the electricity is back, but more intense. "Kristina, do you feel the sparks, electricity, whatever it was like last night?"

"It's like the sparks have grown to fireworks shooting through my body." That's exactly what it's like and it drives me to give her more, unselfishly. More passionate kisses and more of my feelings, all of me, all in.

I lean my forehead against hers and smile uncontrollably, "I'm so fuckin' happy to be in the same place with you, Kristina. Fireworks. High voltage and combustible, my Sweetness." I hold her tight and need more. I roll her underneath me and stroke into her completely, in and out, in and out, feeling her like never before. I want more. She wraps her arms around my neck and pulls herself up to me, kissing me while we fit together in pleasure. I catch her legs and lean down to her to kiss her, taking her legs with me. I push in as deep as I can, wanting to get closer to her and needing to be as close as possible. I hold us together like two perfectly matched puzzle pieces and look at our connection, seeing my hard dick stroke in and out of her perfect little heaven. I see her nerve center, needy and staring back at me, so I touch her softly and she cries out my name.

"Chase! Oh Chase! More."

All I want to do is make her happy. She gets whatever she wants. I increase the pressure on her clit, circling it and teasing it. She arches into me and I feel her get wet at my touch. I stroke into her slowly, but hard and I can see her start to unravel. "You're amazing, Kristina. The things you do to me. Come for me. Come for me hard. Feel the fireworks. Maybe we can see them together." I push into her hard and fast, pounding into her while I have her bent in half and rub her clit harder.

"Tell me, Sweetness. Tell me everything." I whisper with my eyes closed, on the edge of the world and ready to jump off head-first.

"You cut through me. Straight to my heart, Chase." She starts to buck and I lose it completely.

"Fuck, Kristina. Come for me. Come for me now. Come with me." I call out to her even though she's right there with me. I need her to come. I can't finish before her and I'm out of control. "Please! Oh fuck! Oh fuck!" I can't help myself, it's intense and I press down on her hips, holding her in place while I stroke into my paradise found, losing it by the millisecond. I know she's with me, she's right there with me and I hear her scream out.

"Chase! I'm yours!" She squeezes me tight and I come hard as if on queue. She digs her fingers into my back and shoulders, as I push and pull us through knowing I have to leave her for ten days. Knowing we're in the same place. Knowing I'm falling, just like she is. Maybe I already fell.

Chase

We race to get ready and get to the stadium on time. We skipped breakfast and our morning activities still have us running late. I'm not complaining. No, I'm not complaining even a little. Kristina doesn't have to be at the stadium as early as I do, so she'll have time to get her day going. I'll have to settle for whatever is left in the clubhouse, if anything. That's fine. It was worth it. I'm hoping for a few minutes to say goodbye to my girl properly, but I don't know if that's going to happen either—I'd give up food for it. She picks up all of her stuff and tosses it in her bag, so she's ready to go. I toss my duffle bag over my shoulder and get her bag, ready to load up and get out. I see my hoodie that she's been wearing left on my bed and drop the bags. I get the hoodie and give it to Kristina, "Take it with you. You might need it to take care of you while I'm gone." She hugs me tight and I don't think it has anything to do with the hoodie. "I know, Sweetness." I hold her head to my chest and feel it in my heart. "I promise it will be okay and I'll be back looking for you as soon as I get off the plane next Wednesday. How about I pick you up when I get back next Wednesday? We can go out or order in or whatever you want." She half smiles at me. "We will text and talk while I'm gone. I'll call you everyday, Sweetness." I look at her and she's upset. "Trust me, I don't want to leave you. I'm going to miss you." I speak softly and lean my head against hers. I notice the clock and time issues keep getting worse. "We gotta go, Sweetness." She pulls the hoodie on and I grab the bags, ushering us both out to my truck.

We drive to the stadium in silence and she's staring out the passenger window. I get her talking, "Why don't we get to know each other better while I'm gone?"

She turns and glares at me like I'm crazy. "How's that going to work?"

"We text each other and ask questions. Not like Truth or Dare, or anything like that. Little things we want to know about each other. Say three or four each day. Could be fun."

"Okay."

"I was wondering, are you really interested in baking?"

"Yes, I've always wanted to."

"Do you have a mixer and baking stuff, tools, whatever to bake?"

"I have a bowl, a spoon and a little measuring cup."

"Well, Sherry has everything and you will be at her place. You should be good." I laugh, "Remember chocolate chip cookie bars and brownies are my favorite." At least I've got her smiling. We pull into the player's garage to park and I've got no time.

Text to Seno - Cover me... I'm here in the garage... need 5 minutes... please.

I get an immediate response of a thumbs up emoji.

I reach for Kristina's hand, pulling her closer so I can kiss her and she resists. "I only have a few minutes. I'm already late. I just want to give you a kiss, my Sweetness."

"It's better if I just go." She says grumpily.

"No. I'm getting my goodbye kiss. I need to have something to get me through to next week." She rolls her eyes at me and I realize it's part of her defense mechanism. I turn her face to look at me, "You don't need to protect yourself from me. Drop the self-defense. I'll always protect you." I get out of my truck and quickly walk around to the passenger side, opening the door and not giving her a choice. I claim her mouth with mine and wrap my arms around her, pulling her out of my truck in the process. "You're mine. Don't forget it."

"Chase..." I cut her off.

"Yes, my Sweetness. I'm yours, only yours," More than you know and more than I ever thought possible.

"Okay. I like being your girl." My heart sinks at her words and I kiss her again before running off into the stadium. Bad enough to be gone, I'm not going to be gone and scratched from the game.

Kristina

I'm left standing here watching while Chase runs off into stadium. I have a little time before I need to be at work and I don't want anyone to see me right now. I pull on the big hoodie and take off for a walk in the village. Hiding the tears running down my face more than anything else. He doesn't want to hurt me, but he is by simply leaving on the road trip. It's not his fault. It's work.

CHAPTER TWENTY-THREE

Chase

I walk through the stadium thinking to myself about how I can call her and text her. I might even send her dirty pictures and I mean pictures of me at the end of the game when I'm covered in mud and have holes in my uniform... and maybe some abs and happy trail. I want her to be happy while I'm gone and I want to buy her presents.

Text to Sherry - Hey lovey. Heard my girl is going to be hanging out with you to learn to bake. Thought you might order everything she needs to bake and have it delivered to her. You still have my credit card info. I mean every-thing. She only has a bowl, a spoon and a measuring cup. You can use my card for ingredients or whatever she needs. Make sure she learns how to make your brownies and your chocolate chip cookie bars. :) Don't overdo it, relax and make Kristina do everything. Don't worry about Seno, I've got him and we're rooming together this trip. Most important please take care of yourself and Baby Seno.

Text from Sherry - I'll order stuff later today. Love shopping therapy. What color does she like or what color is her kitchen?

Text from Sherry - And it's Baby Girl Seno :)

Text to Sherry - I bet she'll be just like you :) and drive Seno crazy!

Text from Sherry - I think she already has him wrapped around her little finger :)

Text to Sherry - I'll let you know about color later today.

Next on the list...

Text to Carter - Dude, can you get a jersey made up for the intern Kristina for me? My name and number. And an oversized hoodie the same way. Please.

Text to Carter - Can I have something left for her everyday of the road trip? Different jerseys, caps, shirts, hoodies, whatever I can get for her with my name and number on it.

Text from Carter - I can arrange that. Are you sure you want to do that? She was pissed about the things you've had delivered to the control booth.

Text to Carter - Does she have an employee locker or something you can leave it in for her to find?

Text from Carter - She has a small cubicle in the media offices. I can leave things for her there.

Text to Carter - She has a cubicle? Where pictures and stuff can get put on the walls?

Text from Carter - Yea, I guess.

Text to Carter - Leave stuff for her at her cubicle. Thanks.

I hope I don't get in trouble for having gifts left for her everyday, but I think it'll be okay. She's not going to be PA Announcer during that time because there are no home games. She'll get a gift and a reminder of me everyday that I'm gone. Perfect.

Text to Kristina - Waiting on the plane. Thinking about you, my Sweetness. <3

Text to Kristina - What's your favorite color?

Text to Kristina - What's your favorite candy?

Text from Kristina - You didn't forget me yet? :)

Text to Kristina - I'm not going to forget you, beautiful.

Text from Kristina - 10 days is a long time... you'll forget me

Text to Kristina - Stop. No, I won't forget you. I haven't forgotten you since Arizona.

Text from Kristina - Chocolate

Text from Kristina - Tiffany Blue

Text to Sherry - Tiffany Blue... Thank you

Text to Kristina - What kind of chocolate?

Text from Kristina - Milk chocolate... white chocolate is good, but not really chocolate.

Text from Kristina - Chocolate with caramel is good, but not chocolate with anything fruity...that just ruins it.

Text to Kristina - Will you be watching the game tonight?

Text from Kristina - Yes. Not sure if I'll be working or not yet. Michelle and I are planning to go to Sherry's.

Text to Kristina - Cool. Getting ready to take off. Talk to you soon, Sweetness.

My chest feels heavy. I miss her and I haven't even gotten to San Francisco yet.

Seno looks over at me, "Texting the girl?"

"Yea. Dude, I'm lost with her and I think she's right there with me. It's never been like this. I miss her already."

"It's just a new girl. Give it time."

I turn to Seno, irritated and quietly, "Then why does it feel like I have sparks and electricity running through my body when I'm with her? Why was I happy when she was still there in the morning? Why does her touch feel different than all the rest? Why can't I stop thinking about her?"

"Man, you're screwed." Seno chuckles. "Do you keep thinking things and not saying them? Have a hard time putting words together when she touches you? Can't keep your hands off of her? Want to tell her that you love her, but know it sounds crazy?"

"Fuck me! I really am screwed."

"No, you're fine. If it's real, you're lucky." Seno smiles and his eyes shine. "Thank you for telling me to ask Sherry out and getting me to go out." He takes a deep breath, obviously thinking about her. "When it's right, it's right and sometimes you just know. Do what makes you happy. Don't rush it. Get to know her. If that means you have her over every night, so be it. My Dad told me to do whatever I needed to do to make sure my happy didn't get away, that it doesn't matter what anyone else thinks."

"So, I'm not crazy and she didn't drug me or something?"

"I don't think so, but we can have you tested." Seno smiles at me and laughs. "Don't tell her you love her too soon. Might freak her out."

"I don't love her."

"Whatever you say. I'll be here when you need me."

"You think I love her?"

"Give it some time it could be lust." Seno stops and thinks, before continuing, "You miss her, what do you miss?"

"I just want to be close to her. I want to protect her."

"Yea, you're screwed." Seno pats me on the leg and smiles.

"So, is Sherry on the DL for the rest of the season?"

"Probably the rest of the regular season for away games. Everything should be good for the postseason. I expect she'll miss some home games, but not too many. And, yes, we're going to postseason and we're winning. I want a championship ring for the year my girl is born. My girls make me feel like I've already won."

He's so happy, it's crazy. "Does she have a name yet?"

"We're down to a couple, but Sherry can't decide. She's thinking something Hawaiian maybe, but then we found out she's further along than we thought and she already had a girl name picked out. She's due before the end of June."

"That's next month. Dude, that's insane."

Seno nods and sits happily as the plane lands and everybody gets their phones out, texting to check in. I turn on my phone to messages from Kristina.

Text from Kristina - Why me and not one of the other girls?

Text from Kristina - Why won't you forget me?

Text to Kristina - Landed in San Francisco

How am I supposed to answer those questions? This game might have been a bad idea. This isn't a conversation I want to have by text. I want to have it live and in person, not when I'm gone for the next ten days. I know I need to respond.

Text to Kristina - You're the only girl that has ever made me feel this way

Text to Kristina - I think our connection is special and I'm not referring to the sex, but the sex is our own fireworks show.

Text to Kristina - What duty do you have at the stadium today?

Text from Kristina - Just preparing pregame notes and the lineup for the broadcasters and getting it sent over to them in SF. I'll be off in time to go to Sherry's, but I'll be researching stat questions and feeding the information to the broadcasters for the post game.

Text from Kristina - Maybe you should see what it's like with another girl, now that you don't want to fuck every girl you see.

That's it. I call her and I shouldn't. I'm irritated and I'm with the team. The phone rings, but there's no answer. I know she has her phone, she's texting me.

Text to Kristina - Answer your phone.

Text from Kristina - Can't, I'm at work.

Text to Kristina - Answer your phone or I'll call into the stadium and get transferred to you. I'm not having this conversation by text.

Text from Kristina - I'll call you in a couple minutes.

Text to Kristina - Okay.

I'm frustrated. I don't know why she would suggest such a thing, unless she doesn't like me. She keeps trying to push me away, but when we're together she holds on to me.

The team is going directly to the stadium for practice.

Everybody is pumped up and we're ready to keep the winning streak going. My phone isn't ringing and my head is all over the place.

Seno barks at me, "Stop looking at your phone. Shake it off. Everything isn't on your schedule."

He's right. I toss my phone into my locker and go work out, trying my best to leave Kristina in my locker with my phone. I put my earbuds in and escape everybody for a while with my work out playlist on shuffle, it starts with "Turn It Up" by The Wrecks. Working out always gets my head straight, puts me in the right frame of mind for the game. It brings everything into focus for me. Lying on my board out in the ocean is the only place that relaxes me more.

I take batting practice in the cages, enjoying my alone time and I'm driven to swing the bat viciously. I'm seeing the ball and feel like the bat is part of me. Connecting with no effort at all.

I go to my locker, prepared to hit the showers and get ready for the game. My phone is blowing up and I reach for it to turn the sound off, but I can't ignore the activity. Two missed calls and texts, all from Kristina.

Kristina

Why isn't he answering? He told me to call him. Damn it! I told him to be with another girl. He's probably doing it right now. There's always some slut ready for a player. Why did I say that! Answer the phone! My hands are shaking as I try calling him again. Straight to voicemail.

Text to Chase - I called, you didn't answer.

Text to Chase - Where are you?

Text to Chase - My break is almost over.

Text to Chase - Why aren't you answering me?

Text to Chase - I shouldn't have said that. I didn't mean it.

Text to Chase - I don't want you with another girl, not even just to see.

Text from Chase - Don't fuck with me. I don't play those games.

Text from Chase - Do you want me? You want to be with me? Be my girl? You wouldn't suggest another girl if you did.

Text from Chase - I'm all in with you, Sweetness. If you're not, don't fuck with me. Tell me.

Text to Chase - I want to be all in.

Text to Chase - I'm yours, Chase.

Text from Chase - I only want you, Sweetness. I miss you. I don't like being away from you.

Text from Chase - I'm not going to hurt you. Please don't play games with me.

Text to Chase - How do you know you won't hurt me?

Text from Chase - I just know. There's nobody like you. I'll always protect you.

Text to Chase - :)

He can't know he won't hurt me. I'll get hurt. But, pushing him toward another woman is hurting myself. Why do I do these stupid things when I want to be with him?

Chase

I hit the shower and let the hot water roll down over my body. The spray hits my face and I close my eyes. Everything from the world around me washes away and all I can see is her. I can feel her with me. My girl.

Going into the game today, it's going to be extreme. The question is will it be really good or suck. Too many things happening in the club house. First, Seno on the road without Sherry. Second, Mason hasn't stopped talking about Michelle since we got to the stadium. Third, Bravo is off the disabled list and getting texts from a hook up he has in San Francisco that he thought he was rid of.

And then there's me, and I miss Kristina. I'm not even sure that it's missing her, I won't see her tonight and I don't like it. I can't believe she told me to be with another chick. It makes me need to see her and show her she's mine. Since I'm on the road for eight more days, that's not an option. I'm not experienced with chicks. What I mean to say is I'm very experienced with sex, not experienced at all with having one chick all to myself. The part that gets me the most is that I never wanted a chick to be my girl. Fuck their brains out, yes. Protect them, no. I'm not concerned about being tempted or cheating, that's not me. But, Kristina makes me want her and I don't even notice anybody else. I know she'll be watching the game.

The answer is Seno was on point, hitting safely on all his at bats, scoring twice and bringing in three baserunners. Mason was on fire with two home runs. Bravo was brought in as designated hitter in the eighth, hitting a double. Everyone else did as they normally do. Me? I hit a triple and struck out my other two at bats. The real problem was my fielding. I pride myself on my fielding. I will dive for that shit. I will run for it like an Olympic sprinter. I will climb the wall and I will jump into the wall if that's what it takes. Today, well the best way I know how to describe it is from the movie Tin Cup when he got the shanks and his swing felt like an unfolding lawn chair. That was my catching. Awkward at best, if I was able to get to the ball, and I simply missed the ball more than once. I'm surprised Skip didn't pull me sooner than he did, and that was in the sixth. Somehow, we still won 9-7. Not our best showing, but a win is a win.

Kristina

I get to Sherry's to find her and Michelle already sitting in front of the TV watching the pregame. It's funny to see the teacher and student situation with Michelle as the student, she's always the one who knows everything. It must be killing her not knowing baseball, but she'll probably know it better than the rest of us soon. They're discussing the lineup and the impact of the order on the game. I hear them starting with Chase because he's leading off.

"Cross is perfect at lead off because he has the speed and we want him on the bases. Speed matters because he can outrun the ball when a grounder gets hit or he bunts. It's also a benefit for stealing bases, which he has proven with his record of stolen bases," Sherry goes on about my guy.

"His strong, long legs and coordination give him a significant speed advantage. Sometimes these long-legged guys don't have the control. Chase has excellent control," I chime in.

"Perv," Michelle interjects. "Though I do like the dirty uniform and he always seems to get a very dirty uniform."

"That's mostly the stealing and some of the sliding across the outfield to get the ball," Sherry says shaking her head at out interaction. "I'm a bit surprised Mason is hitting second. I suspect they will be moving him toward the clean up spot. He's been coming into his own with his hitting." She turns to Michelle, "That's a good thing. He's getting better and that's a sign of longevity in this game. There's always someone better waiting for the chance to take your spot in the lineup."

The game is starting and Chase is at bat. The first two pitches are balls outside and on the third pitch he smacks it fair up the first base line. The first baseman misses the ball and it bounces off the outfield wall before the right fielder can get to it. Chase is showing us a great example of his long legs and speed. He's turned up to full speed and running. I can see him watching the coaches and trusting their signs, not worrying about the ball or wasting time looking for it himself. He rounds first and second without concern and dives for third, sliding in hot and hooking the base with his foot to maintain contact. Sherry cheers for him and claps. I join her, getting to yell for my guy. I smile uncontrollably at the ability to yell for him freely and the sense of pride that runs through me knowing he's my man. Michelle and Sherry both look at me and smile, like I'm finally getting it. Maybe I am. Maybe I've known longer than any of them have had a clue and I'm good at hiding it.

Mason is up to bat and takes four balls in a row for a walk. "He's starting to get at bats like this because of his hitting. Teams don't want him to connect, but they don't want to give him the intentional walk because they know he won't swing for it out of the zone." Sherry gets this expression on her face that I've only ever seen when she's with Rick, "There's my Rick walking to the batter's box." She beams and yells, "Let's go Seno!" He swings his bat and stands ready for the pitch. The

219

first pitch is low and inside, "See that? They are trying to back him up off the plate." The second pitch is placed the same and he doesn't move. "That's it, my king! Hold your ground!" The third pitch looks like a curve ball that lost its drop and his bat connects with a clean pop. "Yes! Run, baby!" Sherry cheers him on. "Home run! Woooo!" She puts her hand to her belly and smiles, baby must be cheering her daddy on, too. Seno scores, knocking in Mason.

CHAPTER TWENTY-FOUR

Chase

The team gets checked into the hotel and we all plan to meet in the bar. Seno and I get to our room, get our things unpacked and check our phones. He immediately calls Sherry and stretches out on his bed, settling in for what looks like a long call. I have messages and they're not all from Kristina.

Text from Sherry - Kristina and Michelle are here watching the game with me. It's fun.

Text from Sherry - Kristina says she's being stupid and she can't help it. I'm working on it.

Text from Kristina - Thank you for the jersey :) It was left hanging on my cubicle waiting for me before I left the stadium today.

Text to Kristina - :) I didn't want to get in trouble for sending you stuff to the control booth

Text from Kristina - You did good. You would've been in trouble if you called me at the stadium.

Text to Kristina - Don't tell me to be with other chicks and you won't have that problem.

Text to Kristina - Are you still at Sherry's? Want to talk on the phone? I want to hear your voice, Sweetness.

Text from Kristina - Michelle is driving us home right now. I'll call you when we get home, okay?

Text to Kristina - I'm looking forward to it. <3

Seno is obviously happy to stay right where he is and doesn't care if he goes to the bar or not. I'd rather be on the phone with my girl, too. I've never felt like that before. I've always picked on the guys that did it and dragged them out to the bar anyway. Besides, I got enough ribbing in the club house today about my hickeys. I order us dinner from room service and change into a T-shirt and sweatpants. It's kind of nice to relax and hang out in the room. Seno and I always used to room together, so it's like old times except now we both have chicks to talk to. Back then, neither one of us had a girl. I like having him as a roommate, and I finally understand why he spends so much time with Sherry. I get it, I want to be with Kristina, too. I thumb through the magazine in the room while I wait for

Kristina to call and see an ad for an artisan chocolatier in San Francisco, so I go on their website and have a box of chocolate candies sent to her. I check out the options, choosing a box that is all milk chocolate, none of them have anything fruity and about half of the box has caramel. I have it gift wrapped and include a card that says "Sweets for my Sweetness." That's when my phone rings, "Hello?"

"Hi, baby." Her sweet voice coming to me through the phone is heaven to my ears. I love that she calls me baby.

"Hey, Sweetness. How was your day?"

"Good. I'm sorry about my text. My automatic defense mechanism kicks in. The thing is that every relationship I've had, ended. I'm afraid of getting hurt again. But, I really don't want you with anyone else. Only me, Chase." Her words cut right through me and my heart rolls over in my chest like a puppy that wants its tummy rubbed more.

"They were all idiots and didn't know what they had when they had you, Kristina. Besides, those relationships had to end otherwise you wouldn't have been available for me. I feel like a fool because I miss you so much and we only spent a couple days together."

"I guess that's true. I miss you, too. It was a great couple of days." I hear her happiness and daydreamy attitude at thoughts of our time together. "I love your little place on the beach, it's perfect. I think you're what makes it perfect." Fuck me, she kills me.

"I wish I was there with you, Sweetness. I'd show you how much you mean to me."

She giggles, "Tell me."

"I'm better with actions than I am with words."

"Then tell me what your actions would be."

Huh, "I want to hold you close to me and kiss you, until you

223

can feel everything I feel for you." I remember the morning and take a deep breath. "I like waking up with you in my bed, with your arm around me and you using me as your pillow. I like holding you all night long, you between my arms, your hair silky against my skin and the sweet sounds you make while you sleep. No, Kristina, I'll never hurt you. I'll always protect you." I feel like I'm falling as I say the words, knowing that I mean them and realizing the truth.

We talk on the phone until room service delivers dinner and then call back to talk more after we eat. I can hear Seno questioning Sherry about how she feels, making sure she isn't overdoing it, and telling her how much he loves her and misses her. Kristina and I mostly giggle on the phone, still getting to know each other and not wanting to say the wrong thing. Making sure I don't tell her I love her too soon, and I don't know if that's what this feeling is or not, all I know is that I've never felt it before and I want to be with her all the time. The end of our phone call feels weird, like we both want to say more and neither of us do. It doesn't matter. We spent time together on the phone being together and that's good.

Kristina

I love the sound of his voice, it's deep and comforts me. Our phone call reminds me of being a teenager and spending hours on the phone with my boyfriend. Sweet and giggly. I'm never like that anymore. Except, Chase makes it okay. I block out the fact that the guy I was on the phone with back then dumped me and had probably been cheating on me the whole time we were together. That's been over for years. I was young and didn't know any better. Chase will always protect me. I pull the blankets up over my head and pretend I'm in his fluffy bed waiting for him to find me again, replaying his sweet words in my head until I fall asleep happy.

Chase

Road Trip Day 2: Wednesday - Game 2 in San Francisco

The game went well, mostly because I wasn't in the lineup. That's not a good thing. I need to figure out how to get this under control to keep my spot in the lineup. Seals won 6-1. I learned that Kristina really isn't a morning person and doesn't get out of bed any earlier than she has to. I also learned that I love to hear her voice when she wakes up in the morning, it gave me wood. As grumpy as she was, she was still hazy with sleep when my phone call woke her up and if I wasn't sharing a room with Seno, I'd probably have stroked myself. She sent me a couple of text messages throughout the day and we talked on the phone after the game.

Text to Kristina - What toppings do you like on your pizza?

Text to Kristina - What is your favorite restaurant?

Text to Kristina - What's your favorite song?

Text from Kristina - Bacon, sun-dried tomatoes, basil, and garlic

Text from Kristina - I'm not sure I have a favorite. I like to try new places all the time. Usually it's more about what's convenient. Coffee Shops are a creature comfort for me.

Text from Kristina - Like my all time favorite song or my favorite right now?

Text to Kristina - Both

Text from Kristina - My all time favorite is "Just Can't Get Enough" by Depeche Mode.

Text from Kristina - Right now I love "Dive" by Ed Sheeran, I think it's Sherry's fault.

Text from Kristina - Is there a song that makes you think of me?

Text from Kristina - What's your favorite thing to eat?

Text from Kristina - What's your favorite color?

Text to Kristina - There are a few songs that make me think of you.

Text from Kristina - What are they? All of them.

Text to Kristina - "Feels Like the First Time" by Foreigner.

Text to Kristina - "Just Like Heaven" by the Cure.

Text to Kristina - "Won't Stop" by OneRepublic.

Text to Kristina - "Turn It Up" by The Wrecks.

Text to Kristina - Pizza

Text to Kristina - I really like the blue color in my bedroom, but lately I find I'm fond of the warm green I see when I look into your eyes.

She had an oversized hoodie with Cross and the number 17

on the back of it left at her cubicle, she told me she loved it and felt like it was hugging her. She even sent me a picture of her wearing it and nothing else. I managed not to get in trouble today and she didn't tell me to be with another girl, so I think that's progress.

―――――

Kristina

I never thought I'd say this about a guy, but I miss him. I love how he leaves presents for me. He doesn't have to do that. I want to be with him and I'd be happy to have him in a small apartment alone even if he wasn't a baseball player. I don't care if he has money or any of the rest of it. He's all that matters.

The days while the team is away are standard, full of basic prep duties and nothing exciting. It's an early game and a short day for me. I see the lineup and there's no Cross. I guess everyone needs a day off. I wish we could spend our time off together. I wish his arms were around me right now.

―――――

Chase

Road Trip Day 3: Thursday - Game 3 in San Francisco

Luckily, I was back in the lineup. I hated being away from Kristina and not playing. What's the point? We swept the series, winning three out of three games. I hit two home runs, and brought in five of my teammates to score—that's 7 runs batted in. Every single one of us got at least one hit. I'm not usually a home run hitter, but the ball connected with my bat effortlessly. I didn't realize I was a triple away from a cycle until I reviewed my stats after the game. We won 14-2, a total massacre. It was awesome. The only thing that would've made it better is if she was here to celebrate with me. Woah! Who am I? Dude, be cool and give it time. She's yours.

I want to call Kristina in the morning again, but decide not to poke the tiger.

> Text to Kristina - Good Morning, Sweetness. I don't to want to wake you up again. Let me know when you can talk.
> Text from Kristina - You can always call me. :)

I call her and we talk about plans for the day. She's going to Sherry's after work to bake and I hope they save some for me. The game is earlier than normal because it's a getaway day and the team flies to Houston after the game today. One of the reasons I want to talk to her, in case it's too late later. But, that's been vetoed. She wants me to call her either way, no matter how late.

Text to Kristina - What are your favorite flowers?

Text to Kristina - What's the first thing you want to do when I get back?

Text to Kristina - Is there a song that makes you think of me?

Text from Kristina - Daisies

Text from Kristina - 2 songs… "I Want To Hold Your Hand" and "Dive"

Text from Kristina - Right now, I want you to hold me all night and let me spend the night with you. This could change though.

Text to Kristina - I've been hoping you would stay over with me again. I want to hold you every night.

Text from Kristina - Which side of the bed do you prefer to sleep on?

Text from Kristina - What's your favorite home cooked meal?

Text from Kristina - What's the first thing you want to do when you get back?

Text to Kristina - Left Side, closest to the bathroom and the bedroom door.

Text to Kristina - I love pasta and pot roast.

Text to Kristina - Hug you tight and smell your hair.

Text from Kristina - You might get tired of me staying over. I'd invite you to my place, but my roommate has already proven that your place is easier.

Text to Kristina - I'll never get tired of you. I want you with me every night.

Kristina

I never get two short days in a row. It's nice and the fact that I've been sleeping well the last couple of nights makes it better. I'm going to Sherry's right after work for baseball and baking.

> Text from Sherry - I used up some of my baking supplies. I needed cookies. Don't tell Rick I was baking. I only made a small batch for me and the baby.
> Text to Sherry - I'll pick up on my way. What do you need?
> Text from Sherry - Eggs, chocolate chips, peanut butter chips, unsalted butter.
> Text from Sherry - Tamales from the delicatessen would be great, too. :)

I laugh knowing it's a pregnant request.

> Text to Sherry - I'm sure I can manage all of that.
> Text to Sherry - I'll pick up on my way.

I walk into Sherry's with her requested supplies and tamales. The game is already on and she's focused on it with her hand resting on her belly. I put away the groceries and meet her in front of the TV with tamales. She nods at me in appreciation and we enjoy some baseball talk while we spend time with our guys. It's funny, I never thought of it as spending time together when I watch the game until Sherry said it. She's right. In the stadium with them or not, it's experiencing part of their life with them and making it our own. We cheer for them and I don't miss Chase so much when I watch him playing. I love the smile on his face when he looks up to see the ball he hit go out of the park.

I knew he was special, but it may be more than I expected. I want to be what he wants.

Sherry tells me about how she met Rick and how everything went so fast. She's happy and wouldn't change a thing. She never wanted to get married and never considered having a child, but Rick changed those things for her. There's nothing she wants more than the life she has now.

The game is over and it's time to bake. Sherry has a stool in her kitchen where she sits and gives me directions. She goes through everything step by step and I make chocolate chip cookies. I clean up after myself as I go and when I put the cookies in the oven, she instructs me on how to make brownies. It's not hard, but I need to follow instructions and Sherry does everything from memory. I make notes in my phone as we go, so I can try to replicate the process on my own later. The kitchen smells delicious and I made it that way. I can't wait to bake for Chase, I'm leaving these with Sherry.

Kristina

I get home for the night and I haven't heard from Chase. I call him, but he doesn't answer, "Hey baby, I'm home from Sherry's and going to bed. You were great tonight. Please call me. I miss you."

Chase

We land in Houston late. We had to wait on the plane and getting to the hotel took longer than it should've. By the time I call her, she's already asleep and I knew she would be because of the message she left me. I was hoping to hear about baking and get to talk sweet to her when I climbed into bed for the night. She did answer the phone in a quiet voice and I could tell she was sleeping, so I talked sweet to her, "Hey Sweetness. I wish I were there with you. I want to hold you and kiss you. I want to feel your body against mine, our hearts beating together." She made some sweet little noises. "Sleep and remember you're my girl. Goodnight, Sweetness." I made a kiss noise at her through the phone and hung up.

Kristina

I wake up early and feel spoiled as I put on my new Seals T-shirt that says "Cross" on the back. I take a couple selfies, front and back, and send them to Chase. His name on my shirt and cutoff short shorts only covering my ass. Nothing I've ever done before Chase. But this morning I'm happy and nothing can dim the light glowing in my heart. I'm proud to wear his name and waiting impatiently for tonight's game, so I can watch him play and spend some time with him. He's my guy and I'm his. I'm falling for him.

Chase

Road Trip Day 4: Friday - Game 1 in Houston

Friday morning we didn't have practice and didn't have to be at the stadium until noon. We slept in. I woke up to pictures of Kristina wearing the T-shirt with my name and number on the back, eating chocolates and texts. Fuck she's hot in my number.

Text from Kristina - Good morning, baby. :)
Text from Kristina - You don't need to keep giving me things.
Text from Kristina - The chocolates are delicious.
Text from Kristina - We'll talk about Houston and baking tonight.
Text from Kristina - Thank you for the shirt and candy... you really don't need to keep giving me things, but I do like it. :)
Text from Kristina - Which stadium do you like playing in the most?
Text from Kristina - Did you have pets when you were growing up?
Text from Kristina - Have you ever been in love?
Text to Kristina - What's your favorite thing to eat?
Text to Kristina - If you picked my walk up song, what would it be?
Text to Kristina - Did you pick media or is that just what the internship is for?
Text to Kristina - The stadium closest to you.
Text to Kristina - Yes. Two dogs, both Labs. My parents still have one of them.

I don't know how to answer her last question. This is not how I want her to find out I love her. If I say no, that means never and includes now. I don't want to tell her I don't love her, and honestly I think it would be a lie. At the same time, if I say yes, she'll ask me when or who or something. Can I blame it on the dog?

Text from Kristina - I picked Media. It's what I want to do.

Text from Kristina - Comfort food like waffles, pizza, stew, pasta.

Text from Kristina - Walk up song is serious business. It needs to have some intensity to it and some type of meaning. It needs to get you pumped up and send a message to the other team. I love the sentiment behind "I Want To Hold Your Hand," but I think it should be harder rock. Maybe even punk. I need to think about this one.

Text from Kristina - You never answered the third question.

Text to Kristina - Yes, I was in love with my dog when she ran away.

Text from Kristina - I meant with a human being.

Text to Kristina - I don't know.

Text from Kristina - If you don't know, then who does?

Text to Kristina - I meant that I don't know what that kind of love feels like. I just know how I feel.

Text from Kristina - Oh

Text to Kristina - What does love feel like? Is it the sparks and the fireworks? Is it always wanting to be together?

Text to Kristina - Are you asking me how I feel about you? That's not something I'm going to text you about, Sweetness. You know how I feel about you when we're together. You know I miss you and want to hold you.

Text from Kristina - Okay. Chase, you know love when you

feel it. It could be the sparks and fireworks, or it could be something else.

Text to Kristina - When your heart rolls over in your chest helpless and bare because you need someone and want someone so much that it physically hurts?

Text from Kristina - I think it depends on what exactly you need and want.

Text to Kristina - Or, maybe it's just the person and you take whatever you can get just to be with them.

Text from Kristina - *jaw drop*

We go to the stadium and do our workouts. The team is in a good mood because we got the chance to sleep in and relax. The game is going to be a pitcher's duel between Houston's ace and Rhett Clay. I probably won't even see a ball in center field.

Text from Kristina - I'm watching the game with Sherry tonight... Make it a win! ;)

Text to Kristina - Anything for you, Sweetness.

Text to Kristina - Make sure Sherry is relaxing and not doing much, okay?

Text from Kristina - I'm on that... picking up dinner on my way.

Text to Kristina - You're the best. Beautiful inside and out, Sweetness. <3

Walking out onto the field at game time I point my gloved hand at Seno and wink, "Make it a win!" as I stretch and warm up. He smiles and nods. I can see him physically relax at the words and think that I need to say them before every game until Sherry's here.

The game was horrible. It was long, a test of endurance and

patience. I caught myself staring at the stars while I was in the outfield, knowing she's closer than the stars and we'll be under them together soon. I need to stay focused and not let down time in the outfield get the best of me. All four of the balls that make it to the outfield land in my glove. Martin hit a double, knocking in me and Mason in the first inning, but Houston answers back in the second with a single and home run. We're tied at 2 in the second inning and it stays that way until the top of the ninth when I get to be the hero, hitting a home run and driving in Clay and Brandt. We win 5-2. Seno and Clay work the complete game together with precision, the relievers are thankful to get the night off.

Kristina

My day was crazy and all I could think about was Chase. I pick up Sherry's favorite tamales for dinner and get to her place in time for the second inning. I sit down in front of the TV with her and she starts in, obviously searching for something to distract her.

"So, how's things with Chase?"

Not sure how to answer, "Good. We haven't been able to talk much." I turn to her, "I bet you miss Rick."

"I do. I want to be there with him, but I know this is more important to both of us right now." She wraps her arms around her belly and offers a shaky smile.

I'm out of my zone here, but I want to be helpful, "I'm sure he misses you, too. He seems like a great guy."

"He is. He's perfect. I can't imagine being married to anyone else and I wouldn't want a family with anyone, but him." She rambles on, "Family is very important to him and I'm so happy to be giving him something he's wanted for so long. I still have to pinch myself to make sure this is my life. It's been such a roller coaster ride. I'm sure you are starting to see what the professional athlete world is like, being with Chase. You two are young, but when it's right it's right. I wish I'd met Rick sooner. I envy you meeting Chase so young. You two can do anything together and start your lives together."

I black out there for a minute listening to Sherry talk about my life with Chase. Suddenly all I can focus on is that she's pregnant, huge and uncomfortable. I flash back to mounting him bare and not caring about what might happen, simply needing him and having him was all that mattered. How could I be so stupid! I know he says he'll protect me, but he's still a guy. Damn it! I did it myself! It wasn't even him. He tried to stop it. I wanted more. I steer Sherry back to the game and try not to think about it. She needs calm company, I can be that for her tonight. We can cheer for our guys together.

CHAPTER TWENTY-FIVE

Chase

Seno and I have fallen into a routine, phone calls with our women and room service every night. We decide to stick with it since we're on a winning streak and you never fuck with a streak. I hesitate to even think the word streak because it could jinx it. It doesn't matter, we would be in our room and talking to our women even if we'd lost. We both change into sweatpants and dial our women at the same time.

"Hello?"

"Hey, Sweetness. I made it a win for you. Did you see my home run?"

"Yes, baby! It was a moon shot! We were both yelling at the TV!"

"Are you having fun baking and watching baseball with Sherry?"

"Yea, I'm staying with her tonight. Helping her get some things done that are hard for her and we're going to stay up and watch movies, because she's having a hard time sleeping." Her tone is different.

"Is something wrong? Are you okay?"

"Hold on a second."

Text from Kristina - She needs her Mom here or some-body. I don't know about this stuff. She's okay, but she's nervous and worried.

"Sorry, my friend was texting me."

"That was sly."

"I try."

I get Seno's attention across the room and signal for him to cover his phone, "Kristina's staying at your place tonight and thinks Sherry needs someone to stay with her that has more experience with pregnant stuff. Says she's okay, but looks nervous and worried." He nods at me and gives me a thumbs up.

"So, Sweetness, what did you bake? Did you have any surprises left for you at your desk today?"

"There was a baseball cap embroidered with your number on it in the regular team colors left for me today, thank you. I'm starting to feel like I'm getting a whole new wardrobe and everything has your name and number on it. Are you marking me?" She giggles.

"Yes. I want everyone to know you're mine. I'm proud to have you as mine and I don't want anyone else even thinking about having you." Fuck me, I'm starting to sound possessive like Seno. Maybe we shouldn't room together.

"Wow." Her breath hitched, "The way you said that gave me chills."

Fuck me, fuck me, fuck me, "It's simply the truth, Kristina. Good chills?"

"Very good chills." I can't help but smile. "I baked brownies and cookies. She said she'll show me more in the morning."

"Room service just got here. Let me call you back after we eat, okay? Or do you want to call me when you climb into bed, so I can tell you what I want?"

"I'll call you later, baby." I thought she was done. "Chase— I miss you, baby." She hangs up leaving me wishing that I could be with her right now. She misses me. It shouldn't make me feel good that she misses me, but it does. She fits, too. I mean, she belongs with me and fits the team dynamic. She's even helping Sherry, looking out for her and she doesn't have to do that. Shit, I was being selfish and killing to birds with one stone, thinking my girl would learn to bake and Sherry would have someone around—she took it to a whole different level. I love her heart.

Seno and I eat dinner while he calls Sam and she agrees to go stay with Sherry for a few days. I'm happy I ordered us a twelve pack of brews, we're going to need them this weekend. I turn on the TV and flip through channels, while the twelve pack disappears.

I'm stretched out on my bed, half asleep watching an action flick when my phone rings, "Hey, Sweetness."

"Hi, baby... What are you doing?"

"Seno and I are hanging in the room, tossing back some brews."

"Michelle says I have a big box from Amazon waiting for me at home. Do you know anything about that?"

"I guess that depends on what's in the box. Might be a delivery from somebody else."

"So, you did send me something? What is it?"

"You'll have to look for yourself, Sweetness." I don't know

exactly what's in the box, Sherry did that part. I'd rather she be surprised anyway. I wouldn't tell her if I knew.

"You really don't need to keep sending me things."

"I want you to have things. I want you to have the appropriate team gear and things that you need. It makes me happy to give you things." I want to give you everything are the words going through my head and I realize my buzz may be getting the best of me. "So, are you curled up on the couch with a blanket?"

"Yes, and I'm lonely," playing with me in her sweet, soft girly voice.

"Oh, Sweetness, we can't have that. Close your eyes and let me make it better. I'm there with you right now. I lean over the back of the couch and kiss your cheek, your skin's so soft. You turn your head and look at me, I can only imagine the need in my eyes matches the need I find in yours. We claim each other's lips because we can't help it, we need the touch, the electrical contact. I wrap my arms around you and pick you up, bringing you close to my chest and holding you tight, never wanting to let you go. I carry you out to the balcony and you snag your blanket on the way. I sit down on the lounge chair under the night sky with you in my arms and get us both wrapped in the blanket. My hands hold you possessively because you're mine and I'm not going to share. I love the way your body fits perfectly against mine while I hold you and we look at the stars with the faint sound of the ocean in the background. The night sky is so dark that the stars shine and twinkle with more stars than you can imagine. The beauty of the night is breathtaking, but doesn't compare to my woman that I'm holding in my arms, my Kristina, my Sweetness. You make me warm all over. You make my heart beat faster. You make my pulse race. I want to hold you and protect you. You make me think things that I don't understand and want to say things that I know I shouldn't."

I'm interrupted by Seno throwing something at me and mouthing "Shut up! You're drunk!" at me.

I try to get my head straight. I don't even know what I was saying. "Sweetness, what would you do if you were here with me?" Seno gives me a thumbs up.

I hear a sweet sigh and I know she's falling asleep, "I want to be in your arms under the stars. Can't you be here with me under the stars?"

"Yes, my Sweetness. I'm with you under the stars. Tell me what you would do if I was there with you."

"My feet would be nestled between your legs. My arm stretched across your body and holding you at your waist. My head cuddled into your neck with my face resting on your chest. Relaxing to the sound and feel of your heartbeat. Absorbing your warmth and content being near you, I'd kiss your bare chest and move my hand up your torso to hold onto it. You'd kiss me on the forehead because it's the only place you could reach without disturbing our position. I feel tingles just being near you and I'm embarrassed by my attraction because I can't help myself as I lightly rub against your leg. I'm wet for you and I can't control it, when all I want is for you to keep holding me."

"I want to hold you, too, my Sweetness." I shouldn't, but... "Are you really wet for me right now, Sweetness?" No response. "If you're tired, I can let you go to sleep."

"I'm not ready yet. Um, maybe." That's a yes.

"Do you want to tell me about it?"

"Are you, uh, hard?"

"Trust me, as soon as you said wet I got hard."

She giggles and it makes it worse. Seno gets up and stomps across the room, "Horndog," then locks himself in the bathroom and turns the shower on.

"How hard are you?"

"I thought you just wanted me to hold you."

"Mostly, but other things are good, too. Chase, baby, I want you bad."

"What do you want?"

"I want you to hold your cock and tell me how hard it is."

Oh fuck, "It's rock solid, thinking about you."

"I wish you were in me."

"Me, too… Sweetness, what are you wearing? I'm laying shirtless with my hand in my sweatpants."

"You should come out of those sweats and stroke yourself for me. I want to lick your cock and kiss it all over. You'd see my breasts bounce in the skimpy tank top I'm wearing and get a view straight down my shirt. You're so hard that I can only get half of you in my mouth and that's not good enough."

"No, my Sweetness deserves all of me. I pull you up to my lips and kiss you as you slide back onto my hard dick. Oh, Kristina, I can feel you on me and it's amazing."

"Stroke it like I'm on you, baby."

"Are you touching yourself, Sweetness? Please touch yourself. I would touch you and make you feel good if I was there. Do it for me, Sweetness. Reach your hand into your panties and feel how wet you are."

"Are you stroking your dick?"

"Yes, and imagining you on me. I want to make you come and I want to hear you. Find your spot, Sweetness, and rub it for me. Tell me how wet you are. Tell me how you feel."

"My panties are soaked, and I'm slick to the touch. So easy for you to slide in. I need you, Chase. Fuck, I'm falling for you."

"It's okay, Sweetness. I need you, too. Rub it and feel me pushing into you. I'll always protect you, Kristina. Always you,

Sweetness." I hear her whimper softly, sexy. I've heard it before and I know she's with me. "Feel how hard I am for you."

"I sit up straight and ride you hard because I can't help myself. Grinding against you at our connection. I touch our connection and feel how hard you are, filling me, stretching me. Oh!" Her tone changes.

"I'm here with you, Sweetness. You want to come?"

"Yes, oh yes, oh Chase."

"Rub it harder for me, faster, Sweetness. Don't stop, just don't stop. I want you on me. I want to push into you and feel you wet around me. I want you however I can get you." I'm getting close and start to lose my breath.

"Oh, Chase!"

"More, Sweetness. More. Don't stop. I won't stop, push it Sweetness. More."

"Chase!" I hear her cry out my name and whimper. I know the sound and it sets me off instantly.

I groan as I come, "Fuck, Sweetness. How do you do this to me? Oh, fuck... I'm still coming. Tell me you feel it. Tell me you want me in you. Tell me it's only you and me, Kristina."

There's only silence.

"Chase?"

"I'm here, Sweetness."

"I miss you, baby. It's only you and me."

I smile, "I miss you, too. I'm here to catch you if you're falling. I'll always protect you. I promise you're safe with me. I promise. I'm still holding you, Sweetness. All night long." We hang up and sleep, unable to keep our eyes open. My girl. All I can think about and I dream about her now, too.

Kristina

Five minutes ago I was listening to his voice and couldn't keep my eyes open. Now, I can't sleep. I can't believe I told him that I'm falling for him. Shit! This is how I end up pregnant and the size of a house! Plus, bonus! It will be my own fault! I'm the one that slides onto his cock without warning and doesn't want to get off of him. I can't be falling for him. This isn't part of my plan. I need to have a job and be self-sufficient. Being dependent on a man, any man, not an option. The tone in his voice tonight owned me. New, sincere and possessive, it shot right through me. I want him so bad that I had phone sex and fuck if I didn't start it! Yep. This is my end. The life I want goes out the window. I'm controlled by a man. This can't happen. Oh, and his possessive words. He wants us to be living together? He said he wants me in his bed every night. He said it's only me and him. He wants to be like them. He wants to move me in, get married and knock me up. I can't do this. I don't want to get hurt again. He said he'll protect me and I believe him. I believe every word he says.

I get home after no sleep and find the huge Amazon box waiting for me. It's full of everything for baking. Mixer with all the attachments, bowls, measuring cups, everything I could possibly need for baking and not the cheap stuff. I walk into my room to find all of my new Seals wardrobe hanging everywhere. Everything says Cross and has a big 17 on it. He can't buy me and mark me. He doesn't get to own me.

No, I can't do this. I want him. I think I love him, but this isn't me. It's too much.

CHAPTER TWENTY-SIX

Chase

Road Trip Day 5: Saturday - Game 2 in Houston

I wake up thinking about Kristina and I'm somehow satisfied from last night. I reach for my phone to call my girl and tell her good morning, but Seno yells at me from across the room, "Pervert! Keep that shit in your pants and under control. No more beer nights for you. Fuck, at least tell me to take a shower or something before you have phone sex and wack it."

"Sorry, it was her fault. I'll warn you if it happens again. Dude, she says the hottest things. Fuck me." I relax in bed thinking about our conversation, "Hey, she told me she's falling for me."

Seno stares at me, "Is that what you want? Just her? No more girls everywhere waiting for you to fuck them? No more nights with the twins? No more walking away the next day, without even knowing their name?"

"I want her. I know it sounds stupid. I need her. I want to protect her. I told her I'm here to catch her if she falls. I promised I wouldn't hurt her. I mean it. Dude, I understand why you want Sherry with you. The one special one that's yours, that you can share with and just be you, everything is better with them being in the same room or sitting in the stadium during a game."

Seno smiles, "You need to do whatever makes you happy and keeps you that way. Don't tell her you love her over the phone or text or anything stupid, do it in person with no alcohol in your system."

"I can do that."

I have pictures of a mixer and baking stuff from Kristina.

Text from Kristina - You need to stop.
Text from Kristina - I mean, good morning. Thank you for the baking tools and the outrageously expensive mixer with attachments that cost as much as my rent.
Text from Kristina - Sorry, please stop sending me things.
Text from Kristina - I don't think I can do this.

Woah! What the fuck happened? I call her, but she doesn't answer.

Text to Kristina - Good morning.

Text to Kristina - Please answer your phone or call me.

Text to Kristina - I thought you would like it because you wanted to learn how to bake.

Text to Kristina - You're still going to have things left for you at your cubicle everyday until I get back.

Text to Kristina - I'm sorry. Tell me what to do here.

Text to Kristina - You said you're falling for me. This doesn't make any sense.

Text to Kristina - I'll never hurt you. I mean it.

Text to Kristina - We won't end like the rest of them.

Text to Kristina - Don't run scared. Please. I need you.

I turn to Seno, "She froze me out and won't respond. Fuck!"

"Give her a chance to respond and see what happens. You can send her flowers or something if you want."

"No, she told me to stop sending her things."

"Concentrate on baseball. Only five more games until we go home. She'll come around."

We head over to the stadium early to work out and I need to run it off. I need to run her out of my system. Maybe I need to find a hook up tonight and forget about her. But, that's not what I want. Fuck. I want her. I keep checking my phone, but there's nothing new. I've run over ten miles and already spent too much time in the batting cage. I walk into the clubhouse and hang out with the guys, listening to music and playing cards. Trying to get through the day without my Sweetness.

Mason walks in, "What the fuck did you do? Michelle said Kristina freaked out and took off."

"Where'd she go? She's not at the stadium working?" I hear the worry in my voice.

Mason watches Seno drop his head and shake it, "Uh, I'm sure everything is fine."

Seno comments, "Mason, you're an idiot. See if you can find out where she went."

Text to Carter - Can you find out what time Kristina is working today? And if she's there?

Text from Carter - On it

Text from Carter - She called in sick.

Text to Sherry - Any idea where Kristina is?

Text to Kristina - At least tell me you're okay.

Text from Kristina - I'm okay. Please leave me alone.

Text to Kristina - I will do anything you want, except leave you alone.

Text from Sherry - Yes

Text to Sherry - Where is she?

Text from Sherry - She doesn't want you to know.

Text to Sherry - Can you help me? I don't know what to do. I need to know she's safe.

Text from Sherry - She's safe.

I'm completely lost and it's almost time for the game to start. I go through the motions, get ready and go out on the field to stretch and warm up. I don't know what to do, since she won't talk to me. I need to be in the same place with her and bring her back to me, tell her to stop running. I know that's all this is. She's running away because she's scared of getting hurt again. I guess from her view I'm not the best bet, but I'm not that guy. I was, but meeting her saved me. She saved me and made me realize what I was missing. She may be the only one that can save me. Why won't she let me save her?

I try to get the game started right. I walk through the dugout clapping and say "Let's make it a win!" I'm first at bat and as I stand in the on deck circle swinging my bat, I wonder if she's somewhere watching me. The cameraman is watching me and I look directly into the camera as if I'm looking at Kristina, pat my heart and point at her. I step up to the plate and dig in with my cleats. The plan is the same as it always is, get on base and let the team bring me around to score. Keep it simple. Get a base hit. Take a walk. Whatever. Just get on base. It takes ten pitches, but I get the walk and making the pitcher throw ten pitches to the first batter is in our favor. Use the starter up and get into the bullpen early. Mason is at bat next and communicating with me. I steal second successfully and I'm in scoring position with no outs. Mason hits a double off the right field wall and I score. That's how we play baseball. We scored 3 in the first inning. One out in the bottom of the sixth inning and a fly ball is heading toward left center field. I run to make the catch and Simms is running toward me from left field. I call him off because I've got the ball, but he keeps coming at me. I catch the ball as he's grabbing for it and take his elbow to my face, knocking me backwards to the ground. I roll with it into a backwards somersault to help lessen the impact and somehow manage to hold onto the ball for the out. I sit up and Skip waves at me to see if I'm okay, I wave him off. I refuse to look like I'm hurt, even if I am. I'm staying in this game and we're winning. I'm not going on the disabled list and I'm not showing any signs of injury to anybody that might be watching me play. The last thing I need is another reason for Kristina to not want to be with me. Nobody is taking my spot on the team or getting anywhere near my girl, and she's still my girl. I just need to get to her and everything will be fine. Seno hit a homer in the 6th inning and a double in the 9th, driving in four runs. The streak continues, Seals win 7-1.

Kristina

It's stupid, but I find Sherry's is my safe place and I've taken up baking to keep busy. She suggested it, said it helps when she's nervous. She also said she wouldn't mind some cookies. Sam is visiting until the team gets back, so they turn the game on and cheer together. It makes sense, both of them are close to Rick. I'm trying the recipes she taught me on my own without her assistance and watching the game out of the corner of my eye, trying not to pay attention to Chase when he's at bat.

Sherry checks on me, "How are you doing?"

"I think I've got the cookies down. You'll be the test when you taste them."

She examines me, "Everything else okay, too?"

Sam yells out louder than expected when Kris Martin gets a hit and I let it distract me from Sherry's question.

She doesn't push me, "You're always welcome here. You know where to find me if you want to talk." She starts to walk away, but turns and speaks quietly over her shoulder, "Don't give up so easily, things have a way of working out. Cookies smell good."

I don't know how to make this work out. Sam yells again when Kris comes around to score. "What's with cheering for Martin?"

"It's been this way since I met Sam. I think he's her baseball fantasy," she laughs as she goes back to the game in time for Seno to bat.

Baking is my escape tonight. I don't want to think about my life.

Chase

Seno and I get back to our room and he directs me, "Get changed. We're going out with the team. Sam has Sherry and I've been told to go get wasted. You should, too. Hurry up!" He makes a quick check in call to his woman and he's ready in less than five minutes. "Why aren't you ready? Let's go."

"I'm going to stay here."

"I don't know what part of this you don't understand. You're going if I have to drag you with me. Not trying to get you hooked up or anything, I get it. But, we're going out and we're getting wasted. It's a bad decision with an early game tomorrow, and I'm not going to get away with those much longer. Work with me here and get your ass ready."

I start to argue, but realize that he needs this and no matter what, he's always had my back. Time to get wasted.

Seno leads me out of the hotel and we walk a couple blocks to the bar where the team is already drinking. The guys are doing shots and we need to catch up. We order a couple plates of appetizers, a round for the team and a couple extra shots each for us. It's a whiskey night. I know better. Whiskey nights always get me into trouble. I check my phone and it's still radio silence from Kristina. I want to talk to her and that means I need to get rid of my phone or I'll drunk dial her. It would also be a good idea to have a keeper. I know I'm an adult, but me and whiskey usually ends up me and at least one chick in my bed. I haven't tested this since I stopped fucking every chick that wanted me and the fact that Kristina is ignoring me isn't helping. Maybe I should text her before I give up my phone for the night or something. It doesn't matter, she's not going to call me tonight. Fuck it.

Text to Kristina - Seno dragged me out to the bar to get wasted. I'd rather be talking to you, but he insisted and you don't want to talk to me. Maybe wasted will be a good thing.

Three shots in and I'm feeling pretty good. Seno and I have been going shot for shot. We haven't drunk like this since before he met Sherry. It was always a challenge to keep up with him and I refuse to give up. I'm guessing that maybe he hasn't been drinking as much and this is my chance to out drink him. Mason has our backs to make sure we get back to our room safely with no women, he's even holding my phone to keep me from drunk dialing anyone. I think he's entertained by the drinking display and obvious intent to get wasted. It's a different side of Seno and very few of us have seen it. It's always been a few of us drinking when this happens, not the whole team. I mean, of course I'd drink regardless and go for luck, but I was being a kid that knew a chick would be waiting at his hotel room door to fuck him, too. The next two shots arrive together and they're doubles. We shoot them both quickly and hang out with the team.

Mason's looking at a phone and I'm hopeful that Kristina has made contact, but he sees me looking and shakes me off. Most of the team is in pretty good condition. Things are a little hazy for me around the edges. Seno stands up to go to the head and he's wavering, or maybe that's my eyesight. I'd say we both achieved wasted. He turns back to me and smiles, "My daughter's name is going to be Elle. Don't tell her it's because I like doing it in elevators, okay?"

"No problem, dude." He turns and walks away, and I know he's wasted. I smile at the information he provided. Who knew Seno was a kinky bastard! It makes me happy to know he isn't all business like he wants everybody to think. Sherry got extra points with me, too. Lucky dude, got the right woman and she puts out in elevators. I'm happy for him.

It hits me like a brick that I may never talk to Kristina again. I don't really believe that will happen. She works at the stadium. But, the reality is she could be done with me. My chest hurts. I don't think she was using me. I don't think I was a notch on her bedpost or a player conquest to add to her collection. She's not that kind of chick. Yeah, she was at the party in Arizona, but she was working at the stadium there, too. And, she left me hard and wanting, she didn't fuck me. No, she's not that type of girl. Kristina's real. I'm worried about her. I promised I wouldn't hurt her and now I'm wondering if somehow I did without knowing it. I never want to hurt her. I wonder if she knows how much she's hurting me right now. This must be love. I've heard it's a blessing and a curse. Shit, I've seen it. If you love someone it gives them the ability to hurt you. The more love you have for them, the more they can hurt you. Yeah, I love her and I'm in deep. I hope there isn't another dude, that would kill me. I stand up to walk over to Mason and I'm drunk off my ass. I lean on him, "Does anybody know where Kristina is? Is she okay? Is there another dude?"

Mason gives me a painful grin, "I haven't heard anything about another dude. All I can get out of Michelle is that she's safe. I don't get it either."

"Ask for an update." I need more.

"I don't think it's that kind of a thing." He looks at me, not liking where this is going.

"Please." I look at the floor. "I need her to be okay. Do you think she'll talk to me again?"

"Man, you're drunk. Maybe we should get you back to the hotel."

"Just get her on the phone with me." I feel like I'm begging.

"No, that's why you gave me your phone. No drunk dialing." Mason stands his ground.

He's right. I go back to my seat at the table and nibble on the appetizers. Seno comes back and almost misses the chair when he sits down.

Mason comes to us, "She's just a chick. There's always another one. Maybe we should get you guys back to sleep it off."

Seno adds his two cents, "No, she's not just a chick. This fool's totally in love with her. He's not getting over it any time soon." He didn't tell Mason, he announced it loudly to the whole bar in his drunk tone. Fuck me. There were chicks hanging on me within seconds, all offering to help me get over her or show me that they were better for me anyway.

"I'm not interested." I get up and leave the bar. I don't know what direction I'm walking. I don't know which way to get to the hotel. I'm wasted and I hoped that would help numb me, if it's helping then I don't want to be sober because this still hurts. The lights all have a glow around them. The sky is dark and cloudy, not like when I have Kristina and the sky is clear with bright shining stars. I feel empty. I want to call her, but Mason still has my phone. I feel better getting outside and away from everybody. I wish she were with me. The other problem is that I don't have a clue where I am. I see a woman walking toward me and for a few seconds I think it's Kristina. I don't know how she found me. It makes sense because she saved me before, so why wouldn't she find me when I'm lost? Well, she's in San Diego and I'm in Houston, that's why not and I can see that it's not her as the figure walks right by me. I start walking back the direction I came from, thinking maybe I'll find the bar or one of the guys from the team. Maybe I can get another drink before I go back to my room. Nothing looks familiar. I keep walking because I didn't walk that far, or I didn't think I did. I see Mason walking toward me.

"Where did you take off to? You were gone quick and I couldn't find you. Let's get back to the hotel."

"Maybe we could get another drink first."

"You don't need it. Let's get you back. I already got Seno to bed."

"Can I have my phone?"

"No drunk dialing?"

"No drunk dialing." He hands me my phone and a text pops through. He looks at my face, ready to grab the phone back away from me.

"Maybe we should just turn it off for the night and you should go to bed." He tries to slide the phone away from me, but I don't let him.

Text from Kristina - I wasn't looking for a ball player and I don't think I can be in a relationship with one. My heart has been broken too many times and I'm not strong enough for you. Goodbye, Chase.

Damn it! Damn it! Damn it! I want to throw my phone to the ground and watch it splatter into a thousand little pieces.

Text to Kristina - No. This isn't goodbye. You are strong enough. You're everything.

Error this number is not accepting your messages

FUCK! She dumped me in a text and blocked me!

To @Kristeeeeeena - This isn't goodbye. You are strong enough. You're everything.
To @Kristeeeeeena - I'm not letting you go. I'm coming for you.
To @Kristeeeeeena - We're not over. You're still my Sweetness.

"Call Michelle and see if Kristina is there with her." I stare at Mason waiting.

"I can't do that. I'm not putting Michelle in that position with her roommate. I'll call her and let you know if I can find out anything. I know this is killing you."

"Then do it and get a picture of her if you can."

Mason shakes his head and dials. He starts talking to Michelle and finally gets to asking about Kristina. We get to my room and he directs me to go inside while he finishes his conversation, so I leave the door blocked for him to keep the door from locking. I hear him end his call and he comes into my room. "Michelle says that Kristina's a wreck. I was able to confirm that there isn't another guy. Something about a phone conversation you had with her last night, baseball, and Sherry. Honest, it didn't make any sense to me."

I get that we had a pretty deep conversation last night. I know because I felt our connection, too. Was I supposed to tell her I'm falling for her, too? Baseball is my job, I love it and it pays well, but it does have me on the road about ninety days a year, players get hurt and we get traded like commodities. Sherry? I don't get that part. Maybe Sherry was pushing me on her? I know Sherry thinks I'm a great guy. Maybe she was a mean baking coach? Maybe Sherry is in an overly emotional state, missing her man and Kristina decided it's too hard? I don't understand women.

I look at Mason, "Thanks for watching out for me tonight, dude. I appreciate it. Please let me know if you get any more info on Kristina. If you can, please make sure she knows I'm still hers. I'm not giving up on her. I really do love her, Seno wasn't just being a dick. I'm going to tell her when we get home, even if she doesn't want me." Mason pats me on the back and takes off for his room.

Now, I'm sad and my chest still hurts. I admit that I love her and it makes me hurt more. I'm going to tell her when I get back to San Diego. It doesn't matter if she wants me or not, she needs to know. If it's my turn to have a broken heart, so be it. She deserves to know that I love her.

I call room service and order breakfast to be delivered, to make sure we wake up in time to get to the stadium and have coffee waiting for us. It's going to be a challenge and I won't be surprised if one or both of us get scratched from the lineup tomorrow. I'm feeling too much, so I raid the mini bar and throw back three bottles of whiskey. Seno is completely passed out. I open my laptop looking for a distraction and end up watching videos on youtube. Just when I feel like I might be able to sleep, a string of Foreigner videos starts to play and the whiskey has taken control.

Kristina

It's the middle of the night and my Twitter is blowing up. I've been tagged on a few posts and they just keep going. I check notifications knowing I don't have to respond and curious about what's going on. It's Chase. He's posting videos and directing them to me. I know I shouldn't, but I can't help myself and I go watch them as he posts them. No words in his posts, simply the link and video. A string of Foreignor,"Feels Like the First Time," "I Want to Know What Love Is," "Waiting For a Girl Like You," "I Don't Want to Live Without You," and "Say You Will," followed by "Just Like Heaven," "Dive," and "Turn It Up." "I Want to Hold Your Hand" is last and the only one with a message, it says 'please, this is all I want.' His fans are commenting on the tweets, but he's not responding. I'm staying invisible, but that doesn't keep the tears from rolling silently down my cheeks as I watch every single video and realize he's hurting, too.

CHAPTER TWENTY-SEVEN

Chase

Road Trip Day 6: Sunday - Game 3 in Houston

I wake up, startled by room service banging on the door. I sit up and the room spins. Fuck me. Seno speaks, "I got it."

"I ordered last night to make sure we got up and had coffee. I knew it would be bad this morning."

"Good thinking. What were you thinking when you drank the mini bar?" With a chastising tone.

"Fuck me. Dude, the room is spinning." Room service wheels in a cart with breakfast and coffee. Seno tosses the waste basket on my bed and his timing is impeccable. I block rather than catch because everything is moving and blow chunks into the waste basket, as if it was on queue. Seno appears to be just fine and appreciating that I ordered breakfast.

"You need to get it together. We need to get to the stadium."
He looks at me funny, "What were you doing with your laptop
in bed last night? Surfing porn?" He walks toward me and clicks
the touchpad to see what I was doing. "Fuck. What did you do?"

I look over and my laptop is open to twitter. I was tweeting
videos to Kristina and apparently decided to drink more from
the mini bar than I thought, since there are a pile of empty little
bottles on the floor. I can't tell you more than that. It's all I can
do to stop vomiting and I really just want the room to stop
trying to spin.

"Man, you really can't be trusted to control yourself."

"Did she tweet me back?"

"Seriously? You can't get up, probably will be late to the
stadium and end up scratched from the game. And you want to
know if she tweeted you? Fuck, dude. You do have it bad."
Seno tosses the other waste basket my direction and goes off to
shower. I guess I have to look for myself and that's not an
option right now. This has happened in the past. I blame the
whiskey. I know that nobody made me drink it. But, all it takes
is somebody to get me going and last night I didn't want to feel
anything, so I had a few more and then the whiskey took over. I
don't remember going back for more, but I know it was me. It
reminds me of the nights when I would wake up with women in
my bed and not know what I did or what their names were.
Sometimes I didn't know where I was or how I got there. It
reminds me of waking up in Arizona covered in hickeys and
how the minor leaguers knew I was out of control. The night I
was with Kristina and didn't know her name or who she was
and almost lost her completely because I had no way to find her.
The morning I woke up with the tail from the mascot costume
on my floor and all I could remember was the seal. This isn't

me. No, this isn't what I want and it definitely isn't who I want to be.

I think about Kristina's words while I lay in my bed with my eyes closed. She doesn't think she's strong enough. I need to be strong enough for both of us. Whiskey nights are not the way to do that. Whiskey nights are me giving up and running away from the problem. I need to pull it together and get to the stadium. I need an update on my girl. I need strength to make it through three more days and then I'll find her. Yeah, I'll find her and I'll make everything right again. I know she still wants to be mine.

Seno drags me to the stadium and I get there on time, but Skip scratches me anyway. Fuck it. I sit by my locker in the clubhouse and mope, finally getting time to see what I did on social media last night. Videos. I tweeted videos at Kristina. Every Foreigner love song that's been in my head since she spent the night with me and every song we had ever talked about. I scan through what I did, hoping for a response, but all I got was comments from fans—nothing from the only person that matters. Still radio silence.

Seno walks through the clubhouse and glares at me. He sits in front of me and leans in so I'm the only one that can hear him, "You need to pull your shit together. You need to be in the game and not sitting here accepting that Skip scratched you. I don't care how fucked up you are or how shitty you feel. Your hangover is your own fault, suck it up. The girl will be there or she was never there to begin with. Don't waste your time, use it on productive things and get your ass on that field. If nothing else keep busy and get out of your head, the game is your distraction."

"But,…" Seno cuts me off.

"No fuckin' buts! I'm here. I'm playing. I'm not letting the rest of my life get in my head. No, I'm making this about being the best I can be. I want my girls to be proud of me. I know Sherry loves to watch me play, and that's what I'm doing. Don't you think that I'd rather be with my pregnant wife?" He stops and looks me in the eye. "Okay, now get off your ass and start harassing Skip. I want you on the field and I don't want to see you sitting around like an emotional teenage boy." He gets up and goes about his ritual of getting ready for the game.

He's right. Am I acting like an emotional teenage boy? Fuck that, that's totally unacceptable. I find water and start following Skip around, making it my goal to get into the game today. I've seen Seno do it and he may not start, but he usually manages to get into the game. I harass Skip and start working out, bugging Skip every step of the way and showing him I can do this, showing him that he wants me on that field and running the bases.

Skip finally puts me in as a pinch runner in the seventh inning and I end up part of a double switch, hitting in the pitcher's spot. I'm motivated and want to show Skip he's doing the right thing. Brandt is hitting and signs are getting thrown all over the diamond. Brandt and I are communicating with each pitch, I've got a huge lead off of first base and the pitcher throws to first. I dive for the base, making it back just in time. I stretch my lead off of first again and the pitch is wild, I steal second standing. The third base coach wants me to steal third, there's nobody covering second and I'm half way to third when the pitch is thrown. Brandt choppers the ball through the infield and I score on his base hit. The streak continues, we win 4-1.

The team is flying to Chicago tonight, so we're busy and that's good, helps me stay focused. That is until we get on the plane and everybody gets their phones out to call their women, and I can't because she blocked me. I want to call her and talk for a few minutes, like my teammates. Seno sits next to me and ends his call with Sherry. "Good work getting into the game," with an attaboy nod.

"Thanks."

With a deep sigh, "She was baking with Sherry this afternoon and they were watching the game together. So, she's safe and not hiding. Sherry said Kristina's been asking her questions about ball players and I don't think she'd do that if she was ready to be done with you. Give her the few days and when we get back I'll help you find her. But, I want to see you hustling in Chicago. No, whiny ass shit."

"I got it. Thanks for letting me know she's okay."

To @Kristeeeeeena - Flying to Chicago. Miss you.

Seno wakes me up when the plane is landing and I feel much better than I did earlier, I may have shook off the hangover. I'm hungry. We get checked into our room and settled. I take Seno and Mason out for a steak dinner, it's Chicago home of the steakhouse. I figure I owe them since I've been such a punk the last couple of days. We keep it an early night and I make up for my whiskey night by turning in early.

Kristina

"How could you jump in so quick with a baseball player? They're all players in every sense of the word."

Sherry grins, "You'd think that, but it's not true. Rick hadn't been with a woman in two years when I met him. That doesn't mean it wasn't a struggle. Their past isn't their present and they can't control the women that are after them."

"I guess. I don't know. They're gone so much and they could be doing anything," I should think before I speak. The last thing I want is a worried pregnant woman on my hands.

Sherry looks at me funny, "We don't like being apart, so I go on road trips. The rest doesn't matter. It's not a concern because we trust each other."

Do I trust Chase? I think I trusted him the first moment I met him. I hadn't considered him cheating until I told him to try another girl. So fucking stupid. Can it be cheating if I told him to do it? No, he wouldn't cheat. I don't have the luxury of being able to travel with him. I have to work.

"How do you deal with him getting hurt? Doesn't it freak you out when pitchers throw at him?"

"I never want him hurt, but when he got hurt last season it brought us closer together. It pisses me off when they throw at him and I yell at the pitchers when they do it. It's part of the game." She stops and turns to me, "We all have to live. Life has risks."

She doesn't ask me about Chase, she simply continues helping me learn how to bake and let's me do my own thing. She's content and happy sharing her life with a baseball player.

Wanting Chase could be a change to my whole life plan. I don't know if I can have what I want and him. What if he wants more than I'm willing to give?

CHAPTER TWENTY-EIGHT

Chase

The next three days I do my best to stay focused. Mason and Seno share info they get about Kristina— she's safe and still there. I can go find her when I get home and figure it out from there. Baseball is my world. No chicks. No booze. My team, work outs and games.

Monday's game was postponed due to rain. A day wasted. The team got together and went for deep dish Chicago Style pizza. Then I hung out with Mason, who I found out has been spending time alone in his room this whole trip. Well, maybe not quite alone, playing video games online with Michelle and talking to her through the game—basically whispering in her ear the whole time they've been apart. Luckily, she's busy with work today and the team takes over Mason's room with a video game competition. Yes, we played baseball.

I didn't realize Michelle works, but I guess she has to pay rent somehow. She's always available for games and it doesn't matter what time of day or day of the week. Mason has been spending all his free time with her, so I don't know when she's working. "Dude, what does your chick do?"

"She's a freelance contractor of some type. She doesn't go into it. She has some deadlines and mostly knows how much work she has to get done each day to stay on pace for her jobs," Mason shares vaguely.

"So, you don't know?"

"Pretty much. The only part I understand is that she's self-employed."

We all stay up too late for the doubleheader we have tomorrow.

Kristina

Between work and hanging out at Sherry's I haven't been home much. I get home and my apartment is silent, but I know Michelle should be here. "Hello?" I call out.

"SShhhhh… busy," comes through her closed bedroom door.

I've never got that response before. I knock on her door, "Coming in."

She groans and looks up at me as I stand in her doorway.

"Are you behind on work?" Michelle looks ragged, like she hasn't slept.

"No. Busy."

"Busy with what?" I walk over to look at her computer expecting to find she's on a video game binge. "What the…"

"Don't ask. I don't know where it's coming from. I can't help it and I can't sleep and I'm barely keeping up the minimums on my fantasy serials."

"Okay, but you need to get some sleep. What did you tell Jones you do?"

"I'm a self-employed freelance contractor. I got lucky and he didn't ask questions. I've learned to lean in for a kiss and he'll do anything to avoid it."

"I don't know why you put up with that. I can't believe he hasn't kissed you."

"I can't believe you don't claim Chase as your own and stop being stupid," she stares at me with disdain. "It's kind of sweet that Mase is taking it slow. At least that's what I keep telling myself and then I remind myself how amazing his hands feel when he holds me. I'm being patient."

"Whatever."

"Seriously, Kristina, he's a good guy and he's into you. Forget that he's a baseball player for five minutes and think about the man. The hot man with long legs and muscles and always in a dirty uniform. Maybe the uniform part doesn't help, but you get the idea."

"Michelle!"

"He gets my attention. Do you know how many other women are noticing him if I am? You need to get your shit together."

"I'm thinking about it."

"Like, really?"

"Yes."

"Don't think too long. I think you're good until the team gets back. Mase said Chase is going to find you when he gets home. You better know what you want by then."

"So, what's with the project you're working on?"

"It's extra-curricular and we are keeping it to ourselves."

"Um, what about your critique partner?"

"I don't want to have to explain him to Mason."

"That's not what I meant. Does he know about your project?"

"No. I haven't figured that part out yet. This may never get beyond my laptop."

"I doubt that, but whatever."

I walk away and leave her to her project. I have things to think about.

Chase

There's no time for anything other than baseball on Tuesday. We're playing a doubleheader to make up the rain out from yesterday. The lineups for both games are posted at the same time and game one starts at 11:00am. Doubleheaders are a mixed bag. Skip probably won't play the same guys both games and may make some last minute changes between games. Then again, if I'd look at the lineups I'd know.

```
Game 1
1 CF Cross
2 SS Mason
3 1B Martin
4 C Seno
5 3B Lucine
6 2B Brandt
7 RF Rock
8 LF Simms
9 P Grace

Game 2
```

```
1 2B Brandt
2 SS Hart
3 CF Cross
4 LF Mason
5 3B Simms
6 1B Saben
7 RF Bravo
8 C  Stray
9 P  Clay
```

It's going to be a long day for a few of us. I need to be in both games. The less down time the better.

Game one went like most games that have the lineup. We won 12-4 and Seno is pissed about the 4. I told him to take the win, but he doesn't listen. It's a good thing he's sitting game two out. Every single one of us got a hit, even Corey Grace and he hits for shit. Mason, Lucine and Brandt hit homers. I got on base four of my five at bats and my teammates brought me home three times. I stole second base twice, walked twice and caught six balls in the outfield. Center Field is my space.

Game two, I'm concerned it will be wonky. First of all, Bravo is in the lineup and we haven't won a game with Bravo in the lineup all season. Second, Seno and Lucine aren't in the lineup. Third, Mason isn't in the Sherry approved position. I spend the game leaning toward Right Field and covering half of Bravo's zone in addition to my own, pushing him farther right. I've been watching him and he doesn't have the speed or desire to cover all of Right Field. I've got this, and it's a good thing I do because I run for a pop fly in Right Center Field that he never would've caught. It's mostly rookies on the field for game two and they step up to show what they can do. I'm one of them, but I'm the rookie that's been a Seal the longest. Mason is fine in Left Field, but not as sharp as he is at Short Stop. I get the change though, Short Stop for two games would be too much. He hit two doubles and a homer, I won't be surprised to see him in the clean up spot more often. Stray brought his bat with him today, hitting safely at all of his at bats. A double and three singles. Brandt is new to the Seals, but not a rookie. He's good people, a little quiet maybe, and what the team has been looking for at Second Base. He walked twice, popped out and hit a single. Simms is still getting his feet under him, but the progress is there. He seems to be able to handle anything on the left side. He hit two singles, but got caught stealing both times he made it on base. It wasn't spectacular, but we managed to pull out a win. 2-1 Seals.

Wednesday I wake up anxious. I know we go home today and I've never been more ready to go home. It's an early game and we're going to win, keeping our streak intact. We fly home right after the game and I'm going to find my Sweetness. I know Mason has a date with Michelle tonight, Seno wants to go home to Sherry, and Martin is expecting a visit from a special friend. I'm not alone in my desire to get home and it shows in our playing. Shortest game all season at two hours and fifteen minutes, and that's fine—especially when Josh Kranston shuts out Chicago and pitches the complete game in only 80 pitches. Mason hit a homer in the 4th inning that knocked me in. And in the 7th, we strung together three singles and a walk to score a run. 3-0 Seals.

Kristina

It's hard to ignore baseball when you work in baseball media. More specifically, it's hard to forget Chase when he plays hard and he's the star of the game. I'm constantly writing copy and updating stats that surround him. His batting average and on base percentage keep going up, and his fielding percentage is one of the highest in the league. His UBR and UZR are both impressive, but what stands out most to me is his stolen base percentage. He's the best in the division and three of the top five are on the Seals. The problem is Michelle. Something about the dirty pants does it for her and Chase is always dirty. If she acted like this when Jones was around, he'd swear he has competition. And, that makes me think about him. It's hard not to when I know what he's capable of. It's not the sex. We are combustible together, but it's more than that. I'm relaxed around him and I'm never relaxed around anyone. I can't remember the last time I slept as well as I do when I'm with him. Everything melts away. I guess I believe he'll protect me, he takes away my worries. I like being close to him and that seems to turn into sex.

I wanted to get laid. Just once in my life I wanted to be the girl that gave it up to a baseball player that made it to the majors, a professional athlete. Baseball skank for the night. It's not me. But, the environment reminded me of my ex-boyfriend and he didn't make it to the varsity team in college. I'm sure he wouldn't have found out, but somehow it would vindicate me to know I was with a man that made it further than the jerk who cheated on me and therefore he had to be better. The fact that it was a one and done thing would be the icing on the cake. It's what I wanted and I went for it. I knew my target when I got to the party. Everyone knew Cross wanted to get naked and fuck. I didn't stop when he wanted me and I was wearing the mascot costume. I didn't care. But, when we kissed my heart immediately began to pound. I remember vividly how my heartbeat was so strong that I swear you should've been able to see it beating out of my chest. Like in the cartoons when the red cartoon heart flies out of the characters chest pulling the character off of it's feet and it shows it's warm glow out there for everyone to see the cupids and tweety birds flying around it. Completely exposed. He was drunk and I could read his eyes even if he wasn't coherent. He was with me. He wanted me. I wanted him. I still can't believe that I dry humped him in my PJs. He told me he wanted me enough that night and I believe that he did. I ran because I was afraid of the overwhelming emotions. There's no reason I couldn't have taken advantage of the easy ball player and went on my way. No, my fear won and my fear keeps getting in the way. It makes me say things I don't mean and hide from what I want. If I'm being honest with myself, it's not the fear that's the problem. It's how much I want to be with him. The only fear is that I'm not what he really wants or can't be what he really wants. Fear that I love him as much as I do and he doesn't know what love is or will choose not to love me back. I had to leave him. I can't get dumped by another baseball player. Baseball players suck.

CHAPTER TWENTY-NINE

Chase

The plane ride home was a bit rowdy, not uncommon when the next day is an off day. I bug Seno and Mason to see what they can find out about Kristina. I want as much info as I can get, so I can find her. It seems that she was watching the game with Michelle and disappeared as soon as it was over.

When the plane lands, I don't waste any time. I start my search for Kristina.

Always the last place you look, it's where you find what you're looking for. I've been all over town searching for her. I've been all over the stadium, to her apartment, to Seno's, I've even checked a couple places that Michelle suggested. No sign of her, so I go home to regroup. I need a new plan. If she's hiding from me or doesn't want me to find her, I'll never find her. I open up my bungalow to the beach and there she is, my Sweetness is sitting on the beach between the ocean and my patio. She's looking at the waves and the wind off the ocean is blowing her hair back. The sudden relief in my body almost knocks me over. I stay where I am and look at her. The sight of her alone has my blood flowing and my heart beating faster. I have hope. The fact that she's here on my beach, she must want me to find her. She must want to see me. I want to go to her and I realize that I've been waiting for this, I've been waiting for days to see her and hold her. I've been waiting to have her in my arms, so I can tell her that I love her. I don't want to push her or scare her, and I don't want her to think I'm saying it to get her back. It's not a trick. I'm stuck dead in my tracks, not knowing what to do and I hear Seno in my head telling me to do whatever I need to do to keep my happy. All that matters is that she knows I love her.

I kick my shoes off and run out to her on the sand, dropping down to sit in front of her and face her. "Hi." I watch for signs that she's going to get up and leave, or maybe I could somehow get lucky and she would reach for me to kiss me, or, shit, I'd be happy if she smacked me at this point. I get nothing. "I know you don't want to talk to me. I know you want me to leave you alone. I know you said you were falling for me. The only part I want to believe is that you're falling for me. I don't know what made you run from me, but I think you're afraid of us. I want to be with you. We should be together. I want to know what made you run and I will do anything in my power to fix those things. I care about you and I don't want to push you or pressure you. So, I'm going to say what I have to say and then I'm going in my house. You're always welcome and the door will be unlocked." I take a deep breath and gaze out at the ocean with the roaring waves, feeling a kind of peace fill me and I know I'm doing the right thing, "I didn't know how to react on the phone when you said you were falling for me. I'm not falling for you. I can't fall for you because," I gaze into her eyes and palm her head, running my fingers through her silky hair, "Kristina, I love you. I'm in deep. I couldn't say it over the phone, not the first time. You dumped me and it hurt in my chest, like I'd been cracked open and somebody took out everything that was good, leaving me to suffer with my pain alone. But, none of that matters. If you're done with me, I'll have to figure out a way to make you want me again. And, I'll do it. Right now, I want you to know that I love you. You and only you. In my heart, you're my girl and you always will be. I love you and I'll always protect you." She doesn't speak. She doesn't move a muscle. I lean in and kiss her forehead. I release her from my arms, as much as I don't want to and stand up. I walk back to my bungalow, doing my best to not look back and I know in my heart she'll come to me. I'm just not sure how long it will take and I want her now. I leave my sliding door open and walk to my kitchen, sitting at my counter drinking a bottle of water while I watch her sit there and hope she comes to me.

The sunset is taking over the sky and Kristina is still sitting on the beach, no action other than changing her position and stretching out her legs. The breeze off the ocean has kicked up. I run a blanket out to her and place it around her shoulders, returning quickly to my kitchen counter where I continue to watch her. I run in to my bedroom to change into sweats and use the bathroom, and when I return she isn't sitting on the beach anymore—she's gone. I yell out, "Fuck me! Damn it!" and storm around my living room as I search for her on the beach.

"Is something wrong? I can leave." I hear the sweet voice and turn around to find Kristina sitting on my couch.

"No, don't leave. Nothing is wrong. I ran in the other room real quick and then you weren't on the beach anymore, I thought you were gone."

"I'm right here."

"I see that now."

"Tell me again, Chase."

I smile and feel my body start to relax, "I love you, Kristina."

She smiles and it's the most beautiful thing I've ever seen.

I want to know what pushed her over the edge, but I'm afraid to bring it up. I need to know if I'm going to keep it from happening again. "Do you want to tell me what happened? I don't want you having any questions about me or how I feel about you or what I want from you. I want you to be mine and I want you to be happy."

"I don't want to talk about it right now. You're off tomorrow, right?"

"Yes."

"Me, too."

"Do you want to hang out with me tomorrow?"

"I was thinking I could stay here with you until we go to work on Friday."

"That's perfect." I walk to her across the room and press my lips to hers while I wrap my arms around her. She reaches her arms around my neck and holds on as she wraps her legs around my waist. My girl, my Sweetness, is here with me.

I'm in my head and I just want to hold her. I want to spend time with her. Her body wrapped around me and holding onto me like this makes me want more, but that can wait. I could be sliding into her in less than thirty seconds. I don't understand how she can go from wanting me to leave her alone to wrapped around me, and she probably still has me blocked. She confuses me. It doesn't matter. I need to hold her. I grab the blanket off of my couch and walk out to my patio, carrying her with me. I sit down on the lounge chair and she's basically sitting in my lap, facing me with her arms and legs wrapped around me. She takes over our kiss and is pushing me for more. I want her to know that we aren't just sex. "Lay next to me here, Sweetness." She looks at me a little funny and does as I ask. I lean back into the chair and kick my feet up, while she snuggles into my side using my chest as her pillow and burrowing her head in under my chin. She reaches her arm across me and holds my waist. I cradle her from behind and lean down to kiss her forehead, as we entangle our legs and I cover us with the blanket. I look up into the darkness to find the clear night sky, speckled with bright shining stars. "This is perfect, Sweetness. What can I do to make it perfect for you?"

"It's perfect, Chase. You're perfect. Am I still your girl?"

"You'll always be my girl. You're my everything. Please tell me why you think you aren't strong enough to be with me. What happened to make you dump me? What did I do wrong?" I say as sweetly as possible while I have her in my arms and she can't run away.

"I had time to think about being with you and the time we spent together. I've never been so reckless and I didn't even care. You make me lose all rational thought and all I can think about is you, us, together. And you weren't here. I was lost. I went to hang out with Sherry, learn to bake and watch the game. She tells me about meeting Rick, all I can see is that she's the size of a house and I mentally slap myself for being careless. I can't believe how stupid I was."

"I'm so sorry, Sweetness. I told you I would always protect you and I mean it. I should've made sure you were protected. Honestly, I was already lost in you and you do something to me that I don't understand. I couldn't help myself and I've never had another girl bare before. You felt so good around me, fuck, just thinking about it I want you again. Hot, wet and tight around me with nothing in between us." My stomach flips and my groin is doing somersaults. "It's the nothing in between us part that means the most, it's as close to you as I can get. I want to be as close to you as I can get," Comes out raspy and sexy, completely out of my control. "I promise you it won't happen again."

"I started it and I didn't give you any warning. It was all me."

"No. I wanted you just like that and I could've pulled out sooner. It was me, too. Don't blame yourself."

She swallows hard. "I don't want to be like them. I don't want to be living together, married and pregnant that quick. I don't think I can be what you really want."

"Hold on. That's not what I want." She stops and looks at me. "I mean, that's not what I want right now. I want a girl-friend who I love and I want her all to myself. I'm not sharing with any other dudes. I want to take her out. I want to buy her gifts. I want to spoil her. I want a girl who loves me and isn't a slut after a player. I want to spend time together and build a life that we both want. I'd love to have my girl in my bed every night, but that doesn't mean I expect her to move in with me. The other stuff, I don't know. I've never thought about getting married or having kids. How are we supposed to know what we'll want? I just want to have my girl with me and love her. Remember, I'm the guy who's never even had a girlfriend. I have a steep learning curve, but I'm trying."

Kristina smiles at me, "So, you really just want a girlfriend?"

"Well, not just a girlfriend. Someone special, I mean," This is going to go all wrong and I already know it, "I always want to be with you. I don't know what to call it, but I think girlfriend is where it starts. Fuck! I totally screwed that up, didn't I?"

"No, I understand. You want me and only me. You want to

keep me. You love me. You want to protect me. You want a future with me, but we don't know what we want yet."

I smile, "Yeah, does that work for you?" I can tell by the look on her face that I couldn't have done much better. I get the Sherry part of the problem now.

"Yes," She giggles happily. Someday, when I inevitably decide to propose it's exactly how I hope her answer sounds.

"Good. So, my Sweetness, what would you like to do until we go to work on Friday? Can I take you out to dinner? Keep holding you under the stars? Whatever you want, you get."

"Love me under the stars, Chase."

I pull the blanket up over us and maneuver her onto my lap, facing me. I claim her mouth passionately. I know she's mine. I hold her tightly against me and feel what it's like to have her in my arms knowing that I love her. It's different. I know I like her, care for her, that she's special, but feeling what it's like to love her and think I'd lost her. Feeling the pain in my chest. Now I understand because this feeling is so much more and I never want it to end. I run my hands along her body, feeling her and I know she wants more. Our electricity is shooting through me and I know she can feel it, too. I can feel her shaking.

"Chase, please."

Fuck me. I want more, too. I don't have a condom in reach when we are outside on the patio. Obviously, something I may need to resolve for the future. "I want you, too, Sweetness. Have to go inside for a condom."

"No, I need you now. Please." Her tone is needy and pleading. Fuck I want her bad. She reaches into my sweats and frees my dick, stroking it lightly and feeling how hard I am.

"You know I want you. Let's go inside," I plead with her, fighting my own urge to slide her right down on me and come hard inside her. I've always wanted to do that and I know it's not an option.

"Now baby, please. Inside me."

Fuck, fuck, fuck. This is a disaster waiting to happen. I stand up and take her with me, she automatically wraps her legs around me and holds on. "I know you said under the stars, and we'll get there before the night's over. I need you to believe in your heart that I'll always protect you. You need to trust me and giving in to you for this will just make it worse. Sweetness, you need to know that I'd love to just slide into you and not worry about anything. No matter what, I'll always take care of you and it'll always be us. No blame, Sweetness." I get to my bed and sit down with her still in my lap, her legs wrapped around me. She pushes my sweats down and is sliding out of her shorts before I can even reach for a condom. I grab her around the waist and hold her to me tightly, trying to gain control of the situation. "Kristina. Please work with me here." I feel her rubbing against me and it's driving me crazy. I quickly rip open the condom and roll it on, and she's on me instantly. Her heat sliding down over me feels like I found my home and I never want to leave. Fuck me. She needs me, I can feel her need running through her body as she moves on me and I'm thankful that I'm what she needs. "Thank you, Kristina. Thank you for needing me. I love you, my Sweetness." I pull her down to me, slowing her actions and holding her tight. I touch my lips to hers and she opens for me, inviting my tongue to dance with hers. I may have missed kissing her more than anything else. Her soft, full lips and her sweet taste are things I can't get enough of. I run my fingers through her hair and hold her face to mine so I can keep kissing her and kissing her. I see things when I gaze into her eyes that I can feel in my heart. She moves her hips while we kiss and I'm overcome by emotion. I'm not used to this, I've never experienced this before. I, I just want to love her. I touch her face and I trace her features delicately.

"Chase, baby... oh, Chase." She keeps moving on me and buries her face in my neck, kissing and sucking me there. She finds the right places and I grasp her hips, guiding her and meeting her with my own motions. Causing her to shake and shiver with every stroke, whimpering and moaning my name like I'm what she needs to survive.

"Is it too much, Sweetness? Don't worry, I've got you. I'm right here with you. I didn't know how much I need you and how much control your body has over mine. Oh, fuck, how do you make me feel like this?"

"More, Chase... please. I need..." She sits up straight and bounces on my hard dick, grinding against me at every contact.

"Oh, Kristina... Don't stop, Sweetness, you're going to make me come like that, oh fuck me. I can't stop. Come with me."

"I want to make you go first, Chase. Feel me around you. Feel me tight, hot and wet, riding you while you're so hard up in me." I reach for her and feel how hot and wet our connection is and I feel her shiver at my touch. I push up into her, meeting her movements and I'm pounding up into her, I need to come so bad. I touch her clit and she tightens, fuck me. I rub it and feel her get wetter. "Chase, I need you... more... more... please." I want to roll her underneath me and take over, but we're past that.

"I've got you, Sweetness." I rub her clit faster with a light touch, getting harder as I go and she explodes around me.

"Oh, Chase..." I'm pounding in her and my dicks pulsating in pleasure inside her.

"Fuck you're amazing! Oh fuck!" I call out as I'm

completely drained. She collapses on me, hot and sweaty. I hold her tight as I try to catch my breath.

"Chase, do you still love me?"

I don't know where that comes from, "Yes. I'll always love you. Nothing is going to change that. You're my girl. I promise you that I won't break your heart, it's safe with me." Managing to get all the words out on the little breath I have. I squeeze her and kiss every piece of her that I can reach without letting her go.

She rolls out of my arms and I step away to handle business.

"How can you say that? You can't know that for sure. You might feel different when you wake up tomorrow or next week."

I wish I could make her understand. I wish I knew what her past had done to make her this way. "I don't think love is something that goes away."

She cocks her head to the side, considering my words.

"It's the spark, the fireworks, that zing I get when I'm with you. The emptiness when you wouldn't talk to me. The connection we have when we talk on the phone. The undeniable need between us, pulling us together. It's never been that way with anyone else. I don't want to be with anyone else." I don't know why I keep going on. I want her to agree with me. I want her to say she feels those things too. She doesn't need to tell me she loves me, though I'd love to hear the words. I've never had a woman tell me they love me.

She smiles at me, "Okay."

I get back in bed with intentions of showing her how I feel. I've got no clue what I'm doing.

Kristina

Chase is searching my eyes for something and not saying a word. His hazel eyes are darker and almost grey, yet bright against the teal sheets. He's a guy. I know what he wants. Love me or not, they all want the same thing. I can see it in his hooded eyes. He wants sex like all of the rest of them. That's what my ex-boyfriend wanted and as soon as I wasn't there for him, he found it somewhere else. That's not love. It's getting satisfaction.

He leans over me, kissing my lips delicately and pulling back away. The single touch of his lips increases my heart rate as it zings through me. He's focused on me and his smile widens, "I love you." His tone is full of devotion and I don't know why that makes me lust for him. He wraps his arms around me and holds me against him, his heart beating at a nervous pace. I nuzzle against his chest and lightly trace an outline of his muscles from his arm to shoulder, and then to his chest. Repeating the process back to where I started a few times while I lie silently in his strong protective arms. I trace up his neck to his lips and he releases a warm sigh. I kiss his neck and trace his lips again. He meets my finger with his tongue and kisses it. I want his lips. I pull my hand back and climb on top of him, needing my lips on him. I kiss him from his neck to his lips, dragging my tongue and retracing what I'd done with my finger. He meets my kiss willingly with desire. I'm already breathing hard and all I've done is kiss him. This is crazy! I want him so bad. No, I need him. His arms wrap around me and he takes control of our kiss, tugging on my lower lip. I can't help myself, I reach for his cock to guide him in.

"No, Sweetness. Me, not my dick." He takes control of the situation, "Please. Let me love you."

His hands warm and tender on my body, his lips attentively kissing me pull me into him. I want more and I feel his hand at his dick. It excites me. I want him inside me and I push back against him.

"If that's what you want, it's yours." Yet he didn't let me take him in. He sits up, "Hold on." He stands and wraps his king sized comforter around us like a cloak with a hood over our heads. I hold on tight and wrap my legs around him while I kiss his neck, enjoying the private darkness he's made for us. "I love your legs wrapped around me. Your lips on my neck may be my downfall." He turns all the lights off including the patio lights as he walks through his bungalow carrying me. He takes us outside to his patio naked and in the darkness, walking out to the sand so we can see the white caps on the ocean and hear it's roar. He claims my mouth as we stand there in our wide-open solitude. He turns to go back inside, but takes us to the back corner of his patio. He crawls onto a cushioned lounger on all fours as I cling to him. We lie there together, claiming each other with the blanket blocking out the world.

Chase mutters under his breath, "I have no idea what I'm doing. Sex won't prove anything to you." His kiss is aggressive and controlling, "I need you." He settles himself between my legs and keeps kissing me. His hands at my breasts, but then searching for my hands. He intertwines his fingers with mine and everything around us stops for a moment in time, it's just us. Nothing else exists as we gaze into each other's eyes and giggle happily.

"Please, Chase."

"I'm trying."

I don't understand what he means. Trying? I don't get it.

He lies on top of me and whispers in my ear, "You're special to me. You'll always be special to me. I'll never hurt you." He takes a deep breath, and pushes into me a little at a time. Tightening his fingers around mine, "Kristina…" He kisses me softly and open-mouthed. He's blocked everything else from my world, he's the only thing that exists.

He moves slowly, giving me more and more of him until our bodies mash together at our connection. He's buried deep inside me, yet focused on my mouth. He's somehow managing to continuously rub that spot that drives me crazy with little movement. But it's his hands that give everything away. The muscles flexing in his hands and the grip his fingers have on mine. He's not letting me go. He's holding on tight and I find I am, too. I open my eyes and he's looking at me. I try to pull my hands away and he won't let me. "I want to touch you. I'll give my hands back." He kisses me with more need than I've ever felt and loosens his grip. I run my fingers through his hair and wrap my arms around his neck, wishing I could reach around his muscular shoulders. He's hot to the touch and his warm breath is ragged at my ear. The friction between us growing as he moves faster. He pulls out and strokes back into me repeatedly, and completely. He's amazing, huge and hard.

"I need you," he declares on a whisper.

"You have me, Chase. I'm with you, baby."

I feel his grin against my cheek and his hands move to my hips. He caresses my thighs and lifts my legs, catching them with his arms and coming down on me while he strokes into me. "I need to be closer to you. I don't know how. I can only get deeper."

"Oh, Chase!"

He pounds into me wildly, "This isn't what I wanted to do. I can't help myself when I'm with you." He stops and rests his forehead against mine, "I love you. How can I show you I love you? How can I prove it to you?"

"You show me in your touch and in your kiss. You don't have to do anything special, just be you."

He consumes me. I hear the blood rushing through my body, our hearts beating, and our uneven breaths. The heat of his touch controlling me as he takes over my body. I'm hit with the sudden realization that I'm his. I feel my center tighten, spooling toward release. He takes me harder and faster, "You drive me crazy. Tell me what you want."

"More of you," slips from my tongue without a thought.

"I can do that. Tell me if I hurt you. I never want to hurt you."

"All of you, Chase. Harder, baby. Please. Send me to the stars." I don't know where my words come from, but he listens.

He takes my hands back in his, locking his fingers with mine and supporting himself on our hands pressed together into the cushion. He claims my lips and slides his tongue against mine in time to the stroke of his hard length inside me. Pushing into me harder and harder until he's slamming into me on every stroke and unable to get any deeper. I cry out to him with need and want to hold him, but he has my hands, "Chase!" It drives him further, faster. I'm suddenly ready to explode and see light flickering behind my closed eyelids. He feels so good, I'm calling out his name on every stroke. "I need you," escapes me and I'm out of control.

"I've got you." He releases my hands and wraps his arms around me, holding me tight to him. "You're amazing around me. Custom fit, Sweetness."

He keeps slamming into me, harder and harder. The flickering turns to a full-on fireworks display exploding just for me as I come harder than ever before. I tighten quickly around him and I'm reminded of his size as I scream out his name, "Chase, oh Chase! So big!" He slams into me again over and over, I come even harder.

He reaches between my legs, "I think that was two."

"Uh huh. Oh Chase."

He finds my clit and teases it, "I didn't give this any attention."

And I'm lost, coming a third time at his hand with him still buried in me. He's in complete control.

"I need to come. I'm so hard for you. I could stay this way all night. Do you want to come again first?"

"Come for me." All the words I can manage. He pounds into me with his fist around the base of his cock and then lets go and gives me all of him again. My orgasm rolls on and on. I'm out of control, flying through the stars.

"Kristina! Kristina! Oh fuck, Sweetness."

Suddenly he's there with me, holding my hand as I float through space looking at the stars. His arm around me, holding me against him in the starlit night.

CHAPTER THIRTY

Kristina

I wake up snuggled against him on his patio, lying side by side on the lounger. We're still covered, but we can see the sky through an opening in the blanket. I have no idea what time it is, but it's dark out. I move my hands to his chest.

"Are you back with me?" He asks.

"Yeah."

"Is this okay, or do you want me to take you back inside?"

"I want to stay right here."

"I lost you there for a while, are you okay?"

"There were fireworks and you held my hand while we floated through the stars."

"I was there, too. You were already in the stars when I got there. I'll try not to let you go there alone next time," He smiles at me content with himself.

We lie there together until I fall asleep in his arms.

Chase

When the sun comes up I take my woman to my bed and lock up the house. The sunrise is beautiful, but on the beach with the early morning surfers probably isn't the place to sleep naked. I don't know what she does to me, if it's how I feel about her or what, but I want to slide right back into her and claim her as mine again. I want to keep her. I hope she wants me to keep her. She already owns me. She was sleeping and didn't wake up when I brought her to bed. I hold her and go back to sleep.

Kristina

"Chase?" My eyes are closed and it's dark. He's holding me.

His arms tighten around me, "I'm right here."

I roll into him and kiss his chest, still half asleep. My hands wander his body, exploring his adonis belt. We're both naked. My hands travel farther south and I drag a finger along the hard long length of his cock. I wrap my hand around him and I can't reach all the way around. He's holding me close and I stroke him lightly, more of a caress. I kiss his neck and he leans in to meet my lips with his. Tracing my lips with the tip of his tongue, then kissing my upper lip, then my lower lip. Everything in slow motion. He rolls me underneath him and holds me with his arms around me. He kisses me, worshiping my lips and I'm lost in him. I'm falling for him. I knew it would be like this when I kissed him the first time. I love him and he makes me want to do crazy things. I rock my hips up at him while he's kissing me and I feel him hard at my entrance. "I trust you, Chase. I want to be closer to you."

290

He bends my knees and spreads my legs, his lips never leaving mine. He takes my hand and wraps it around his bare cock. "I want to be closer to you, too. I want to be bare with you, no condom separating us. I won't take you that way, you have to give yourself to me."

I feel him in my hand. I stroke him and his body shivers. I rub his tip against me and I'm wet for him. He groans under his breath at the feel of me. I push against his tip, taking him in. "I'm yours, Chase."

He takes control pushing all the way in quickly, "I love you, Kristina." He moves slowly and his kiss becomes more passionate. "Thank you, love. You mean everything to me," he whispers in my ear.

I should tell him that I love him, but I haven't said that to a man since my high school boyfriend. Honestly, nothing has ever felt like this and I'm not referring to his peen, though it is in it's own league. There's something about Chase. I've tried to fight it, but I find myself asking "why fight it if it's what I want?" He makes me want to take a chance. I believe him when he says he loves me. I believe every word he says. I trust him completely, more than I trust myself. "Chase, baby, tell me again."

He smiles against my lips, "I love you, Sweetness."

He doesn't expect a response or anything in return. He starts to move with long slow strokes, over and over. I squeeze him and cry out his name in pure pleasure.

Chase

The way she says my name, it's like she's saying she's mine. I can feel it in her body and hear the thoughts she has running through her head. I'm trying to clear them all away and be everything in her existence, like she is for me. "You feel amazing around me. I want you to come with me deep inside you. I want to feel you get wet for me and tighten around me. I want to feel that you're mine."

She nods, breathless as I kiss her neck.

"I want to be closer to you. Tell me if I hurt you. I never want to hurt you. I need to be deeper inside you. Do you feel my love?" I spread her legs further and push in as far as I can, holding myself deep against her. It's not enough. I lift her legs, bringing her knees to her chest and push in further. She squeals and I brush the hair out of her face, watching to make sure I don't hurt her.

"Yes, Chase. I know you love me. I feel it everywhere."

"Ready for more?"

"Please. More."

I pound into her hard. Watching my hard dick slam into her bare, over and over. Her tight little heaven, hot and wet around me. I'm not sure I deserve her this way. I'll ruin her for everyone else. It doesn't matter. She's not a fuck. I'm keeping her. There's nothing like this direct contact. Just us and nothing in the way. Nothing keeping us apart.

"Oh, Chase!" she cries out on every stroke into her. "You make me so full. You're so hard. Oh! Oh!" She starts to scream and I wrap my arm around her, muffling her cries with my kiss.

"Almost, Sweetness. You feel so good, just a little more. I've got you." I keep slamming her tight hole and I don't want to stop. She's coming hard around me. I feel her orgasm hit her. I'm not giving this up. I've wanted her for too long and to have her bare, fuck me. Fuck! I want to come inside. I want to come in deep with my tip pressing against her wall. Fuck. Fuck. Control! I want to stay inside her. I could go for hours, until she whimpers my name all sweet and sexy. It's my downfall and I try to make it last. I lean into her ear. "I want to see the stars with you, take me with you."

She arches into me, "You're the only one for me. It's okay, come inside. I want you. I know you want to."

I want to, but I can't, "We can't take that risk. I promised I'd protect you."

"Please, Chase, I want to feel you come inside me. I want to feel you hard and pulsating."

Fuck me. I want to so bad. Maybe it would be okay this once. Only once. She's so hot and tight, I want to stay inside her as long as I can. I'm pushing and pulling myself closer to the edge, while I listen to her sexy little cries.

"Nobody compares to you, baby." She starts to moan and I'm done.

I can't control myself any longer. I grab my dick and pull out quick, trying not to get any near her heaven. No stroking necessary. Fuck, I'm a fucking fire hose. I collapse on top of her and give it a quick last tug.

Kristina

Waking up in his arms, happy and content. I wonder why I ever questioned being with him. I love him. I want to make him as happy as he makes me. I'm all in. We can figure this out together.

I want to do something for him. I get up quietly, trying not to disturb him in his deep sleep. I wander to his kitchen, hoping he has the ingredients to make cookies. No such luck, but I do find what I need to make French toast. I mix up soaking liquid the best I can with what I have to work with and search further for more flavor. I layer the French toast in a small baking dish with chocolate bits and bake it. When it's done, I plate up a few pieces. I add more chocolate bits and dust the plate with powdered sugar as I hear Chase call out my name.

CHAPTER THIRTY-ONE

Chase

I wake up the next day and I'm alone in my bed. I remember our early morning rendezvous and hope she didn't run. I did and said some stupid shit. I know better than to push the boundaries with her.

"Kristina?" I call out.

"Just a second. I'm almost ready."

That's when I notice the delicious smell. I stretch and sit up with the blanket pulled up to my waist, keeping my good bits covered. I straighten the sheets and put my hands on the back of my head as I lean back against my headboard. I don't remember ever feeling this content.

"Good morning," she smiles at me as she carries in a big plate with two forks and a glass of milk. "I hope you don't mind, I went through your kitchen. I didn't find everything I needed to make cookies, so I hope you like French toast. You don't have syrup so I added chocolate bits and extra powdered sugar."

"You cooked for me?"

"Yeah." She giggles, "Sherry taught me some things. I wanted to make chocolate chip cookie bars, but you don't have the ingredients."

I take the plate from her and set it on my nightstand. I grab her around the waist and pull her into bed with me. "We will get whatever you want for the kitchen today."

"Chase, umm. I need to talk to you about something."

Oh fuck. "Okay."

"I'm sorry about earlier. You make me lose my mind. Thank you for doing the right thing and protecting me."

"I'll always protect you. I'm sorry I got carried away last night. It won't happen again."

"It's okay as long as it's you. It will always be us." She kisses me sweetly and rests her hands on my shoulders, "I'll do anything for you, Chase. I'm yours. I love you."

I'm surprised by her words. My smile takes over all the way into my cheeks and I feel my eyes light up. "Tell me again."

"I love you, Chase."

"You love me? Are you sure?"

She laughs, "Yes! I'll always love you. Nobody compares to you."

"I love you, too." I take her in my arms, kissing her and loving her. She's the only one for me.

PLAYLIST

"Hearts Don't Break Around Here" by Ed Sheeran
"Train in Vain" by The Clash
"Tonight & Forever" by The Damnwells
"I Will Keep the Bad Things From You" by The Damnwells
"Graceless" by The Damnwells
"Favorite Liar" by The Wrecks
"I Don't Like You" by The Wrecks
"Turn It Up" by The Wrecks
"Automatic" by The Subways
"Rock & Roll Queen" by The Subways
"She Sun" by the Subways
"Blasphemous Rumors" by Depeche Mode
"Strangelove" by Depeche Mode
"Just Can't Get Enough" by Depeche Mode
"People Are People" by Depeche Mode
"Return of Mack" by Mark Morrison
"Cake By the Ocean" by DNCE
"I Want to Hold Your Hand" by The Beatles
"Kiss is on My List" by Hall and Oates

"Kristina" by Rick Springfield

"Waiting For a Girl Like You" by Foreigner

"Feels Like the First Time" by Foreigner

"Something So Strong" by Crowded House

"Won't Stop" by OneRepublic

"Dive" by Ed Sheeran

"I Want To Know What Love Is" by Foreigner

"Just Like Heaven" by The Cure

"Last of the Real Ones" by Fall Out Boy

"Sweetness" by Jimmy Eat World

"1950" by King Princess

THE CLOSER

AN ALL ABOUT THE DIAMOND ROMANCE BOOK 5

Houck

It's been a shitty week and it's only Thursday. I've blown two saves and my girlfriend dumped me. She said I use her for sex and don't care about her. Neither are true, but I compare everyone to Angie and nobody comes close. I never should've let her walk away from me. I didn't know any better and she didn't want to traipse around the country following a minor league player. Why would she? We were friends and nothing more. We were college kids. She had her own goals and she achieved them without me. She never needed me, not the way I need her. They say the last person you think about when you go to bed and the first person you think about when you wake up is the one who's most important to you, it's always been Angie. Nights like this when I've blown the save, I wish I had her with me. The girlfriends come and go. I keep hoping there's one out there for me, I just haven't met her yet.

I swear Angie has a sixth sense. Most times I have her on

my mind, she calls or something within a few days. Tonight a text comes in and it's not her typical fun message.

Text from Angie - I need to see you

Text from Angie - Already checked your schedule

Text to Angie - You want to get together over the All-Star Break?

Text from Angie - Just landed in San Diego

FINALLY IN FOCUS

A NOVELLA

I want Kade. I've wanted him since high school, but it made no sense to be interested in a guy who never went to class and always had extra cash. What teenager ever had extra cash? It had to be bad news or illegal. His overgrown light brown hair hanging down into his eyes. His T-shirts were worn, old, and faded, sometimes not long enough to meet the jeans at his waist, and always stretched perfectly across his shoulders. He wore old school button-fly jeans, none of those relaxed fit or skinny jeans or anything stylish, and in fact he still wears those, but now it's usually topped with a black polo shirt (varying degrees of black, since it appears he doesn't care if they fade). Yes, I saw him recently. Shit. I see him all the time. Fine. I know where to find him when I want a glimpse. He's predictable and I'm good with patterns. I haven't spoke to him since senior ditch day, which was the longest conversation I've ever had with him. He had surprised me with his passion and intelligence. He hated school and the drama of everything it encompassed. He was on the home study program, but spent most of his time in the photography lab on campus. I remember learning about his schedule and being hit with my misconception, he wasn't ditching at all. I admired his mouth when he talked to me, and his hands as he used them to describe his words. He had passion in his hands when he held his camera and creativity shining in his hazel eyes. Yeah, I've dreamt about Kade since ditch day. What would it feel like for those hands to touch me? Would his mouth kiss with the same passion?

ACKNOWLEDGMENTS

Thank you to all of the readers who have given me a chance over the last year. It has been a whirlwind, and Chase is finally here. My sixth release since my first book, The Sweet Spot, came out last June when you first met Rick Seno and his buddy the rookie—Chase Cross. Book seven, The Closer, will be following soon.

Thank you to the best author friends a girl could have, especially Tonya Clark for dragging me kicking and screaming (not) into her photography world and adding Model Hunter to my resume.

Thank you to my Naughties for your support and feedback, and putting up with my late night messages. I love how you have taken ownership of my books by character, just as I have. Alisa, you can't have Chase (share nicely, you already have Danny). Sam, you make the Naughties world right. Megs, Mary, Jann, Carolyn, Jaime, Shenanigans—my special brand of crazy wouldn't be complete without you.

ABOUT THE AUTHOR

Naomi Springthorp is an emerging author. Star-Crossed in the Outfield is her sixth release, and An All About the Diamond Romance, Book 5. She's also writing other contemporary romance novels and novellas featuring music, firemen, and more.

Naomi is a born and raised Southern California girl. She lives with her husband and her feline fur babies. She believes that life has a soundtrack and half of the year should be spent cheering for her favorite baseball team.

Join her newsletter at
www.naomispringthorp.com/sign-up

ALSO BY NAOMI SPRINGTHORP

An All About the Diamond Romance

The Sweet Spot

King of Diamonds

Diamonds in Paradise (a novella)

Star Crossed in the Outfield

The Closer (a novella)… coming soon

Up to Bat… coming soon

Stalking Second… coming soon

Novellas and standalone novels

Muffin Man (a novella)

Confessions of an Online Junkie… coming soon

Finally in Focus (a novella)… coming soon

Betting on Love (Vegas Romance)

Just a California Girl

Jacks!… coming in November 2019

33988919R00192

Made in the USA
San Bernardino, CA
29 April 2019